HEIDI

Johanna Spyri

Om Books International

Reprinted in 2023 by

Om Books International

Corporate & Editorial Office
A-12, Sector 64, Noida 201 301
Uttar Pradesh, India
Phone: +91 120 477 4100
Email: editorial@ombooks.com
Website: www.ombooksinternational.com

Sales Office
107, Ansari Road, Darya Ganj,
New Delhi 110 002, India
Phone: +91 11 4000 9000
Email: sales@ombooks.com
Website: www.ombooks.com

ISBN: 978-93-5276-647-5

Printed in India

10 9 8 7 6 5 4 3 2

Contents

Chapter 1

Up The Mountain To Alm-Uncle

From the old and pleasantly situated village of Mayenfeld, a footpath winds through green and shady meadows to the foot of the mountains, which on this side look down from their stern and lofty heights upon the valley below. The land grows gradually wilder as the path ascends, and the climber has not gone far before he begins to inhale the fragrance of the short grass and sturdy mountain-plants, for the way is steep and leads directly up to the summits above.

On a clear sunny morning in June two figures might be seen climbing the narrow mountain path; one, a tall strong-looking girl, the other a child whom she was leading by the hand, and whose little checks were so aglow with heat that the crimson colour could be seen even through the dark, sunburnt skin. And this was hardly to be wondered at, for in spite of the hot June sun the child was clothed as if to keep off the bitterest frost. She did not look more than five years old, if as much, but what her natural figure was like, it would have been hard to say, for she had apparently two, if not three dresses, one above the other, and over these a thick red woollen shawl wound round about her, so that the little body presented a shapeless appearance, as, with its small feet shod in thick, nailed mountain-shoes, it slowly and laboriously plodded its way up in the heat. The two must have left the valley a good hour's walk behind them, when they came to the hamlet known as Dörfli, which is situated half-way up the mountain. Here the wayfarers met with greetings from all sides, some calling to them from windows, some from open doors, others from outside, for the elder girl was now in her old home. She did not, however, pause in her walk to respond to her friends' welcoming cries and questions, but passed on without stopping for a moment until she reached the last of the scattered houses of the hamlet. Here a voice called to her from the door: "Wait a moment, Dete; if you are going up higher, I will come with you."

The girl thus addressed stood still, and the child immediately let go her hand and seated herself on the ground.

"Are you tired, Heidi?" asked her companion.

"No, I am hot," answered the child.

"We shall soon get to the top now. You must walk bravely on a little longer, and take good long steps, and in another hour we shall be there," said Dete in an encouraging voice.

They were now joined by a stout, good-natured-looking woman, who walked on ahead with her old acquaintance, the two breaking forth at once into lively conversation about everybody and everything in Dörfli and its surroundings, while the child wandered behind them.

"And where are you off to with the child?" asked the one who had just joined the party. "I suppose it is the child your sister left?"

"Yes," answered Dete. "I am taking her up to Uncle, where she must stay."

"The child stay up there with Alm-Uncle! You must be out of your senses, Dete! How can you think of such a thing! The old man, however, will soon send you and your proposal packing off home again!"

"He cannot very well do that, seeing that he is her grandfather. He must do something for her. I have had the charge of the child till now, and I can tell you, Barbel, I am not going to give up the chance which has just fallen to me of getting a good place, for her sake. It is for the grandfather now to do his duty by her."

"That would be all very well if he were like other people," asseverated stout Barbel warmly, "but you know what he is. And what can he do with a child, especially with one so young! The child cannot possibly live with him. But where are you thinking of going yourself?"

"To Frankfurt, where an extra good place awaits me," answered Dete. "The people I am going to were down at the Baths last summer, and it was part of my duty to attend upon their rooms. They would have liked then to take me away with them, but I could not leave. Now they are there again and have repeated their offer, and I intend to go with them, you may make up your mind to that!"

"I am glad I am not the child!" exclaimed Barbel, with a gesture of horrified pity. "Not a creature knows anything about the old man up there! He will have nothing to do with anybody, and never sets his foot inside a church from one year's end to another. When he does come down once in a while, everybody clears out of the way of him and his big stick. The mere sight of him, with his bushy grey eyebrows and his immense beard, is alarming enough. He looks like any old heathen or Indian, and few would care to meet him alone."

"Well, and what of that?" said Dete, in a defiant voice, "he is the grandfather all the same, and must look after the child. He is not likely to do her any harm, and if he does, he will be answerable for it, not I."

"I should very much like to know," continued Barbel, in an inquiring tone of voice, "what the old man has on his conscience that he looks as he does, and lives up there on the mountain like a hermit, hardly ever allowing himself to be seen. All kinds of things are said about him. You, Dete, however, must certainly have learnt a good deal concerning him from your sister—am I not right?"

"You are right, I did, but I am not going to repeat what I heard; if it should come to his ears I should get into trouble about it."

Now Barbel had for long past been most anxious to ascertain particulars about Alm-Uncle, as she could not understand why he seemed to feel such hatred towards his fellow-creatures, and insisted on living all alone, or why people spoke about him half in whispers, as if afraid to say anything against him, and yet unwilling to take his Part. Moreover, Barbel was in ignorance as to why all the people in Dörfli called him Alm-Uncle, for he could not possibly be uncle to everybody living there. As, however, it was the custom, she did like the rest and called the old man Uncle. Barbel had only lived in Dörfli since her marriage, which had taken place not long before. Previous to that her home had been below in Prättigau, so that she was not well acquainted with all the events that had ever taken place, and with all the people who had ever lived in Dörfli and its neighbourhood. Dete, on the contrary, had been born in Dörfli, and had lived there with her mother until the death of the latter the year before, and had then gone over to the Baths at Ragatz and taken service in the large hotel there as chambermaid. On the morning of this day she had come all the way from Ragatz with the child, a friend having given them a lift in a hay-cart as far as Mayenfeld. Barbel was therefore determined not to lose this good opportunity of satisfying her curiosity. She put her arm through Dete's in a confidential sort of way, and said: "I know I can find out the real truth from you, and the meaning of all these tales that are afloat about him. I believe you know the whole story. Now do just tell me what is wrong with the old man, and if he was always shunned as he is now, and was always such a misanthrope."

"How can I possibly tell you whether he was always the same, seeing I am only six-and-twenty and he at least seventy years of age; so you can hardly expect me to know much about his youth. If I was sure, however, that what I tell you would not go the whole round of Prättigau, I could relate all kinds of things about him; my mother came from Domleschg, and so did he."

"Nonsense, Dete, what do you mean?" replied Barbel, somewhat offended, "gossip has not reached such a dreadful pitch in Prättigau as all that, and I am also quite capable of holding my tongue when it is necessary."

"Very well then, I will tell you—but just wait a moment," said Dete in a warning voice, and she looked back to make sure that the child was not near enough to hear all she was going to relate; but the child was nowhere to be seen, and must have turned aside from following her companions some time before, while these were too eagerly occupied with their conversation to notice it. Dete stood still and looked around her in all directions. The footpath wound a little here and there, but could nevertheless be seen along its whole length nearly to Dörfli; no one, however, was visible upon it at this moment.

"I see where she is," exclaimed Barbel, "look over there!" and she pointed to a spot far away from the footpath. "She is climbing up the slope yonder with the goatherd and his goats. I wonder why he is so late today bringing them up. It happens well, however, for us, for he can now see after the child, and you can the better tell me your tale."

"Oh, as to the looking after," remarked Dete, "the boy need not put himself out about that; she is not by any means stupid for her five years, and knows how to use her eyes. She notices all that is going on, as I have often had occasion to remark, and this will stand her in good stead some day, for the old man has nothing beyond his two goats and his hut."

"Did he ever have more?" asked Barbel.

"He? I should think so indeed," replied Dete with animation; "he was owner once of one of the largest farms in Domleschg. He was the elder of two brothers; the younger was a quiet, orderly man, but nothing would please the other but to play the grand gentleman and go driving about the country and mixing with bad company, strangers that nobody knew. He drank and gambled away the whole of his property, and when this became known to his mother and father they died, one shortly after the other, of sorrow. The younger brother, who was also reduced to beggary, went off in his anger, no one knew whither, while Uncle himself, having nothing now left to him but his bad name, also disappeared. For some time his whereabouts were unknown, then some one found out that he had gone to Naples as a soldier; after that nothing more was heard of him for twelve or fifteen years. At the end of that time he reappeared in Domleschg, bringing with him a young child, whom he tried to place with some of his kinspeople. Every door, however, was shut in his face, for no one wished to have any more to do with him. Embittered by this treatment, he vowed never to set foot in Domleschg again, and he then came to Dörfli, where he continued to live with his little boy. His wife was probably a native of the Grisons, whom he had met down there, and who died soon after their marriage. He could not have been entirely without money, for he apprenticed his son, Tobias, to a carpenter. He was a steady lad, and kindly received by every one in Dörfli. The old man was, however, still looked upon with suspicion, and it was even rumoured that he had been forced to make his escape from Naples, or it might have gone badly with him, for that he had killed a man, not in fair fight, you understand, but in some brawl. We, however, did not refuse to acknowledge our relationship with him, my great-grandmother on my mother's side having been sister to his grandmother. So we called him Uncle, and as through my father we are also related to nearly every family in Dörfli, he became known all over the place as Uncle, and since he went to live on the mountain side he has gone everywhere by the name of Alm-Uncle."

"And what happened to Tobias?" asked Barbel, who was listening with deep interest.

"Wait a moment, I am coming to that, but I cannot tell you everything at once," replied Dete. "Tobias was taught his trade in Mels, and when he had served his apprenticeship he came back to Dörfli and married my sister Adelaide. They had always been fond of one another, and they got on very well together after they were married. But their happiness did not last long. Her husband met with his death only two years after their marriage, a beam falling upon him as he was working, and killing him on the spot. They carried him home, and when Adelaide saw the poor disfigured body of her husband she was so overcome with horror and grief that she fell into a fever from which she never recovered. She had always been rather delicate and subject to curious attacks, during which no one knew whether she was awake or sleeping. And so two months after Tobias had been carried to the grave, his wife followed him. Their sad fate was the talk of everybody far and near, and both in private and public the general opinion was expressed that it was a punishment which Uncle had deserved for the godless life he had led. Some went so far even as to tell him so to his face. Our minister endeavored to awaken his conscience and exhorted him to repentance, but the old man grew only more wrathful and obdurate and would not speak to a soul, and every one did their best to keep out of his way. All at once we heard that he had gone to live up the Alm and did not intend ever to come down again, and since then he has led his solitary life on the mountain side at enmity with God and man.

Mother and I took Adelaide's little one, then only a year old, into our care. When mother died last year, and I went down to the Baths to earn some money, I paid old Ursel, who lives in the village just above, to keep and look after the child. I stayed on at the Baths through the winter, for as I could sew and knit I had no difficulty in finding plenty of work, and early in the spring the same family I had waited on before returned from Frankfurt, and again asked me to go back with them. And so we leave the day after tomorrow, and I can assure you, it is an excellent place for me."

"And you are going to give the child over to the old man up there? It surprises me beyond words that you can think of doing such a thing, Dete," said Barbel, in a voice full of reproach.

"What do you mean?" retorted Dete. "I have done my duty by the child, and what would you have me do with it now? I cannot certainly take a child of five years old with me to Frankfurt. But where are you going to yourself, Barbel; we are now half way up the Alm?"

"We have just reached the place I wanted," answered Barbel. "I had something to say to the goatherd's wife, who does some spinning for me in the winter. So goodbye, Dete, and good luck to you!"

Dete shook hands with her friend and remained standing while Barbel went towards a small, dark brown hut, which stood a few steps away from the path in a hollow that afforded it some protection from the mountain wind. The hut was situated half way up the Alm, reckoning from Dörfli, and it was well that it was provided with some shelter, for it was so broken-down and dilapidated that even then it must have been very unsafe as a habitation, for when the stormy south wind came sweeping over the mountain, everything inside it, doors and windows, shook and rattled, and all the rotten old beams creaked and trembled. On such days as this, had the goatherd's dwelling been standing above on the exposed mountain side, it could not have escaped being blown straight down into the valley without a moment's warning.

Here lived Peter, the eleven-year-old boy, who every morning went down to Dörfli to fetch his goats and drive them up on to the mountain, where they were free to browse till evening on the delicious mountain plants.

Then Peter, with his light-footed animals, would go running and leaping down the mountain again till he reached Dörfli, and there he would give a shrill whistle through his fingers, whereupon all the owners of the goats would come out to fetch home the animals that belonged to them. It was generally the small boys and girls who ran in answer to Peter's whistle, for they were none of them afraid of the gentle goats, and this was the only hour of the day through all the summer months that Peter had any opportunity of seeing his young friends, since the rest of his time was spent alone with the goats. He had a mother and a blind grandmother at home, it is true, but he was always obliged to start off very early in the morning, and only got home late in the evening from Dörfli, for he always stayed as long as he could talking and playing with the other children; and so he had just time enough at home, and that was all, to swallow down his bread and milk in the morning, and again in the evening to get through a similar meal, lie down in bed and go to sleep. His father, who had been known also as the goatherd, having earned his living as such when younger, had been accidentally killed while cutting wood some years before. His mother, whose real name was Brigitta, was always called the goatherd's wife, for the sake of old association, while the blind grandmother was just "grandmother" to all the old and young in the neighbourhood.

Dete had been standing for a good ten minutes looking about her in every direction for some sign of the children and the goats. Not a glimpse of them, however, was to be seen, so she climbed to a higher spot, whence she could get a fuller view of the mountain as it sloped beneath her to the valley, while, with ever-increasing anxiety on her face and in her movements, she continued to scan the surrounding slopes. Meanwhile the children were climbing up by a far and roundabout way, for Peter knew many spots where all kinds of good food, in the shape of shrubs and plants, grew for his goats, and he was in the habit of leading his flock aside from the beaten track. The child, exhausted with the heat and weight of her thick armor of clothes, panted and struggled after him at first with some difficulty. She said nothing, but her little eyes kept watching first Peter, as he sprang nimbly hither and thither on his bare feet, clad only in his short light breeches, and then the slim-legged goats that went leaping over rocks and shrubs and up the steep ascents with even greater ease. All at once she sat herself down on the ground, and as fast as her little fingers could move, began pulling off her shoes and stockings. This done she rose, unwound the hot red shawl and threw it away, and then proceeded to undo her frock. It was off in a second, but there was still another to unfasten, for Dete had put the Sunday frock on over the everyday one, to save the trouble of carrying it. Quick as lightning the everyday frock followed the other, and now the child stood up, clad only in her light short-sleeved under garment, stretching out her little bare arms with glee. She put all her clothes together in a tidy little heap, and then went jumping and climbing up after Peter and the goats as nimbly as any one of the party. Peter had taken no heed of what the child was about when she stayed behind, but when she ran up to him in her new attire, his face broke into a grin, which grew broader still as he looked back and saw the small heap of clothes lying on the ground, until his mouth stretched almost from ear to ear; he said nothing, however. The child, able now to move at her ease, began to enter into conversation with Peter, who had many questions to answer, for his companion wanted to know how many goats he had, where he was going to with them, and what he had to do when he arrived there. At last, after some time, they and the goats approached the hut and came within view of Cousin Dete. Hardly had the latter caught sight of the little company climbing up towards her when she shrieked out: "Heidi, what have you been doing! What a sight you have made of yourself! And where are your two frocks and the red wrapper? And the new shoes I bought, and the new stockings I knitted for you—everything gone! not a thing left! What can you have been thinking of, Heidi; where are all your clothes?"

The child quietly pointed to a spot below on the mountain side and answered, "Down there." Dete followed the direction of her finger; she could just distinguish something lying on the ground, with a spot of red on the top of it which she had no doubt was the woollen wrapper.

"You good-for-nothing little thing!" exclaimed Dete angrily, "what could have put it into your head to do like that? What made you undress yourself? What do you mean by it?"

"I don't want any clothes," said the child, not showing any sign of repentance for her past deed.

"You wretched, thoughtless child! Have you no sense in you at all?" continued Dete, scolding and lamenting. "Who is going all that way down to fetch them; it's a good half-hour's walk! Peter, you go off and fetch them for me as quickly as you can, and don't stand there gaping at me, as if you were rooted to the ground!"

"I am already past my time," answered Peter slowly, without moving from the spot where he had been standing with his hands in his pockets, listening to Dete's outburst of dismay and anger.

"Well, you won't get far if you only keep on standing there with your eyes staring out of your head," was Dete's cross reply; "but see, you shall have something nice," and she held out a bright new piece of money to him that sparkled in the sun. Peter was immediately up and off down the steep mountain side, taking the shortest cut, and in an incredibly short space of time had reached the little heap of clothes, which he gathered up under his arm, and was back again so quickly that even Dete was obliged to give him a word of praise as she handed him the promised money. Peter promptly thrust it into his pocket and his face beamed with delight, for it was not often that he was the happy possessor of such riches.

"You can carry the things up for me as far as Uncle's, as you are going the same way," went on Dete, who was preparing to continue her climb up the mountain side, which rose in a steep ascent immediately behind the goatherd's hut. Peter willingly undertook to do this, and followed after her on his bare feet, with his left arm round the bundle and the right swinging his goatherd's stick, while Heidi and the goats went skipping and jumping joyfully beside him. After a climb of more than three-quarters of an hour they reached the top of the Alm mountain. Uncle's hut stood on a projection of the rock, exposed indeed to the winds, but where every ray of sun could rest upon it, and a full view could be had of the valley beneath. Behind the hut stood three old fir trees, with long, thick, unlopped branches. Beyond these rose a further wall of mountain, the lower heights still overgrown with beautiful grass and plants, above which were stonier slopes, covered only with scrub, that led gradually up to the steep, bare rocky summits.

Against the hut, on the side looking towards the valley, Uncle had put up a seat. Here he was sitting, his pipe in his mouth and his hands on his knees, quietly looking out, when the children, the goats and Cousin Dete suddenly clambered into view. Heidi was at the top first. She went straight up to the old man, put out her hand, and said, "Good evening, Grandfather."

"So, so, what is the meaning of this?" he asked gruffly, as he gave the child an abrupt shake of the hand, and gazed long and scrutinisingly at her from under his bushy eyebrows. Heidi stared steadily back at him in return with unflinching gaze, for the grandfather, with his long beard and thick grey eyebrows that grew together over his nose and looked just like a bush, was such a remarkable appearance, that Heidi was unable to take her eyes off him. Meanwhile Dete had come up, with Peter after her, and the latter now stood still a while to watch what was going on.

"I wish you good day, Uncle," said Dete, as she walked towards him, "and I have brought you Tobias and Adelaide's child. You will hardly recognise her, as you have never seen her since she was a year old."

"And what has the child to do with me up here?" asked the old man curtly. "You there," he then called out to Peter, "be off with your goats, you are none too early as it is, and take mine with you."

Peter obeyed on the instant and quickly disappeared, for the old man had given him a look that made him feel that he did not want to stay any longer.

"The child is here to remain with you," Dete made answer. "I have, I think, done my duty by her for these four years, and now it is time for you to do yours."

"That's it, is it?" said the old man, as he looked at her with a flash in his eye. "And when the child begins to fret and whine after you, as is the way with these unreasonable little beings, what am I to do with her then?"

"That's your affair," retorted Dete. "I know I had to put up with her without complaint when she was left on my hands as an infant, and with enough to do as it was for my mother and self. Now I have to go and look after my own earnings, and you are the next of kin to the child. If you cannot arrange to keep her, do with her as you like. You will be answerable for the result if harm happens to her, though you have hardly need, I should think, to add to the burden already on your conscience."

Now Dete was not quite easy in her own conscience about what she was doing, and consequently was feeling hot and irritable, and said more than she had intended. As she uttered her last words, Uncle rose from his seat. He looked at her in a way that made her draw back a step or two, then flinging out his arm, he said to her in a commanding voice: "Be off with you this instant, and get back as quickly as you can to the place whence you came, and do not let me see your face again in a hurry."

Dete did not wait to be told twice. "Goodbye to you then, and to you too, Heidi," she called, as she turned quickly away and started to descend the mountain at a running pace, which she did not slacken till she found herself safely again at Dörfli, for some inward agitation drove her forwards as if a steam-engine was at work inside her. Again questions came raining down upon her from all sides, for every one knew Dete, as well as all particulars of the birth and former history of the child, and all wondered what she had done with it. From every door and window came voices calling: "Where is the child?" "Where have you left the child, Dete?" and more and more reluctantly Dete made answer, "Up there with Alm-Uncle!" "With Alm-Uncle, have I not told you so already?"

Then the women began to hurl reproaches at her; first one cried out, "How could you do such a thing!" then another, "To think of leaving a helpless little thing up there,"—while again and again came the words, "The poor mite! The poor mite!" pursuing her as she went along. Unable at last to bear it any longer Dete ran forward as fast as she could until she was beyond reach of their voices. She was far from happy at the thought of what she had done, for the child had been left in her care by her dying mother. She quieted herself, however, with the idea that she would be better able to do something for the child if she was earning plenty of money, and it was a relief to her to think that she would soon be far away from all these people who were making such a fuss about the matter, and she rejoiced further still that she was at liberty now to take such a good place.

Chapter 2

At Home With Grandfather

As soon as Dete had disappeared the old man went back to his bench, and there he remained seated, staring on the ground without uttering a sound, while thick curls of smoke floated upward from his pipe. Heidi, meanwhile, was enjoying herself in her new surroundings; she looked about till she found a shed, built against the hut, where the goats were kept; she peeped in, and saw it was empty. She continued her search and presently came to the fir trees behind the hut. A strong breeze was blowing through them, and there was a rushing and roaring in their topmost branches, Heidi stood still and listened. The sound growing fainter, she went on again, to the farther corner of the hut, and so round to where her grandfather was sitting. Seeing that he was in exactly the same position as when she left him, she went and placed herself in front of the old man, and putting her hands behind her back, stood and gazed at him. Her grandfather looked up, and as she continued standing there without moving, "What is it you want?" he asked.

"I want to see what you have inside the house," said Heidi.

"Come then!" and the grandfather rose and went before her towards the hut.

"Bring your bundle of clothes in with you," he bid her as she was following.

"I shan't want them any more," was her prompt answer.

The old man turned and looked searchingly at the child, whose dark eyes were sparkling in delighted anticipation of what she was going to see inside. "She is certainly not wanting in intelligence," he murmured to himself. "And why shall you not want them any more?" he asked aloud.

"Because I want to go about like the goats with their thin light legs."

"Well, you can do so if you like," said her grandfather, "but bring the things in, we must put them in the cupboard."

Heidi did as she was told. The old man now opened the door and Heidi stepped inside after him; she found herself in a good-sized room, which covered the whole ground floor of the hut. A table and a chair were the only furniture; in one corner stood the grandfather's bed, in another was the hearth with a large kettle hanging above it; and on the further side was a large door in the wall—this was the cupboard. The grandfather opened it; inside were his clothes, some hanging up, others, a couple of shirts, and some socks and handkerchiefs, lying on a shelf; on a second shelf were some plates and cups and glasses, and on a higher one still, a round loaf, smoked meat, and cheese, for everything that Alm-Uncle needed for his food and clothing was kept in this cupboard. Heidi, as soon as it was opened, ran quickly forward and thrust in her bundle of clothes, as far back behind her grandfather's things as possible, so that they might not easily be found again. She then looked carefully round the room, and asked, "Where am I to sleep, grandfather?"

"Wherever you like," he answered.

Heidi was delighted, and began at once to examine all the nooks and corners to find out where it would be pleasantest to sleep. In the corner near her grandfather's bed she saw a short ladder against the wall; up she climbed and found herself in the hayloft. There lay a large heap of fresh sweet-smelling hay, while through a round window in the wall she could see right down the valley.

"I shall sleep up here, grandfather," she called down to him, "It's lovely, up here. Come up and see how lovely it is!"

"Oh, I know all about it," he called up in answer.

"I am getting the bed ready now," she called down again, as she went busily to and fro at her work, "but I shall want you to bring me up a sheet; you can't have a bed without a sheet, you want it to lie upon."

"All right," said the grandfather, and presently he went to the cupboard, and after rummaging about inside for a few minutes he drew out a long, coarse piece of stuff, which was all he had to do duty for a sheet. He carried it up to the loft, where he found Heidi had already made quite a nice bed. She had put an extra heap of hay at one end for a pillow, and had so arranged it that, when in bed, she would be able to see comfortably out through the round window.

"That is capital," said her grandfather; "now we must put on the sheet, but wait a moment first," and he went and fetched another large bundle of hay to make the bed thicker, so that the child should not feel the hard floor under her—"there, now bring it here." Heidi had got hold of the sheet, but it was almost too heavy for her to carry; this was a good thing, however, as the close thick stuff would prevent the sharp stalks of the hay running through and pricking her. The two together now spread the sheet over the bed, and where it was too long or too broad, Heidi quickly tucked it in under the hay. It looked now as tidy and comfortable a bed as you could wish for, and Heidi stood gazing thoughtfully at her handiwork.

"We have forgotten something now, grandfather," she said after a short silence.

"What's that?" he asked.

"A coverlid; when you get into bed, you have to creep in between the sheets and the coverlid."

"Oh, that's the way, is it? But suppose I have not got a coverlid?" said the old man.

"Well, never mind, grandfather," said Heidi in a consoling tone of voice, "I can take some more hay to put over me," and she was turning quickly to fetch another armful from the heap, when her grandfather stopped her. "Wait a moment," he said, and he climbed down the ladder again and went towards his bed. He returned to the loft with a large, thick sack, made of flax, which he threw down, exclaiming, "There, that is better than hay, is it not?"

Heidi began tugging away at the sack with all her little might, in her efforts to get it smooth and straight, but her small hands were not fitted for so heavy a job. Her grandfather came to her assistance, and when they had got it tidily spread over the bed, it all looked so nice and warm and comfortable that Heidi stood gazing at it in delight. "That is a splendid coverlid," she said, "and the bed looks lovely altogether! I wish it was night, so that I might get inside it at once."

"I think we might have something to eat first," said the grandfather, "what do you think?"

Heidi in the excitement of bed-making had forgotten everything else; but now when she began to think about food she felt terribly hungry, for she had had nothing to eat since the piece of bread and little cup of thin coffee that had been her breakfast early that morning before starting on her long, hot journey. So she answered without hesitation, "Yes, I think so too."

"Let us go down then, as we both think alike," said the old man, and he followed the child down the ladder. Then he went up to the hearth, pushed the big kettle aside, and drew forward the little one that was hanging on the chain, and seating himself on the round-topped, three-legged stool before the fire, blew it up into a clear bright flame. The kettle soon began to boil, and meanwhile the old man held a large piece of cheese on a long iron fork over the fire, turning it round and round till it was toasted a nice golden yellow colour on each side. Heidi watched all that was going on with eager curiosity. Suddenly some new idea seemed to come into her head, for she turned and ran to the cupboard, and then began going busily backwards and forwards. Presently the grandfather got up and came to the table with a jug and the cheese, and there he saw it already tidily laid with the round loaf and two plates and two knives each in its right place; for Heidi had taken exact note that morning of all that there was in the cupboard, and she knew which things would be wanted for their meal.

"Ah, that's right," said the grandfather, "I am glad to see that you have some ideas of your own," and as he spoke he laid the toasted cheese on a layer of bread, "but there is still something missing."

Heidi looked at the jug that was steaming away invitingly, and ran quickly back to the cupboard. At first she could only see a small bowl left on the shelf, but she was not long in perplexity, for a moment later she caught sight of two glasses further back, and without an instant's loss of time she returned with these and the bowl and put them down on the table.

"Good, I see you know how to set about things; but what will you do for a seat?" The grandfather himself was sitting on the only chair in the room. Heidi flew to the hearth, and dragging the three-legged stool up to the table, sat herself down upon it.

"Well, you have managed to find a seat for yourself, I see, only rather a low one I am afraid," said the grandfather, "but you would not be tall enough to reach the table even if you sat in my chair; the first thing now, however, is to have something to eat, so come along."

With that he stood up, filled the bowl with milk, and placing it on the chair, pushed it in front of Heidi on her little three-legged stool, so that she now had a table to herself.

Then he brought her a large slice of bread and a piece of the golden cheese, and told her to eat. After which he went and sat down on the corner of the table and began his own meal. Heidi lifted the bowl with both hands and drank without pause till it was empty, for the thirst of all her long hot journey had returned upon her. Then she drew a deep breath—in the eagerness of her thirst she had not stopped to breathe—and put down the bowl.

"Was the milk nice?" asked her grandfather.

"I never drank any so good before," answered Heidi.

"Then you must have some more," and the old man filled her bowl again to the brim and set it before the child, who was now hungrily beginning her bread having first spread it with the cheese, which after being toasted was soft as butter; the two together tasted deliciously, and the child looked the picture of content as she sat eating, and at intervals taking further draughts of milk. The meal being over, the grandfather went outside to put the goat-shed in order, and Heidi watched with interest while he first swept it out, and then put fresh straw for the goats to sleep upon. Then he went to the little well-shed, and there he cut some long round sticks, and a small round board; in this he bored some holes and stuck the sticks into them, and there, as if made by magic, was a three-legged stool just like her grandfather's, only higher. Heidi stood and looked at it, speechless with astonishment.

"What do you think that is?" asked her grandfather.

"It's my stool, I know, because it is such a high one; and it was made all of a minute," said the child, still lost in wonder and admiration.

"She understands what she sees, her eyes are in the right place," remarked the grandfather to himself, as he continued his way round the hut, knocking in a nail here and there, or making fast some part of the door, and so with hammer and nails and pieces of wood going from spot to spot, mending or clearing away wherever work of the kind was needed. Heidi followed him step by step, her eyes attentively taking in all that he did, and everything that she saw was a fresh source of pleasure to her.

And so the time passed happily on till evening. Then the wind began to roar louder than ever through the old fir trees; Heidi listened with delight to the sound, and it filled her heart so full of gladness that she skipped and danced round the old trees, as if some unheard of joy had come to her. The grandfather stood and watched her from the shed.

Suddenly a shrill whistle was heard. Heidi paused in her dancing, and the grandfather came out. Down from the heights above the goats came springing one after another, with Peter in their midst. Heidi sprang forward with a cry of joy and rushed among the flock, greeting first one and then another of her old friends of the morning. As they neared the hut the goats stood still, and then two of their number, two beautiful slender animals, one white and one brown, ran forward to where the grandfather was standing and began licking his hands, for he was holding a little salt which he always had ready for his goats on their return home. Peter disappeared with the remainder of his flock. Heidi tenderly stroked the two goats in turn, running first to one side of them and then the other, and jumping about in her glee at the pretty little animals. "Are they ours, grandfather? Are they both ours? Are you going to put them in the shed? Will they always stay with us?"

Heidi's questions came tumbling out one after the other, so that her grandfather had only time to answer each of them with "Yes, yes." When the goats had finished licking up the salt her grandfather told her to go and fetch her bowl and the bread.

Heidi obeyed and was soon back again. The grandfather milked the white goat and filled her basin, and then breaking off a piece of bread, "Now eat your supper," he said, "and then go up to bed. Cousin Dete left another little bundle for you with a nightgown and other small things in it, which you will find at the bottom of the cupboard if you want them. I must go and shut up the goats, so be off and sleep well."

"Good night, grandfather! Good night. What are their names, grandfather, what are their names?" she called out as she ran after his retreating figure and the goats.

"The white one is named Little Swan, and the brown one Little Bear," he answered.

"Good night, Little Swan, good night, Little Bear!" she called again at the top of her voice, for they were already inside the shed. Then she sat down on the seat and began to eat and drink, but the wind was so strong that it almost blew her away; so she made haste and finished her supper and then went indoors and climbed up to her bed, where she was soon lying as sweetly and soundly asleep as any young princess on her couch of silk.

Not long after, and while it was still twilight, the grandfather also went to bed, for he was up every morning at sunrise, and the sun came climbing up over the mountains at a very early hour during these summer months. The wind grew so tempestuous during the night, and blew in such gusts against the walls, that the hut trembled and the old beams groaned and creaked. It came howling and wailing down the chimney like voices of those in pain, and it raged with such fury among the old fir trees that here and there a branch was snapped and fell. In the middle of the night the old man got up. "The child will be frightened," he murmured half aloud. He mounted the ladder and went and stood by the child's bed.

Outside the moon was struggling with the dark, fast-driving clouds, which at one moment left it clear and shining, and the next swept over it, and all again was dark. Just now the moonlight was falling through the round window straight on to Heidi's bed. She lay under the heavy coverlid, her cheeks rosy with sleep, her head peacefully resting on her little round arm, and with a happy expression on her baby face as if dreaming of something pleasant. The old man stood looking down on the sleeping child until the moon again disappeared behind the clouds and he could see no more, then he went back to bed.

Chapter 3

Out With The Goats

Heidi was awakened early the next morning by a loud whistle; the sun was shining through the round window and falling in golden rays on her bed and on the large heap of hay, and as she opened her eyes everything in the loft seemed gleaming with gold. She looked around her in astonishment and could not imagine for a while where she was. But her grandfather's deep voice was now heard outside, and then Heidi began to recall all that had happened: how she had come away from her former home and was now on the mountain with her grandfather instead of with old Ursula. The latter was nearly stone deaf and always felt cold, so that she sat all day either by the hearth in the kitchen or by the sitting-room stove, and Heidi had been obliged to stay close to her, for the old woman was so deaf that she could not tell where the child was if out of her sight. And Heidi, shut up within the four walls, had often longed to be out of doors. So she felt very happy this morning as she woke up in her new home and remembered all the many new things that she had seen the day before and which she would see again that day, and above all she thought with delight of the two dear goats. Heidi jumped quickly out of bed and a very few minutes sufficed her to put on the clothes which she had taken off the night before, for there were not many of them. Then she climbed down the ladder and ran outside the hut. There stood Peter already with his flock of goats, and the grandfather was just bringing his two out of the shed to join the others. Heidi ran forward to wish good-morning to him and the goats.

"Do you want to go with them on to the mountain?" asked her grandfather. Nothing could have pleased Heidi better, and she jumped for joy in answer.

"But you must first wash and make yourself tidy. The sun that shines so brightly overhead will else laugh at you for being dirty; see, I have put everything ready for you," and her grandfather pointed as he spoke to a large tub full of water, which stood in the sun before the door. Heidi ran to it and began splashing and rubbing, till she quite glistened with cleanliness. The grandfather meanwhile went inside the hut, calling to Peter to follow him and bring in his wallet. Peter obeyed with astonishment, and laid down the little bag which held his meagre dinner.

"Open it," said the old man, and inside it he put a large piece of bread and an equally large piece of cheese, which made Peter open his eyes, for each was twice the size of the two portions which he had for his own dinner.

"There, now there is only the little bowl to add," continued the grandfather, "for the child cannot drink her milk as you do from the goat; she is not accustomed to that. You must milk two bowlfuls for her when she has her dinner, for she is going with you and will remain with you till you return this evening; but take care she does not fall over any of the rocks, do you hear?"

Heidi now came running in. "Will the sun laugh at me now, grandfather?" she asked anxiously. Her grandfather had left a coarse towel hanging up for her near the tub, and with this she had so thoroughly scrubbed her face, arms, and neck, for fear of the sun, that as she stood there she was as red all over as a lobster. He gave a little laugh.

"No, there is nothing for him to laugh at now," he assured her. "But I tell you what—when you come home this evening, you will have to get right into the tub, like a fish, for if you run about like the goats you will get your feet dirty. Now you can be off."

She started joyfully for the mountain. During the night the wind had blown away all the clouds; the dark blue sky was spreading overhead, and in its midst was the bright sun shining down on the green slopes of the mountain, where the flowers opened their little blue and yellow cups, and looked up to him smiling. Heidi went running hither and thither and shouting with delight, for here were whole patches of delicate red primroses, and there the blue gleam of the lovely gentian, while above them all laughed and nodded the tender-leaved golden cistus. Enchanted with all this waving field of brightly-coloured flowers, Heidi forgot even Peter and the goats. She ran on in front and then off to the side, tempted first one way and then the other, as she caught sight of some bright spot of glowing red or yellow. And all the while she was plucking whole handfuls of the flowers which she put into her little apron, for she wanted to take them all home and stick them in the hay, so that she might make her bedroom look just like the meadows outside. Peter had therefore to be on the alert, and his round eyes, which did not move very quickly, had more work than they could well manage, for the goats were as lively as Heidi; they ran in all directions, and Peter had to follow whistling and calling and swinging his stick to get all the runaways together again.

"Where have you got to now, Heidi?" he called out somewhat crossly.

"Here," called back a voice from somewhere. Peter could see no one, for Heidi was seated on the ground at the foot of a small hill thickly overgrown with sweet smelling prunella; the whole air seemed filled with its fragrance, and Heidi thought she had never smelt anything so delicious. She sat surrounded by the flowers, drawing in deep breaths of the scented air.

"Come along here!" called Peter again. "You are not to fall over the rocks, your grandfather gave orders that you were not to do so."

"Where are the rocks?" asked Heidi, answering him back. But she did not move from her seat, for the scent of the flowers seemed sweeter to her with every breath of wind that wafted it towards her.

"Up above, right up above. We have a long way to go yet, so come along! And on the topmost peak of all the old bird of prey sits and croaks."

That did it. Heidi immediately sprang to her feet and ran up to Peter with her apron full of flowers.

"You have got enough now," said the boy as they began climbing up again together. "You will stay here forever if you go on picking, and if you gather all the flowers now there will be none for tomorrow."

This last argument seemed a convincing one to Heidi, and moreover her apron was already so full that there was hardly room for another flower, and it would never do to leave nothing to pick for another day. So she now kept with Peter, and the goats also became more orderly in their behaviour, for they were beginning to smell the plants they loved that grew on the higher slopes and clambered up now without pause in their anxiety to reach them. The spot where Peter generally halted for his goats to pasture and where he took up his quarters for the day lay at the foot of the high rocks, which were covered for some distance up by bushes and fir trees, beyond which rose their bare and rugged summits. On one side of the mountain the rock was split into deep clefts, and the grandfather had reason to warn Peter of danger. Having climbed as far as the halting-place, Peter unslung his wallet and put it carefully in a little hollow of the ground, for he knew what the wind was like up there and did not want to see his precious belongings sent rolling down the mountain by a sudden gust. Then be threw himself at full length on the warm ground, for he was tired after all his exertions.

Heidi meanwhile had unfastened her apron and rolling it carefully round the flowers laid it beside Peter's wallet inside the hollow; she then sat down beside his outstretched figure and looked about her. The valley lay far below bathed in the morning sun. In front of her rose a broad snow-field, high against the dark-blue sky, while to the left was a huge pile of rocks on either side of which a bare lofty peak, that seemed to pierce the blue, looked frowningly down upon, her. The child sat without moving, her eyes taking in the whole scene, and all around was a great stillness, only broken by soft, light puffs of wind that swayed the light bells of the blue flowers, and the shining gold heads of the cistus, and set them nodding merrily on their slender stems. Peter had fallen asleep after his fatigue and the goats were climbing about among the bushes overhead. Heidi had never felt so happy in her life before. She drank in the golden sunlight, the fresh air, the sweet smell of the flowers, and wished for nothing better than to remain there forever. So the time went on, while to Heidi, who had so often looked up from the valley at the mountains above, these seemed now to have faces, and to be looking down at her like old friends. Suddenly she heard a loud harsh cry overhead and lifting her eyes she saw a bird, larger than any she had ever seen before, with great, spreading wings, wheeling round and round in wide circles, and uttering a piercing, croaking kind of sound above her.

"Peter, Peter, wake up!" called out Heidi. "See, the great bird is there—look, look!"

Peter got up on hearing her call, and together they sat and watched the bird, which rose higher and higher in the blue air till it disappeared behind the grey mountain-tops.

"Where has it gone to?" asked Heidi, who had followed the bird's movements with intense interest.

"Home to its nest," said Peter.

"Is his home right up there? Oh, how nice to be up so high! Why does he make that noise?"

"Because he can't help it," explained Peter.

"Let us climb up there and see where his nest is," proposed Heidi.

"Oh! Oh! Oh!" exclaimed Peter, his disapproval of Heidi's suggestion becoming more marked with each ejaculation, "why even the goats cannot climb as high as that, besides didn't Uncle say that you were not to fall over the rocks?"

Peter now began suddenly whistling and calling in such a loud manner that Heidi could not think what was happening; but the goats evidently understood his voice, for one after the other they came springing down the rocks until they were all assembled on the green plateau, some continuing to nibble at the juicy stems, others skipping about here and there or pushing at each other with their horns for pastime.

Heidi jumped up and ran in and out among them, for it was new to her to see the goats playing together like this and her delight was beyond words as she joined in their frolics; she made personal acquaintance with them all in turn, for they were like separate individuals to her, each single goat having a particular way of behaviour of its own. Meanwhile Peter had taken the wallet out of the hollow and placed the pieces of bread and cheese on the ground in the shape of a square, the larger two on Heidi's side and the smaller on his own, for he knew exactly which were hers and which his. Then he took the little bowl and milked some delicious fresh milk into it from the white goat, and afterwards set the bowl in the middle of the square. Now he called Heidi to come, but she wanted more calling than the goats, for the child was so excited and amused at the capers and lively games of her new playfellows that she saw and heard nothing else. But Peter knew how to make himself heard, for he shouted till the very rocks above echoed his voice, and at last Heidi appeared, and when she saw the inviting repast spread out upon the ground she went skipping round it for joy.

"Leave off jumping about, it is time for dinner," said Peter; "sit down now and begin."

Heidi sat down. "Is the milk for me?" she asked, giving another look of delight at the beautifully arranged square with the bowl as a chief ornament in the centre.

"Yes," replied Peter, "and the two large pieces of bread and cheese are yours also, and when you have drunk up that milk, you are to have another bowlful from the white goat, and then it will be my turn."

"And which do you get your milk from?" inquired Heidi.

"From my own goat, the piebald one. But go on now with your dinner," said Peter, again reminding her it was time to eat. Heidi now took up the bowl and drank her milk, and as soon as she had put it down empty Peter rose and filled it again for her. Then she broke off a piece of her bread and held out the remainder, which was still larger than Peter's own piece, together with the whole big slice of cheese to her companion, saying, "You can have that, I have plenty."

Peter looked at Heidi, unable to speak for astonishment, for never in all his life could he have said and done like that with anything he had. He hesitated a moment, for he could not believe that Heidi was in earnest; but the latter kept on holding out the bread and cheese, and as Peter still did not take it, she laid it down on his knees. He saw then that she really meant it; he seized the food, nodded his thanks and acceptance of her present, and then made a more splendid meal than he had known ever since he was a goat-herd. Heidi the while still continued to watch the goats. "Tell me all their names," she said.

Peter knew these by heart, for having very little else to carry in his head he had no difficulty in remembering them. So he began, telling Heidi the name of each goat in turn as he pointed it out to her. Heidi listened with great attention, and it was not long before she could herself distinguish the goats from one another and could call each by name, for every goat had its own peculiarities which could not easily be mistaken; only one had to watch them closely, and this Heidi did. There was the great Turk with his big horns, who was always wanting to butt the others, so that most of them ran away when they saw him coming and would have nothing to do with their rough companion. Only Greenfinch, the slender nimble little goat, was brave enough to face him, and would make a rush at him, three or four times in succession, with such agility and dexterity, that the great Turk often stood still quite astounded not venturing to attack her again, for Greenfinch was fronting him, prepared for more warlike action, and her horns were sharp. Then there was little White Snowflake, who bleated in such a plaintive and beseeching manner that Heidi already had several times run to it and taken its head in her hands to comfort it. Just at this moment the pleading young cry was heard again, and Heidi jumped up running and, putting her arms round the little creature's neck, asked in a sympathetic voice, "What is it, little Snowflake? Why do you call like that as if in trouble?" The goat pressed closer to Heidi in a confiding way and left off bleating. Peter called out from where he was sitting—for he had not yet got to the end of his bread and cheese, "She cries like that because the old goat is not with her; she was sold at Mayenfeld the day before yesterday, and so will not come up the mountain any more."

"Who is the old goat?" called Heidi back.

"Why, her mother, of course," was the answer.

"Where is the grandmother?" called Heidi again.

"She has none."

"And the grandfather?"

"She has none."

"Oh, you poor little Snowflake!" exclaimed Heidi, clasping the animal gently to her, "but do not cry like that any more; see now, I shall come up here with you every day, so that you will not be alone any more, and if you want anything you have only to come to me."

The young animal rubbed its head contentedly against Heidi's shoulder, and no longer gave such plaintive bleats. Peter now having finished his meal joined Heidi and the goats, Heidi having by this time found out a great many things about these. She had decided that by far the handsomest and best-behaved of the goats were undoubtedly the two belonging to her grandfather; they carried themselves with a certain air of distinction and generally went their own way, and as to the great Turk they treated him with indifference and contempt.

The goats were now beginning to climb the rocks again, each seeking for the plants it liked in its own fashion, some jumping over everything they met till they found what they wanted, others going more carefully and cropping all the nice leaves by the way, the Turk still now and then giving the others a poke with his horns. Little Swan and Little Bear clambered lightly up and never failed to find the best bushes, and then they would stand gracefully poised on their pretty legs, delicately nibbling at the leaves. Heidi stood with her hands behind her back, carefully noting all they did.

"Peter," she said to the boy who had again thrown himself down on the ground, "the prettiest of all the goats are Little Swan and Little Bear."

"Yes, I know they are," was the answer. "Alm-Uncle brushes them down and washes them and gives them salt, and he has the nicest shed for them."

All of a sudden Peter leaped to his feet and ran hastily after the goats. Heidi followed him as fast as she could, for she was too eager to know what had happened to stay behind. Peter dashed through the middle of the flock towards that side of the mountain where the rocks fell perpendicularly to a great depth below, and where any thoughtless goat, if it went too near, might fall over and break all its legs. He had caught sight of the inquisitive Greenfinch taking leaps in that direction, and he was only just in time, for the animal had already sprung to the edge of the abyss. All Peter could do was to throw himself down and seize one of her hind legs. Greenfinch, thus taken by surprise, began bleating furiously, angry at being held so fast and prevented from continuing her voyage of discovery. She struggled to get loose, and endeavored so obstinately to leap forward that Peter shouted to Heidi to come and help him, for he could not get up and was afraid of pulling out the goat's leg altogether.

Heidi had already run up and she saw at once the danger both Peter and the animal were in. She quickly gathered a bunch of sweet-smelling leaves, and then, holding them under Greenfinch's nose, said coaxingly, "Come, come, Greenfinch, you must not be naughty! Look, you might fall down there and break your leg, and that would give you dreadful pain!"

The young animal turned quickly, and began contentedly eating the leaves out of Heidi's hand. Meanwhile Peter got on to his feet again and took hold of Greenfinch by the band round her neck from which her bell was hung, and Heidi taking hold of her in the same way on the other side, they led the wanderer back to the rest of the flock that had remained peacefully feeding. Peter, now he had his goat in safety, lifted his stick in order to give her a good beating as punishment, and Greenfinch seeing what was coming shrank back in fear. But Heidi cried out, "No, no, Peter, you must not strike her; see how frightened she is!"

"She deserves it," growled Peter, and again lifted his stick. Then Heidi flung herself against him and cried indignantly, "You have no right to touch her, it will hurt her, let her alone!"

Peter looked with surprise at the commanding little figure, whose dark eyes were flashing, and reluctantly he let his stick drop. "Well I will let her off if you will give me some more of your cheese tomorrow," he said, for he was determined to have something to make up to him for his fright.

"You shall have it all, tomorrow and every day, I do not want it," replied Heidi, giving ready consent to his demand. "And I will give you bread as well, a large piece like you had today; but then you must promise never to beat Greenfinch, or Snowflake, or any of the goats."

"All right," said Peter, "I don't care," which meant that he would agree to the bargain. He now let go of Greenfinch, who joyfully sprang to join her companions.

And thus imperceptibly the day had crept on to its close, and now the sun was on the point of sinking out of sight behind the high mountains. Heidi was again sitting on the ground, silently gazing at the blue bell-shaped flowers, as they glistened in the evening sun, for a golden light lay on the grass and flowers, and the rocks above were beginning to shine and glow. All at once she sprang to her feet, "Peter! Peter! Everything is on fire! All the rocks are burning, and the great snow mountain and the sky! O look, look! The high rock up there is red with flame! O the beautiful, fiery snow! Stand up, Peter! See, the fire has reached the great bird's nest! Look at the rocks! Look at the fir trees! Everything, everything is on fire!"

"It is always like that," said Peter composedly, continuing to peel his stick; "but it is not really fire."

"What is it then?" cried Heidi, as she ran backwards and forwards to look first one side and then the other, for she felt she could not have enough of such a beautiful sight. "What is it, Peter, what is it?" she repeated.

"It gets like that of itself," explained Peter.

"Look, look!" cried Heidi in fresh excitement, "now they have turned all rose colour! Look at that one covered with snow, and that with the high, pointed rocks! What do you call them?"

"Mountains have not any names," he answered.

"O how beautiful, look at the crimson snow! And up there on the rocks there are ever so many roses! Oh! now they are turning grey! Oh! Oh! Now all the colour has died away! it's all gone, Peter." And Heidi sat down on the ground looking as full of distress as if everything had really come to an end.

"It will come again tomorrow," said Peter. "Get up, we must go home now." He whistled to his goats and together they all started on their homeward way.

"Is it like that every day, shall we see it every day when we bring the goats up here?" asked Heidi, as she clambered down the mountain at Peter's side; she waited eagerly for his answer, hoping that he would tell her it was so.

"It is like that most days," he replied.

"But will it be like that tomorrow for certain?" Heidi persisted.

"Yes, yes, tomorrow for certain," Peter assured her in answer.

Heidi now felt quite happy again, and her little brain was so full of new impressions and new thoughts that she did not speak any more until they had reached the hut. The grandfather was sitting under the fir trees, where he had also put up a seat, waiting as usual for his goats which returned down the mountain on this side.

Heidi ran up to him followed by the white and brown goats, for they knew their own master and stall. Peter called out after her, "Come with me again tomorrow! Good night!" For he was anxious for more than one reason that Heidi should go with him the next day.

Heidi ran back quickly and gave Peter her hand, promising to go with him, and then making her way through the goats she once more clasped Snowflake round the neck, saying in a gentle soothing voice, "Sleep well, Snowflake, and remember that I shall be with you again tomorrow, so you must not bleat so sadly any more." Snowflake gave her a friendly and grateful look, and then went leaping joyfully after the other goats.

Heidi returned to the fir-trees. "O grandfather," she cried, even before she had come up to him, "it was so beautiful. The fire, and the roses on the rocks, and the blue and yellow flowers, and look what I have brought you!" And opening the apron that held her flowers she shook them all out at her grandfather's feet. But the poor flowers, how changed they were! Heidi hardly knew them again. They looked like dry bits of hay, not a single little flower cup stood open. "O grandfather, what is the matter with them?" exclaimed Heidi in shocked surprise, "they were not like that this morning, why do they look so now?"

"They like to stand out there in the sun and not to be shut up in an apron," said her grandfather.

"Then I will never gather any more. But, grandfather, why did the great bird go on croaking so?" she continued in an eager tone of inquiry.

"Go along now and get into your bath while I go and get some milk; when we are together at supper I will tell you all about it."

Heidi obeyed, and when later she was sitting on her high stool before her milk bowl with her grandfather beside her, she repeated her question, "Why does the great bird go on croaking and screaming down at us, grandfather?"

"He is mocking at the people who live down below in the villages, because they all go huddling and gossiping together, and encourage one another in evil talking and deeds. He calls out, 'If you would separate and each go your own way and come up here and live on a height as I do, it would be better for you!'" There was almost a wildness in the old man's voice as he spoke, so that Heidi seemed to hear the croaking of the bird again even more distinctly.

"Why haven't the mountains any names?" Heidi went on.

"They have names," answered her grandfather, "and if you can describe one of them to me that I know I will tell you what it is called."

Heidi then described to him the rocky mountain with the two high peaks so exactly that the grandfather was delighted. "Just so, I know it," and he told her its name. "Did you see any other?"

Then Heidi told him of the mountain with the great snow-field, and how it had been on fire, and had turned rosy-red and then all of a sudden had grown quite pale again and all the colour had disappeared.

"I know that one too," he said, giving her its name. "So you enjoyed being out with the goats?"

Then Heidi went on to give him an account of the whole day, and of how delightful it had all been, and particularly described the fire that had burst out everywhere in the evening. And then nothing would do but her grandfather must tell how it came, for Peter knew nothing about it.

The grandfather explained to her that it was the sun that did it. "When he says good night to the mountains he throws his most beautiful colours over them, so that they may not forget him before he comes again the next day."

Heidi was delighted with this explanation, and could hardly bear to wait for another day to come that she might once more climb up with the goats and see how the sun bid good night to the mountains. But she had to go to bed first, and all night she slept soundly on her bed of hay, dreaming of nothing but of shining mountains with red roses all over them, among which happy little Snowflake went leaping in and out.

Chapter 4

The Visit To Grandmother

The next morning the sun came out early as bright as ever, and then Peter appeared with the goats, and again the two children climbed up together to the high meadows, and so it went on day after day till Heidi, passing her life thus among the grass and flowers, was burnt brown with the sun, and grew so strong and healthy that nothing ever ailed her. She was happy too, and lived from day to day as free and lighthearted as the little birds that make their home among the green forest trees. Then the autumn came, and the wind blew louder and stronger, and the grandfather would say sometimes, "Today you must stay at home, Heidi; a sudden gust of the wind would blow a little thing like you over the rocks into the valley below in a moment."

Whenever Peter heard that he must go alone he looked very unhappy, for he saw nothing but mishaps of all kinds ahead, and did not know how he should bear the long dull day without Heidi. Then, too, there was the good meal he would miss, and besides that the goats on these days were so naughty and obstinate that he had twice the usual trouble with them, for they had grown so accustomed to Heidi's presence that they would run in every direction and refuse to go on unless she was with them. Heidi was never unhappy, for wherever she was she found something to interest or amuse her. She liked best, it is true, to go out with Peter up to the flowers and the great bird, where there was so much to be seen, and so many experiences to go through among the goats with their different characters; but she also found her grandfather's hammering and sawing and carpentering very entertaining, and if it should chance to be the day when the large round goat's-milk cheese was made she enjoyed beyond measure looking on at this wonderful performance, and watching her grandfather, as with sleeves rolled back, he stirred the great cauldron with his bare arms. The thing which attracted her most, however, was the waving and roaring of the three old fir trees on these windy days. She would run away repeatedly from whatever she might be doing, to listen to them, for nothing seemed so strange and wonderful to her as the deep mysterious sound in the tops of the trees. She would stand underneath them and look up, unable to tear herself away, looking and listening while they bowed and swayed and roared as the mighty wind rushed through them. There was no longer now the warm bright sun that had shone all through the summer, so Heidi went to the cupboard and got out her shoes and stockings and dress, for it was growing colder every day, and when Heidi stood under the fir trees the wind blew through her as if she was a thin little leaf, but still she felt she could not stay indoors when she heard the branches waving outside.

Then it grew very cold, and Peter would come up early in the morning blowing on his fingers to keep them warm. But he soon left off coming, for one night there was a heavy fall of snow and the next morning the whole mountain was covered with it, and not a single little green leaf was to be seen anywhere upon it. There was no Peter that day, and Heidi stood at the little window looking out in wonderment, for the snow was beginning again, and the thick flakes kept falling till the snow was up to the window, and still they continued to fall, and the snow grew higher, so that at last the window could not be opened, and she and her grandfather were shut up fast within the hut. Heidi thought this was great fun and ran from one window to the other to see what would happen next, and whether the snow was going to cover up the whole hut, so that they would have to light a lamp although it was broad daylight. But things did not get as bad as that, and the next day, the snow having ceased, the grandfather went out and shovelled away the snow round the house, and threw it into such great heaps that they looked like mountains standing at intervals on either side the hut. And now the windows and door could be opened, and it was well it was so, for as Heidi and her grandfather were sitting one afternoon on their three-legged stools before the fire there came a great thump at the door followed by several others, and then the door opened. It was Peter, who had made all that noise knocking the snow off his shoes; he was still white all over with it, for he had had to fight his way through deep snowdrifts, and large lumps of snow that had frozen upon him still clung to his clothes. He had been determined, however, not to be beaten and to climb up to the hut, for it was a week now since he had seen Heidi.

"Good evening," he said as he came in; then he went and placed himself as near the fire as he could without saying another word, but his whole face was beaming with pleasure at finding himself there. Heidi looked on in astonishment, for Peter was beginning to thaw all over with the warmth, so that he had the appearance of a trickling waterfall.

"Well, General, and how goes it with you?" said the grandfather, "now that you have lost your army you will have to turn to your pen and pencil."

"Why must he turn to his pen and pencil?" asked Heidi immediately, full of curiosity.

"During the winter he must go to school," explained her grandfather, "and learn how to read and write; it's a bit hard, although useful sometimes afterwards. Am I not right, General?"

"Yes, indeed," assented Peter.

Heidi's interest was now thoroughly awakened, and she had so many questions to put to Peter about all that was to be done and seen and heard at school, and the conversation took so long that Peter had time to get thoroughly dry. Peter had always great difficulty in putting his thoughts into words, and he found his share of the talk doubly difficult today, for by the time he had an answer ready to one of Heidi's questions she had already put two or three more to him, and generally such as required a whole long sentence in reply.

The grandfather sat without speaking during this conversation, only now and then a twitch of amusement at the corners of his mouth showed that he was listening.

"Well, now, General, you have been under fire for some time and must want some refreshment, come and join us," he said at last, and as he spoke he rose and went to fetch the supper out of the cupboard, and Heidi pushed the stools to the table. There was also now a bench fastened against the wall, for as he was no longer alone the grandfather had put up seats of various kinds here and there, long enough to hold two persons, for Heidi had a way of always keeping close to her grandfather whether he was walking, sitting or standing. So there was comfortable place for them all three, and Peter opened his round eyes very wide when he saw what a large piece of meat Alm-Uncle gave him on his thick slice of bread. It was a long time since Peter had had anything so nice to eat. As soon as the pleasant meal was over Peter began to get ready for returning home, for it was already growing dark. He had said his "good night" and his thanks, and was just going out, when he turned again and said, "I shall come again next Sunday, this day week, and Grandmother sent word that she would like you to come and see her one day."

It was quite a new idea to Heidi that she should go and pay anybody a visit, and she could not get it out of her head; so the first thing she said to her grandfather the next day was, "I must go down to see the grandmother today; she will be expecting me."

"The snow is too deep," answered the grandfather, trying to put her off. But Heidi had made up her mind to go, since the grandmother had sent her that message. She stuck to her intention and not a day passed but what in the course of it she said five or six times to her grandfather, "I must certainly go today, the grandmother will be waiting for me."

On the fourth day, when with every step one took the ground crackled with frost and the whole vast field of snow was hard as ice, Heidi was sitting on her high stool at dinner with the bright sun shining in upon her through the window, and again repeated her little speech, "I must certainly go down to see the grandmother today, or else I shall keep her waiting too long."

The grandfather rose from table, climbed up to the hay-loft and brought down the thick sack that was Heidi's coverlid, and said, "Come along then!" The child skipped out gleefully after him into the glittering world of snow.

The old fir trees were standing now quite silent, their branches covered with the white snow, and they looked so lovely as they glittered and sparkled in the sunlight that Heidi jumped for joy at the sight and kept on calling out, "Come here, come here, grandfather! The fir trees are all silver and gold!" The grandfather had gone into the shed and he now came out dragging a large hand-sleigh along with him; inside it was a low seat, and the sleigh could be pushed forward and guided by the feet of the one who sat upon it with the help of a pole that was fastened to the side. After he had been taken round the fir trees by Heidi that he might see their beauty from all sides, he got into the sleigh and lifted the child on to his lap; then he wrapped her up in the sack, that she might keep nice and warm, and put his left arm closely round her, for it was necessary to hold her tight during the coming journey. He now grasped the pole with his right hand and gave the sleigh a push forward with his two feet. The sleigh shot down the mountain side with such rapidity that Heidi thought they were flying through the air like a bird, and shouted aloud with delight. Suddenly they came to a standstill, and there they were at Peter's hut. Her grandfather lifted her out and unwrapped her. "There you are, now go in, and when it begins to grow dark you must start on your way home again." Then he left her and went up the mountain, pulling his sleigh after him.

Heidi opened the door of the hut and stepped into a tiny room that looked very dark, with a fireplace and a few dishes on a wooden shelf; this was the little kitchen. She opened another door, and now found herself in another small room, for the place was not a herdsman's hut like her grandfather's, with one large room on the ground floor and a hay-loft above, but a very old cottage, where everything was narrow and poor and shabby. A table was close to the door, and as Heidi stepped in she saw a woman sitting at it, putting a patch on a waistcoat which Heidi recognised at once as Peter's. In the corner sat an old woman, bent with age, spinning. Heidi was quite sure this was the grandmother, so she went up to the spinning-wheel and said, "Good day, Grandmother, I have come at last; did you think I was a long time coming?"

The woman raised her head and felt for the hand that the child held out to her, and when she found it, she passed her own over it thoughtfully for a few seconds, and then said, "Are you the child who lives up with Alm-Uncle, are you Heidi?"

"Yes, yes," answered Heidi, "I have just come down in the sleigh with grandfather."

"Is it possible! Why your hands are quite warm! Brigitta, did Alm-Uncle come himself with the child?"

Peter's mother had left her work and risen from the table and now stood looking at Heidi with curiosity, scanning her from head to foot. "I do not know, mother, whether Uncle came himself; it is hardly likely, the child probably makes a mistake."

But Heidi looked steadily at the woman, not at all as if in any uncertainty, and said, "I know quite well who wrapped me in my bedcover and brought me down in the sleigh: it was grandfather."

"There was some truth then perhaps in what Peter used to tell us of Alm-Uncle during the summer, when we thought he must be wrong," said Grandmother; "but who would ever have believed that such a thing was possible? I did not think the child would live three weeks up there. What is she like, Brigitta?"

The latter had so thoroughly examined Heidi on all sides that she was well able to describe her to her mother.

"She has Adelaide's slenderness of figure, but her eyes are dark and her hair curly like her father's and the old man's up there: she takes after both of them, I think."

Heidi meanwhile had not been idle; she had made the round of the room and looked carefully at everything there was to be seen. All of a sudden she exclaimed, "Grandmother, one of your shutters is flapping backwards and forwards; grandfather would put a nail in and make it all right in a minute, or else it will break one of the panes some day; look, look, how it keeps on banging!"

"Ah, dear child," said the old woman, "I am not able to see it, but I can hear that and many other things besides the shutter. Everything about the place rattles and creaks when the wind is blowing, and it gets inside through all the cracks and holes. The house is going to pieces, and in the night, when the two others are asleep, I often lie awake in fear and trembling, thinking that the whole place will give way and fall and kill us. And there is not a creature to mend anything for us, for Peter does not understand such work."

"But why cannot you see, Grandmother, that the shutter is loose. Look, there it goes again, see, that one there!" And Heidi pointed to the particular shutter.

"Alas, child, it is not only that I cannot see—I can see, nothing, nothing," said the grandmother in a voice of lamentation.

"But if I were to go outside and put back the shutter so that you had more light, then you could see, Grandmother?"

"No, no, not even then, no one can make it light for me again."

"But if you were to go outside among all the white snow, then surely you would find it light; just come with me, Grandmother, and I will show you." Heidi took hold of the old woman's hand to lead her along, for she was beginning to feel quite distressed at the thought of her being without light.

"Let me be, dear child; it is always dark for me now; whether in snow or sun, no light can penetrate my eyes."

"But surely it does in summer, Grandmother," said Heidi, more and more anxious to find some way out of the trouble, "when the hot sun is shining down again, and he says good night to the mountains, and they all turn on fire, and the yellow flowers shine like gold, then, you will see, it will be bright and beautiful for you again."

"Ah, child, I shall see the mountains on fire or the yellow flowers no more; it will never be light for me again on earth, never."

At these words Heidi broke into loud crying. In her distress she kept on sobbing out, "Who can make it light for you again? Can no one do it? Isn't there any one who can do it?"

The grandmother now tried to comfort the child, but it was not easy to quiet her. Heidi did not often weep, but when she did she could not get over her trouble for a long while. The grandmother had tried all means in her power to allay the child's grief, for it went to her heart to hear her sobbing so bitterly. At last she said, "Come here, dear Heidi, come and let me tell you something. You cannot think how glad one is to hear a kind word when one can no longer see, and it is such a pleasure to me to listen to you while you talk. So come and sit beside me and tell me something; tell me what you do up there, and how grandfather occupies himself. I knew him very well in old days; but for many years now I have heard nothing of him, except through Peter, who never says much."

This was a new and happy idea to Heidi; she quickly dried her tears and said in a comforting voice, "Wait, Grandmother, till I have told grandfather everything, he will make it light for you again, I am sure, and will do something so that the house will not fall; he will put everything right for you."

The grandmother was silent, and Heidi now began to give her a lively description of her life with the grandfather, and of the days she spent on the mountain with the goats, and then went on to tell her of what she did now during the winter, and how her grandfather was able to make all sorts of things, seats and stools, and mangers where the hay was put for Little Swan and Little Bear, besides a new large water-tub for her to bathe in when the summer came, and a new milk-bowl and spoon, and Heidi grew more and more animated as she enumerated all the beautiful things which were made so magically out of pieces of wood; she then told the grandmother how she stood by him and watched all he did, and how she hoped some day to be able to make the same herself.

The grandmother listened with the greatest attention, only from time to time addressing her daughter, "Do you hear that, Brigitta? Do you hear what she is saying about Uncle?"

The conversation was all at once interrupted by a heavy thump on the door, and in marched Peter, who stood stock-still, opening his eyes with astonishment, when he caught sight of Heidi; then his face beamed with smiles as she called out, "Good evening, Peter."

"What, is the boy back from school already?" exclaimed the grandmother in surprise. "I have not known an afternoon pass so quickly as this one for years. How is the reading getting on, Peter?"

"Just the same," was Peter's answer.

The old woman gave a little sigh. "Ah, well," she said, "I hoped you would have something different to tell me by this time, as you are going to be twelve years old this February."

"What was it that you hoped he would have to tell you?" asked Heidi, interested in all the grandmother said.

"I mean that he ought to have learnt to read a bit by now," continued the grandmother. "Up there on the shelf is an old prayer-book, with beautiful songs in it which I have not heard for a long time and cannot now remember to repeat to myself, and I hoped that Peter would soon learn enough to be able to read one of them to me sometimes; but he finds it too difficult."

"I must get a light, it is getting too dark to see," said Peter's mother, who was still busy mending his waistcoat. "I feel too as if the afternoon had gone I hardly know how."

Heidi now jumped up from her low chair, and holding out her hand hastily to the grandmother said, "Good night, Grandmother, if it is getting dark I must go home at once," and bidding goodbye to Peter and his mother she went towards the door. But the grandmother called out in an anxious voice, "Wait, wait, Heidi; you must not go alone like that, Peter must go with you; and take care of the child, Peter, that she does not fall, and don't let her stand still for fear she should get frozen, do you hear? Has she got anything warm to put around her throat?"

"I have not anything to put on," called back Heidi, "but I am sure I shall not be cold," and with that she ran outside and went off at such a pace that Peter had difficulty in overtaking her. The grandmother, still in distress, called out to her daughter, "Run after her, Brigitta; the child will be frozen to death on such a night as this; take my shawl, run quickly!"

Brigitta ran out. But the children had taken but a few steps before they saw the grandfather coming down to meet them, and in another minute his long strides had brought him to their side.

"That's right, Heidi; you have kept your word," said the grandfather, and then wrapping the sack firmly round her he lifted her in his arms and strode off with her up the mountain. Brigitta was just in time to see him do all this, and on her return to the hut with Peter expressed her astonishment to the grandmother. The latter was equally surprised, and kept on saying, "God be thanked that he is good to the child, God be thanked! Will he let her come to me again, I wonder! the child has done me so much good. What a loving little heart it is, and how merrily she tells her tale!" And she continued to dwell with delight on the thought of the child until she went to bed, still saying now and again, "If only she will come again! Now I have really something left in the world to take pleasure in." And Brigitta agreed with all her mother said, and Peter nodded his head in approval each time his grandmother spoke, saying, with a broad smile of satisfaction, "I told you so!"

Meanwhile Heidi was chattering away to her grandfather from inside her sack; her voice, however, could not reach him through the many thick folds of her wrap, and as therefore it was impossible to understand a word she was saying, he called to her, "Wait till we get home, and then you can tell me all about it." They had no sooner got inside the hut than Heidi, having been released from her covering, at once began what she had to say, "Grandfather, tomorrow we must take the hammer and the long nails and fasten Grandmother's shutter, and drive in a lot more nails in other places, for her house shakes and rattles all over."

"We must, must we? Who told you that?" asked her grandfather.

"Nobody told me, but I know it for all that," replied Heidi, "for everything is giving way, and when the grandmother cannot sleep, she lies trembling for fear at the noise, for she thinks that every minute the house will fall down on their heads; and everything now is dark for Grandmother, and she does not think any one can make it light for her again, but you will be able to, I am sure, grandfather. Think how dreadful it is for her to be always in the dark, and then to be frightened at what may happen, and nobody can help her but you. Tomorrow we must go and help her; we will, won't we, grandfather?"

The child was clinging to the old man and looking up at him in trustful confidence. The grandfather looked down at Heidi for a while without speaking, and then said, "Yes, Heidi, we will do something to stop the rattling, at least we can do that; we will go down about it tomorrow!"

The child went skipping round the room for joy, crying out, "We shall go tomorrow! We shall go tomorrow!"

The grandfather kept his promise. On the following afternoon he brought the sleigh out again, and as on the previous day, he set Heidi down at the door of the grandmother's hut and said, "Go in now, and when it grows dark, come out again." Then he put the sack in the sleigh and went round the house.

Heidi had hardly opened the door and sprung into the room when the grandmother called out from her corner, "It's the child again! Here she comes!" And in her delight she let the thread drop from her fingers, and the wheel stood still as she stretched out both her hands in welcome. Heidi ran to her, and then quickly drew the little stool close up to the old woman, and seating herself upon it, began to tell and ask her all kinds of things. All at once came the sound of heavy blows against the wall of the hut and the grandmother gave such a start of alarm that she nearly upset the spinning-wheel, and cried in a trembling voice, "Ah, my God, now it is coming, the house is going to fall upon us!" But Heidi caught her by the arm, and said soothingly, "No, no, Grandmother, do not be frightened, it is only grandfather with his hammer; he is mending up everything, so that you shan't have such fear and trouble."

"Is it possible! Is it really possible! So the dear God has not forgotten us!" exclaimed the grandmother. "Do you hear, Brigitta, what that noise is? Did you hear what the child says? Now, as I listen, I can tell it is a hammer; go outside, Brigitta, and if it is Alm-Uncle, tell him he must come inside a moment that I may thank him."

Brigitta went outside and found Alm-Uncle in the act of fastening some heavy pieces of new wood along the wall. She stepped up to him and said, "Good evening, Uncle, mother and I have to thank you for doing us such a kind service, and she would like to tell you herself how grateful she is; I do not know who else would have done it for us; we shall not forget your kindness, for I am sure—"

"That will do," said the old man, interrupting her.

"I know what you think of Alm-Uncle without your telling me. Go indoors again, I can find out for myself where the mending is wanted."

Brigitta obeyed on the spot, for Uncle had a way with him that made few people care to oppose his will. He went on knocking with his hammer all round the house, and then mounted the narrow steps to the roof, and hammered away there, until he had used up all the nails he had brought with him. Meanwhile it had been growing dark, and he had hardly come down from the roof and dragged the sleigh out from behind the goat-shed when Heidi appeared outside. The grandfather wrapped her up and took her in his arms as he had done the day before, for although he had to drag the sleigh up the mountain after him, he feared that if the child sat in it alone her wrappings would fall off and that she would be nearly if not quite frozen, so he carried her warm and safe in his arms.

So the winter went by. After many years of joyless life, the blind grandmother had at last found something to make her happy; her days were no longer passed in weariness and darkness, one like the other without pleasure or change, for now she had always something to which she could look forward. She listened for the little tripping footstep as soon as day had come, and when she heard the door open and knew the child was really there, she would call out, "God be thanked, she has come again!" And Heidi would sit by her and talk and tell her everything she knew in so lively a manner that the grandmother never noticed how the time went by, and never now as formerly asked Brigitta, "Isn't the day done yet?" but as the child shut the door behind her on leaving, would exclaim, "How short the afternoon has seemed; don't you think so, Brigitta?" And this one would answer, "I do indeed; it seems as if I had only just cleared away the mid-day meal." And the grandmother would continue, "Pray God the child is not taken from me, and that Alm-Uncle continues to let her come! Does she look well and strong, Brigitta?" And the latter would answer, "She looks as bright and rosy as an apple."

And Heidi had also grown very fond of the old grandmother, and when at last she knew for certain that no one could make it light for her again, she was overcome with sorrow; but the grandmother told her again that she felt the darkness much less when Heidi was with her, and so every fine winter's day the child came travelling down in her sleigh. The grandfather always took her, never raising any objection, indeed he always carried the hammer and sundry other things down in the sleigh with him, and many an afternoon was spent by him in making the goatherd's cottage sound and tight. It no longer groaned and rattled the whole night through, and the grandmother, who for many winters had not been able to sleep in peace as she did now, said she should never forget what the Uncle had done for her.

Chapter 5

Two Visits And What Came Of Them

Quickly the winter passed, and still more quickly the bright glad summer, and now another winter was drawing to its close. Heidi was still as light-hearted and happy as the birds, and looked forward with more delight each day to the coming spring, when the warm south wind would roar through the fir trees and blow away the snow, and the warm sun would entice the blue and yellow flowers to show their heads, and the long days out on the mountain would come again, which seemed to Heidi the greatest joy that the earth could give. Heidi was now in her eighth year; she had learnt all kinds of useful things from her grandfather; she knew how to look after the goats as well as any one, and Little Swan and Bear would follow her like two faithful dogs, and give a loud bleat of pleasure when they heard her voice. Twice during the course of this last winter Peter had brought up a message from the schoolmaster at Dörfli, who sent word to Alm-Uncle that he ought to send Heidi to school, as she was over the usual age, and ought indeed to have gone the winter before. Uncle had sent word back each time that the schoolmaster would find him at home if he had anything he wished to say to him, but that he did not intend to send Heidi to school, and Peter had faithfully delivered his message.

When the March sun had melted the snow on the mountain side and the snowdrops were peeping out all over the valley, and the fir trees had shaken off their burden of snow and were again merrily waving their branches in the air, Heidi ran backwards and forwards with delight first to the goat-shed then to the fir trees, and then to the hut-door, in order to let her grandfather know how much larger a piece of green there was under the trees, and then would run off to look again, for she could hardly wait till everything was green and the full beautiful summer had clothed the mountain with grass and flowers. As Heidi was thus running about one sunny March morning, and had just jumped over the water-trough for the tenth time at least, she nearly fell backwards into it with fright, for there in front of her, looking gravely at her, stood an old gentleman dressed in black. When he saw how startled she was, he said in a kind voice, "Don't be afraid of me, for I am very fond of children. Shake hands! You must be the Heidi I have heard of; where is your grandfather?"

"He is sitting by the table, making round wooden spoons," Heidi informed him, as she opened the door.

He was the old village pastor from Dörfli who had been a neighbour of Uncle's when he lived down there, and had known him well. He stepped inside the hut, and going up to the old man, who was bending over his work, said, "Good-morning, neighbour."

The grandfather looked up in surprise, and then rising said, "Good-morning" in return. He pushed his chair towards the visitor as he continued, "If you do not mind a wooden seat there is one for you."

The pastor sat down. "It is a long time since I have seen you, neighbour," he said.

"Or I you," was the answer.

"I have come today to talk over something with you," continued the pastor. "I think you know already what it is that has brought me here," and as he spoke he looked towards the child who was standing at the door, gazing with interest and surprise at the stranger.

"Heidi, go off to the goats," said her grandfather. "You take them a little salt and stay with them till I come."

Heidi vanished on the spot.

"The child ought to have been at school a year ago, and most certainly this last winter," said the pastor. "The schoolmaster sent you word about it, but you gave him no answer. What are you thinking of doing with the child, neighbour?"

"I am thinking of not sending her to school," was the answer.

The visitor, surprised, looked across at the old man, who was sitting on his bench with his arms crossed and a determined expression about his whole person.

"How are you going to let her grow up then?" he asked.

"I am going to let her grow up and be happy among the goats and birds; with them she is safe, and will learn nothing evil."

"But the child is not a goat or a bird, she is a human being. If she learns no evil from these comrades of hers, she will at the same time learn nothing; but she ought not to grow up in ignorance, and it is time she began her lessons. I have come now that you may have leisure to think over it, and to arrange about it during the summer. This is the last winter that she must be allowed to run wild; next winter she must come regularly to school every day."

"She will do no such thing," said the old man with calm determination.

"Do you mean that by no persuasion can you be brought to see reason, and that you intend to stick obstinately to your decision?" said the pastor, growing somewhat angry. "You have been about the world, and must have seen and learnt much, and I should have given you credit for more sense, neighbour."

"Indeed," replied the old man, and there was a tone in his voice that betrayed a growing irritation on his part too, "and does the worthy pastor really mean that he would wish me next winter to send a young child like that some miles down the mountain on ice-cold mornings through storm and snow, and let her return at night when the wind is raging, when even one like ourselves would run a risk of being blown down by it and buried in the snow? And perhaps he may not have forgotten the child's mother, Adelaide? She was a sleepwalker, and had fits. Might not the child be attacked in the same way if obliged to over-exert herself? And some one thinks they can come and force me to send her? I will go before all the courts of justice in the country, and then we shall see who will force me to do it!"

"You are quite right, neighbour," said the pastor in a friendly tone of voice. "I see it would have been impossible to send the child to school from here. But I perceive that the child is dear to you; for her sake do what you ought to have done long ago: come down into Dörfli and live again among your fellowmen. What sort of a life is this you lead, alone, and with bitter thoughts towards God and man! If anything were to happen to you up here who would there be to help you? I cannot think but what you must be half-frozen to death in this hut in the winter, and I do not know how the child lives through it!"

"The child has young blood in her veins and a good roof over her head, and let me further tell the pastor, that I know where wood is to be found, and when is the proper time to fetch it; the pastor can go and look inside my wood-shed; the fire is never out in my hut the whole winter through. As to going to live below that is far from my thoughts; the people despise me and I them; it is therefore best for all of us that we live apart."

"No, no, it is not best for you; I know what it is you lack," said the pastor in an earnest voice. "As to the people down there looking on you with dislike, it is not as bad as you think. Believe me, neighbour; seek to make your peace with God, pray for forgiveness where you need it, and then come and see how differently people will look upon you, and how happy you may yet be."

The pastor had risen and stood holding out his hand to the old man as he added with renewed earnestness, "I will wager, neighbour, that next winter you will be down among us again, and we shall be good neighbours as of old. I should be very grieved if any pressure had to be put upon you; give me your hand and promise me that you will come and live with us again and become reconciled to God and man."

Alm-Uncle gave the pastor his hand and answered him calmly and firmly, "You mean well by me I know, but as to that which you wish me to do, I say now what I shall continue to say, that I will not send the child to school nor come and live among you."

"Then God help you!" said the pastor, and he turned sadly away and left the hut and went down the mountain.

Alm-Uncle was out of humor. When Heidi said as usual that afternoon, "Can we go down to Grandmother now?" he answered, "Not today." He did not speak again the whole of that day, and the following morning when Heidi again asked the same question, he replied, "We will see." But before the dinner bowls had been cleared away another visitor arrived, and this time it was Cousin Dete. She had a fine feathered hat on her head, and a long trailing skirt to her dress which swept the floor, and on the floor of a goatherd's hut there are all sorts of things that do not belong to a dress.

The grandfather looked her up and down without uttering a word. But Dete was prepared with an exceedingly amiable speech and began at once to praise the looks of the child. She was looking so well she should hardly have known her again, and it was evident that she had been happy and well-cared for with her grandfather; but she had never lost sight of the idea of taking the child back again, for she well understood that the little one must be much in his way, but she had not been able to do it at first. Day and night, however, she had thought over the means of placing the child somewhere, and that was why she had come today, for she had just heard of something that would be a lucky chance for Heidi beyond her most ambitious hopes. Some immensely wealthy relatives of the people she was serving, who had the most splendid house almost in Frankfurt, had an only daughter, young and an invalid, who was always obliged to go about in a wheeled chair; she was therefore very much alone and had no one to share her lessons, and so the little girl felt dull. Her father had spoken to Dete's mistress about finding a companion for her, and her mistress was anxious to help in the matter, as she felt so sympathetic about it. The lady-housekeeper had described the sort of child they wanted, simple-minded and unspoilt, and not like most of the children that one saw nowadays. Dete had thought at once of Heidi and had gone off without delay to see the lady-housekeeper, and after Dete had given her a description of Heidi, she had immediately agreed to take her. And no one could tell what good fortune there might not be in store for Heidi, for if she was once with these people and they took a fancy to her, and anything happened to their own daughter—one could never tell, the child was so weakly—and they did not feel they could live without a child, why then the most unheard of luck—

"Have you nearly finished what you had to say?" broke in Alm-Uncle, who had allowed her to talk on uninterruptedly so far.

"Ugh!" exclaimed Dete, throwing up her head in disgust, "one would think I had been talking to you about the most ordinary matter; why there is not one person in all Prättigau who would not thank God if I were to bring them such a piece of news as I am bringing you."

"You may take your news to anybody you like, I will have nothing to do with it."

But now Dete leaped up from her seat like a rocket and cried, "If that is all you have to say about it, why then I will give you a bit of my mind. The child is now eight years old and knows nothing, and you will not let her learn. You will not send her to church or school, as I was told down in Dörfli, and she is my own sister's child. I am responsible for what happens to her, and when there is such a good opening for a child, as this which offers for Heidi, only a person who cares for nobody and never wishes good to any one would think of not jumping at it. But I am not going to give in, and that I tell you; I have everybody in Dörfli on my side; there is not one person there who will not take my part against you; and I advise you to think well before bringing it into court, if that is your intention; there are certain things which might be brought up against you which you would not care to hear, for when one has to do with law-courts there is a great deal raked up that had been forgotten."

"Be silent!" thundered the Uncle, and his eyes flashed with anger. "Go and be done with you! And never let me see you again with your hat and feather, and such words on your tongue as you come with today!" And with that he strode out of the hut.

"You have made Grandfather angry," said Heidi, and her dark eyes had anything but a friendly expression in them as she looked at Dete.

"He will soon be all right again; come now," said Dete hurriedly, "and show me where your clothes are."

"I am not coming," said Heidi.

"Nonsense," continued Dete; then altering her tone to one half-coaxing, half-cross, "Come, come, you do not understand any better than your grandfather; you will have all sorts of good things that you never dreamed of." Then she went to the cupboard and taking out Heidi's things rolled them up in a bundle. "Come along now, there's your hat; it is very shabby but will do for the present; put it on and let us make haste off."

"I am not coming," repeated Heidi.

"Don't be so stupid and obstinate, like a goat; I suppose it's from the goats you have learnt to be so. Listen to me: you saw your grandfather was angry and heard what he said, that he did not wish to see us ever again; he wants you now to go away with me and you must not make him angrier still. You can't think how nice it is at Frankfurt, and what a lot of things you will see, and if you do not like it you can come back again; your grandfather will be in a good temper again by that time."

"Can I return at once and be back home again here this evening?" asked Heidi.

"What are you talking about, come along now! I tell you that you can come back here when you like. Today we shall go as far as Mayenfeld, and early tomorrow we shall start in the train, and that will bring you home again in no time when you wish it, for it goes as fast as the wind."

Dete had now got the bundle under her arm and the child by the hand, and so they went down the mountain together.

As it was still too early in the year to take his goats out, Peter continued to go to school at Dörfli, but now and again he stole a holiday, for he could see no use in learning to read, while to wander about a bit and look for stout sticks which might be wanted some day he thought a far better employment. As Dete and Heidi neared the grandmother's hut they met Peter coming round the corner; he had evidently been well rewarded that day for his labors, for he was carrying an immense bundle of long thick hazel sticks on his shoulders. He stood still and stared at the two approaching figures; as they came up to him, he exclaimed, "Where are you going, Heidi?"

"I am only just going over to Frankfurt for a little visit with Dete," she replied; "but I must first run in to grandmother, she will be expecting me."

"No, no, you must not stop to talk; it is already too late," said Dete, holding Heidi, who was struggling to get away, fast by the hand. "You can go in when you come back, you must come along now," and she pulled the child on with her, fearing that if she let her go in Heidi might take it into her head again that she did not wish to come, and that the grandmother might stand by her. Peter ran into the hut and banged against the table with his bundle of sticks with such violence that everything in the room shook, and his grandmother leaped up with a cry of alarm from her spinning-wheel. Peter had felt that he must give vent to his feelings somehow.

"What is the matter? What is the matter?" cried the frightened old woman, while his mother, who had also started up from her seat at the shock, said in her usual patient manner, "What is it, Peter? Why do you behave so roughly?"

"Because she is taking Heidi away," explained Peter.

"Who? Who? Where to, Peter, where to?" asked the grandmother, growing still more agitated; but even as she spoke she guessed what had happened, for Brigitta had told her shortly before that she had seen Dete going up to Alm-Uncle. The old woman rose hastily and with trembling hands opened the window and called out beseechingly, "Dete, Dete, do not take the child away from us! Do not take her away!"

The two who were hastening down the mountain heard her voice, and Dete evidently caught the words, for she grasped Heidi's hand more firmly. Heidi struggled to get free, crying, "Grandmother is calling, I must go to her."

But Dete had no intention of letting the child go, and quieted her as best she could; they must make haste now, she said, or they would be too late and not able to go on the next day to Frankfurt, and there the child would see how delightful it was, and Dete was sure would not wish to go back when she was once there. But if Heidi wanted to return home she could do so at once, and then she could take something she liked back to Grandmother. This was a new idea to Heidi, and it pleased her so much that Dete had no longer any difficulty in getting her along.

After a few minutes' silence, Heidi asked, "What could I take back to her?"

"We must think of something nice," answered Dete; "a soft roll of white bread; she would enjoy that, for now she is old she can hardly eat the hard, black bread."

"No, she always gives it back to Peter, telling him it is too hard, for I have seen her do it myself," affirmed Heidi. "Do let us make haste, for then perhaps we can get back soon from Frankfurt, and I shall be able to give her the white bread today." And Heidi started off running so fast that Dete with the bundle under her arm could scarcely keep up with her. But she was glad, nevertheless, to get along so quickly, for they were nearing Dörfli, where her friends would probably talk and question in a way that might put other ideas into Heidi's head. So she went on straight ahead through the village, holding Heidi tightly by the hand, so that they might all see that it was on the child's account she was hurrying along at such a rate. To all their questions and remarks she made answer as she passed "I can't stop now, as you see, I must make haste with the child as we have yet some way to go."

"Are you taking her away?" "Is she running away from Alm-Uncle?" "It's a wonder she is still alive!" "But what rosy cheeks she has!" Such were the words which rang out on all sides, and Dete was thankful that she had not to stop and give any distinct answers to them, while Heidi hurried eagerly forward without saying a word.

From that day forward Alm-Uncle looked fiercer and more forbidding than ever when he came down and passed through Dörfli. He spoke to no one, and looked such an ogre as he came along with his pack of cheeses on his back, his immense stick in his hand, and his thick, frowning eyebrows, that the women would call to their little ones, "Take care! Get out of Alm-Uncle's way or he may hurt you!"

The old man took no notice of anybody as he strode through the village on his way to the valley below, where he sold his cheeses and bought what bread and meat he wanted for himself. After he had passed the villagers all crowded together looking after him, and each had something to say about him; how much wilder he looked than usual, how now he would not even respond to anybody's greeting, while they all agreed that it was a great mercy the child had got away from him, and had they not all noticed how the child had hurried along as if afraid that her grandfather might be following to take her back? Only the blind grandmother would have nothing to say against him, and told those who came to her to bring her work, or take away what she had spun, how kind and thoughtful he had been with the child, how good to her and her daughter, and how many afternoons he had spent mending the house which, but for his help, would certainly by this time have fallen down over their heads. And all this was repeated down in Dörfli; but most of the people who heard it said that Grandmother was too old to understand, and very likely had not heard rightly what was said; as she was blind she was probably also deaf.

Alm-Uncle went no more now to the grandmother's house, and it was well that he had made it so safe, for it was not touched again for a long time. The days were sad again now for the old blind woman, and not one passed but what she would murmur complainingly, "Alas! All our happiness and pleasure have gone with the child, and now the days are so long and dreary! Pray God, I see Heidi again once more before I die!"

Chapter 6

A New Chapter About New Things

In her home at Frankfurt, Clara, the little daughter of Herr Sesemann, was lying on the invalid couch on which she spent her whole day, being wheeled in it from room to room. Just now she was in what was known as the study, where, to judge by the various things standing and lying about, which added to the cosy appearance of the room, the family was fond of sitting. A handsome bookcase with glass doors explained why it was called the study, and here evidently the little girl was accustomed to have her lessons.

Clara's little face was thin and pale, and at this moment her two soft blue eyes were fixed on the clock, which seemed to her to go very slowly this day, and with a slight accent of impatience, which was very rare with her, she asked, "Isn't it time yet, Fräulein Rottenmeier?"

This lady was sitting very upright at a small work-table, busy with her embroidery. She had on a mysterious-looking loose garment, a large collar or shoulder-cape that gave a certain solemnity to her appearance, which was enhanced by a very lofty dome-shaped head dress. For many years past, since the mistress of the house had died, the housekeeping and the superintendence of the servants had been entrusted by Herr Sesemann to Fräulein Rottenmeier. He himself was often away from home, and he left her in sole charge, with the condition only that his little daughter should have a voice in all matters, and that nothing should be done against her wish.

As Clara was putting her impatient question for the second time, Dete and Heidi arrived at the front door, and the former inquired of the coachman, who had just got down from his box, if it was too late to see Fräulein Rottenmeier.

"That's not my business," grumbled the coachman; "ring the bell in the hall for Sebastian."

Dete did so, and Sebastian came downstairs; he looked astonished when he saw her, opening his eyes till they were nearly as big as the large round buttons on his coat.

"Is it too late for me to see Fräulein Rottenmeier?" Dete asked again.

"That's not my business," answered the man; "ring that other bell for the maid Tinette," and without troubling himself any farther Sebastian disappeared.

Dete rang again. This time Tinette appeared with a spotless white cap perched on the top of her head and a mocking expression of face.

"What is it?" she called from the top of the stairs. Dete repeated her question. Tinette disappeared, but soon came back and called down again to Dete, "Come up, she is expecting you."

Dete and Heidi went upstairs and into the study, Tinette following. Dete remained standing politely near the door, still holding Heidi tightly by the hand, for she did not know what the child might take it into her head to do amid these new surroundings.

Fräulein Rottenmeier rose slowly and went up to the little new companion for the daughter of the house, to see what she was like. She did not seem very pleased with her appearance. Heidi was dressed in her plain little woollen frock, and her hat was an old straw one bent out of shape. The child looked innocently out from beneath it, gazing with unconcealed astonishment at the lady's towering head dress.

"What is your name?" asked Fräulein Rottenmeier, after scrutinisingly examining the child for some minutes, while Heidi in return kept her eyes steadily fixed upon the lady.

"Heidi," she answered in a clear, ringing voice.

"What? What? That's no Christian name for a child; you were not christened that. What name did they give you when you were baptized?" continued Fräulein Rottenmeier.

"I do not remember," replied Heidi.

"What a way to answer!" said the lady, shaking her head. "Dete, is the child a simpleton or only saucy?"

"If the lady will allow me, I will speak for the child, for she is very unaccustomed to strangers," said Dete, who had given Heidi a silent poke for making such an unsuitable answer. "She is certainly not stupid nor yet saucy, she does not know what it means even; she speaks exactly as she thinks. Today she is for the first time in a gentleman's house and she does not know good manners; but she is docile and very willing to learn, if the lady will kindly make excuses for her. She was christened Adelaide, after her mother, my sister, who is now dead."

"Well, that's a name that one can pronounce," remarked Fräulein Rottenmeier. "But I must tell you, Dete, that I am astonished to see so young a child. I told you that I wanted a companion of the same age as the young lady of the house, one who could share her lessons, and all her other occupations. Fräulein Clara is now over twelve; what age is this child?"

"If the lady will allow me," began Dete again, in her usual fluent manner, "I myself had lost count of her exact age; she is certainly a little younger, but not much; I cannot say precisely, but I think she is ten, or thereabouts."

"Grandfather told me I was eight," put in Heidi. Dete gave her another poke, but as the child had not the least idea why she did so she was not at all confused.

"What—only eight!" cried Fräulein Rottenmeier angrily. "Four years too young! Of what use is such a child! And what have you learnt? What books did you have to learn from?"

"None," said Heidi.

"How? What? How then did you learn to read?" continued the lady.

"I have never learnt to read, or Peter either," Heidi informed her.

"Mercy upon us! You do not know how to read! Is it really so?" exclaimed Fräulein Rottenmeier, greatly horrified. "Is it possible—not able to read? What have you learnt then?"

"Nothing," said Heidi with unflinching truthfulness.

"Young woman," said the lady to Dete, after having paused for a minute or two to recover from her shock, "this is not at all the sort of companion you led me to suppose; how could you think of bringing me a child like this?"

But Dete was not to be put down so easily, and answered warmly, "If the lady will allow me, the child is exactly what I thought she required; the lady described what she wished for, a child unlike all other children, and I could find no other to suit, for the greater number I know are not peculiar, but one very much the same as the other, and I thought this child seemed as if made for the place. But I must go now, for my mistress will be waiting for me; if the lady will permit I will come again soon and see how she is getting on." And with a bow Dete quickly left the room and ran downstairs. Fräulein Rottenmeier stood for a moment taken aback and then ran after Dete. If the child was to stop she had many things yet to say and ask about her, and there the child was, and what was more, Dete, as she plainly saw, meant to leave her there.

Heidi remained by the door where she had been standing since she first came in. Clara had looked on during the interview without speaking; now she beckoned to Heidi and said, "Come here!"

Heidi went up to her.

"Would you rather be called Heidi or Adelaide?" asked Clara.

"I am never called anything but Heidi," was the child's prompt answer.

"Then I shall always call you by that name," said Clara, "it suits you. I have never heard it before, but neither have I ever seen a child like you before. Have you always had that short curly hair?"

"Yes, I think so," said Heidi.

"Are you pleased to come to Frankfurt?" went on Clara.

"No, but I shall go home tomorrow and take Grandmother a white loaf," explained Heidi.

"Well, you are a funny child!" exclaimed Clara. "You were expressly sent for to come here and to remain with me and share my lessons; there will be some fun about them now as you cannot read, something new to do, for often they are dreadfully dull, and I think the morning will never pass away. You know my tutor comes every morning at about ten o'clock, and then we go on with lessons till two, and it does seem such a long time. Sometimes he takes up the book and holds it close up to his face, as if he was very short-sighted, but I know it's only because he wants so dreadfully to gape, and Fräulein Rottenmeier takes her large handkerchief out also now and then and covers her face with it, as if she was moved by what we had been reading, but that is only because she is longing to gape too. And I myself often want to gape, but I am obliged to stop myself, for if Fräulein Rottenmeier sees me gaping she runs off at once and fetches the cod-liver oil and says I must have a dose, as I am getting weak again, and the cod-liver oil is horrible, so I do my best not to gape. But now it will be much more amusing, for I shall be able to lie and listen while you learn to read."

Heidi shook her head doubtfully when she heard of learning to read.

"Oh, nonsense, Heidi, of course you must learn to read, everybody must, and my tutor is very kind, and never cross, and he will explain everything to you. But mind, when he explains anything to you, you won't be able to understand; but don't ask any questions, or else he will go on explaining and you will understand less than ever. Later when you have learnt more and know about things yourself, then you will begin to understand what he meant."

Fräulein Rottenmeier now came back into the room; she had not been able to overtake Dete, and was evidently very much put out; for she had wanted to go into more details concerning the child, and to convince Dete how misleading she had been, and how unfit Heidi was as a companion for Clara; she really did not know what to be about, or how to undo the mischief, and it made her all the more angry that she herself was responsible for it, having consented to Heidi being fetched. She ran backwards and forwards in a state of agitation between the study and the dining-room, and then began scolding Sebastian, who was standing looking at the table he had just finished laying to see that nothing was missing.

"You can finish your thoughts tomorrow morning; make haste, or we shall get no dinner today at all."

Then hurrying out she called Tinette, but in such an ill-tempered voice that the maid came tripping forward with even more mincing steps than usual, but she looked so pert that even Fräulein Rottenmeier did not venture to scold her, which only made her suppressed anger the greater.

"See that the room is prepared for the little girl who has just arrived," said the lady, with a violent effort at self-control. "Everything is ready; it only wants dusting."

"It's worth my troubling about," said Tinette mockingly as she turned away.

Meanwhile Sebastian had flung open the folding doors leading into the dining-room with rather more noise than he need, for he was feeling furious, although he did not dare answer back when Fräulein Rottenmeier spoke to him; he then went up to Clara's chair to wheel her into the next room. As he was arranging the handle at the back preparatory to doing so, Heidi went near and stood staring at him. Seeing her eyes fixed upon him, he suddenly growled out, "Well, what is there in me to stare at like that?" which he would certainly not have done if he had been aware that Fräulein Rottenmeier was just then entering the room. "You look so like Peter," answered Heidi. The lady-housekeeper clasped her hands in horror. "Is it possible!" she stammered half-aloud, "she is now addressing the servant as if he were a friend! I never could have imagined such a child!"

Sebastian wheeled the couch into the dining-room and helped Clara on to her chair. Fräulein Rottenmeier took the seat beside her and made a sign to Heidi to take the one opposite. They were the only three at table, and as they sat far apart there was plenty of room for Sebastian to hand his dishes. Beside Heidi's plate lay a nice white roll, and her eyes lighted up with pleasure as she saw it. The resemblance which Heidi had noticed had evidently awakened in her a feeling of confidence towards Sebastian, for she sat as still as a mouse and without moving until he came up to her side and handed her the dish of fish; then she looked at the roll and asked, "Can I have it?" Sebastian nodded, throwing a side glance at Fräulein Rottenmeier to see what effect this request would have upon her. Heidi immediately seized the roll and put it in her pocket. Sebastian's face became convulsed, he was overcome with inward laughter but knew his place too well to laugh aloud. Mute and motionless he still remained standing beside Heidi; it was not his duty to speak, nor to move away until she had helped herself. Heidi looked wonderingly at him for a minute or two, and then said, "Am I to eat some of that too?" Sebastian nodded again. "Give me some then," she said, looking calmly at her plate. At this Sebastian's command of his countenance became doubtful, and the dish began to tremble suspiciously in his hands.

"You can put the dish on the table and come back presently," said Fräulein Rottenmeier with a severe expression of face. Sebastian disappeared on the spot. "As for you, Adelaide, I see I shall have to teach you the first rules of behaviour," continued the lady-housekeeper with a sigh. "I will begin by explaining to you how you are to conduct yourself at table," and she went on to give Heidi minute instructions as to all she was to do. "And now," she continued, "I must make you particularly understand that you are not to speak to Sebastian at table, or at any other time, unless you have an order to give him, or a necessary question to put to him; and then you are not to address him as if he was some one belonging to you. Never let me hear you speak to him in that way again! It is the same with Tinette, and for myself you are to address me as you hear others doing. Clara must herself decide what you are to call her."

"Why, Clara, of course," put the latter. Then followed a long list of rules as to general behaviour, getting up and going to bed, going in and out of the room, shutting the doors, keeping everything tidy, during the course of which Heidi's eyes gradually closed, for she had been up before five o'clock that morning and had had a long journey. She leant back in her chair and fell fast asleep. Fräulein Rottenmeier having at last come to the end of her sermonizing said, "Now remember what I have said, Adelaide! Have you understood it all?"

"Heidi has been asleep for ever so long," said Clara, her face rippling all over with amusement, for she had not had such an entertaining dinner for a long time.

"It is really insupportable what one has to go through with this child," exclaimed Fräulein Rottenmeier, in great indignation, and she rang the bell so violently that Tinette and Sebastian both came running in and nearly tumbling over one another; but no noise was sufficient to wake Heidi, and it was with difficulty they could rouse her sufficiently to get her along to her bedroom, to reach which she had to pass first through the study, then through Clara's bedroom, then through Fräulein Rottenmeier's sitting-room, till she came to the corner room that had been set apart for her.

Chapter 7

Fräulein Rottenmeier Spends An Uncomfortable Day

When Heidi opened her eyes on her first morning in Frankfurt she could not think where she was. Then she rubbed them and looked about her. She was sitting up in a high white bed, on one side of a large, wide room, into which the light was falling through very, very long white curtains; near the window stood two chairs covered with large flowers, and then came a sofa with the same flowers, in front of which was a round table; in the corner was a washstand, with things upon it that Heidi had never seen in her life before. But now all at once she remembered that she was in Frankfurt; everything that had happened the day before came back to her, and finally she recalled clearly the instructions that had been given her by the lady-housekeeper, as far as she had heard them. Heidi jumped out of bed and dressed herself; then she ran first to one window and then another; she wanted to see the sky and country outside; she felt like a bird in a cage behind those great curtains. But they were too heavy for her to put aside, so she crept underneath them to get to the window. But these again were so high that she could only just get her head above the sill to peer out. Even then she could not see what she longed for. In vain she went first to one and then the other of the windows—she could see nothing but walls and windows and again walls and windows. Heidi felt quite frightened. It was still early, for Heidi was accustomed to get up early and run out at once to see how everything was looking, if the sky was blue and if the sun was already above the mountains, or if the fir trees were waving and the flowers had opened their eyes. As a bird, when it first finds itself in its bright new cage, darts hither and thither, trying the bars in turn to see if it cannot get through them and fly again into the open, so Heidi continued to run backwards and forwards, trying to open first one and then the other of the windows, for she felt she could not bear to see nothing but walls and windows, and somewhere outside there must be the green grass, and the last unmelted snows on the mountain slopes, which Heidi so longed to see. But the windows remained immovable, try what Heidi would to open them, even endeavoring to push her little fingers under them to lift them up; but it was all no use. When after a while Heidi saw that her efforts were fruitless, she gave up trying, and began to think whether she would not go out and round the house till she came to the grass, but then she remembered that the night before she had only seen stones in front of the house. At that moment a knock came to the door, and immediately after Tinette put her head inside and said, "Breakfast is ready." Heidi had no idea what an invitation so worded meant, and Tinette's face did not encourage any questioning on Heidi's part, but rather the reverse. Heidi was sharp enough to read its expression, and acted accordingly. So she drew the little stool out from under the table, put it in the corner and sat down upon it, and there silently awaited what would happen next. Shortly after, with a good deal of rustling and bustling Fräulein Rottenmeier appeared, who again seemed very much put out and called to Heidi, "What is the matter with you, Adelheid? Don't you understand what breakfast is? Come along at once!"

Heidi had no difficulty in understanding now and followed at once. Clara had been some time at the breakfast table and she gave Heidi a kindly greeting, her face looking considerably more cheerful than usual, for she looked forward to all kinds of new things happening again that day. Breakfast passed off quietly; Heidi ate her bread and butter in a perfectly correct manner, and when the meal was over and Clara wheeled back into the study, Fräulein Rottenmeier told her to follow and remain with Clara until the tutor should arrive and lessons begin.

As soon as the children were alone again, Heidi asked, "How can one see out from here, and look right down on to the ground?"

"You must open the window and look out," replied Clara amused.

"But the windows won't open," responded Heidi sadly.

"Yes, they will," Clara assured her. "You cannot open them, nor I either, but when you see Sebastian you can ask him to open one."

It was a great relief to Heidi to know that the windows could be opened and that one could look out, for she still felt as if she was shut up in prison. Clara now began to ask her questions about her home, and Heidi was delighted to tell her all about the mountain and the goats, and the flowery meadows which were so dear to her.

Meanwhile her tutor had arrived; Fräulein Rottenmeier, however, did not bring him straight into the study but drew him first aside into the dining-room, where she poured forth her troubles and explained to him the awkward position in which she was placed, and how it had all come about. It appeared that she had written some time back to Herr Sesemann to tell him that his daughter very much wished to have a companion, and had added how desirable she thought it herself, as it would be a spur to Clara at her lessons and an amusement for her in her playtime. Fräulein Rottenmeier had privately wished for this arrangement on her own behalf, as it would relieve her from having always to entertain the sick girl herself, which she felt at times was too much for her. The father had answered that he was quite willing to let his daughter have a companion, provided she was treated in every way like his own child, as he would not have any child tormented or put upon, "which was a very unnecessary remark," put in Fräulein Rottenmeier, "for who wants to torment children!" But now she went on to explain how dreadfully she had been taken in about the child, and related all the unimaginable things of which she had already been guilty, so that not only would he have to begin with teaching her the A B C, but would have to start with the most rudimentary instruction as regarded everything to do with daily life. She could see only one way out of this disastrous state of affairs, and that was for the tutor to declare that it was impossible for the two to learn together without detriment to Clara, who was so far ahead of the other; that would be a valid excuse for getting rid of the child, and Herr Sesemann would be sure to agree to the child being sent home again, but she dared not do this without his order, since he was aware that by this time the companion had arrived. But the tutor was a cautious man and not inclined to take a partial view of matters. He tried to calm Fräulein Rottenmeier, and gave it as his opinion that if the little girl was backward in some things she was probably advanced in others, and a little regular teaching would soon set the balance right. When Fräulein Rottenmeier saw that he was not ready to support her, and evidently quite ready to undertake teaching the alphabet, she opened the study door, which she quickly shut again as soon as he had gone through, remaining on the other side herself, for she had a perfect horror of the A B C. She walked up and down the dining-room, thinking over in her own mind how the servants were to be told to address Adelaide. The father had written that she was to be treated exactly like his own daughter, and this would especially refer, she imagined, to the servants. She was not allowed, however, a very long interval of time for consideration, for suddenly the sound of a frightful crash was heard in the study, followed by frantic cries for Sebastian. She rushed into the room. There on the floor lay in a confused heap, books, exercise-books, inkstand, and other articles with the table-cloth on the top, while from beneath them a dark stream of ink was flowing all across the floor. Heidi had disappeared.

"Here's a state of things!" exclaimed Fräulein Rottenmeier, wringing her hands. "Table-cloth, books, work-basket, everything lying in the ink! It was that unfortunate child, I suppose!"

The tutor was standing looking down at the havoc in distress; there was certainly only one view to be taken of such a matter as this and that an unfavorable one. Clara meanwhile appeared to find pleasure in such an unusual event and in watching the results. "Yes, Heidi did it," she explained, "but quite by accident; she must on no account be punished; she jumped up in such violent haste to get away that she dragged the tablecloth along with her, and so everything went over. There were a number of vehicles passing, that is why she rushed off like that; perhaps she has never seen a carriage."

"Is it not as I said? She has not the smallest notion about anything! Not the slightest idea that she ought to sit still and listen while her lessons are going on. But where is the child who has caused all this trouble? Surely she has not run away! What would Herr Sesemann say to me?" She ran out of the room and down the stairs. There, at the bottom, standing in the open doorway, was Heidi, looking in amazement up and down the street.

"What are you doing? What are you thinking of to run away like that?" called Fräulein Rottenmeier.

"I heard the sound of the fir trees, but I cannot see where they are, and now I cannot hear them any more," answered Heidi, looking disappointedly in the direction whence the noise of the passing carriages had reached her, and which to Heidi had seemed like the blowing of the south wind in the trees, so that in great joy of heart she had rushed out to look at them.

"Fir trees! Do you suppose we are in a wood? What ridiculous ideas are these? Come upstairs and see the mischief you have done!"

Heidi turned and followed Fräulein Rottenmeier upstairs; she was quite astonished to see the disaster she had caused, for in her joy and haste to get to the fir trees she had been unaware of having dragged everything after her.

"I excuse you doing this as it is the first time, but do not let me know you doing it a second time," said Fräulein Rottenmeier, pointing to the floor. "During your lesson time you are to sit still and attend. If you cannot do this I shall have to tie you to your chair. Do you understand?"

"Yes," replied Heidi, "but I will certainly not move again," for now she understood that it was a rule to sit still while she was being taught.

Sebastian and Tinette were now sent for to clear up the broken articles and put things in order again; the tutor said good morning and left, as it was impossible to do any more lessons that day; there had been certainly no time for gaping this morning.

Clara had to rest for a certain time during the afternoon, and during this interval, as Fräulein Rottenmeier informed Heidi, the latter might amuse herself as she liked. When Clara had been placed on her couch after dinner, and the lady-housekeeper had retired to her room, Heidi knew that her time had come to choose her own occupation. It was just what she was longing for, as there was something she had made up her mind to do; but she would require some help for its accomplishment, and in view of this she took her stand in the hall in front of the dining-room door in order to intercept the person she wanted. In a few minutes up came Sebastian from the kitchen with a tray of silver tea-things, which he had to put away in the dining-room cupboard. As he reached the top stairs Heidi went up to him and addressed him in the formal manner she had been ordered to use by Fräulein Rottenmeier.

Sebastian looked surprised and said somewhat curtly, "What is it you want, miss?"

"I only wished to ask you something, but it is nothing bad like this morning," said Heidi, anxious to conciliate him, for she saw that Sebastian was rather in a cross temper, and quite thought that it was on account of the ink she had spilt on the floor.

"Indeed, and why, I should first like to know, do you address me like that?" replied Sebastian, evidently still put out.

"Fräulein Rottenmeier told me always to speak to you like that," said Heidi.

Then Sebastian laughed, which very much astonished Heidi, who had seen nothing amusing in the conversation, but Sebastian, now he understood that the child was only obeying orders, added in a friendly voice, "What is it then that miss wants?"

It was now Heidi's turn to be a little put out, and she said, "My name is not miss, it is Heidi."

"Quite so, but the same lady has ordered me to call you miss," explained Sebastian.

"Has she? Oh, then I must be called so," said Heidi submissively, for she had already noticed that whatever Fräulein Rottenmeier said was law. "Then now I have three names," she added with a sigh.

"What was it little miss wished to ask?" said Sebastian as he went on into the dining-room to put away his silver.

"How can a window be opened?"

"Why, like that!" and Sebastian flung up one of the large windows.

Heidi ran to it, but she was not tall enough to see out, for her head only reached the sill.

"There, now miss can look out and see what is going on below," said Sebastian as he brought her a high wooden stool to stand on.

Heidi climbed up, and at last, as she thought, was going to see what she had been longing for. But she drew back her head with a look of great disappointment on her face.

"Why, there is nothing outside but the stony streets," she said mournfully; "but if I went right round to the other side of the house what should I see there, Sebastian?"

"Nothing but what you see here," he told her.

"Then where can I go to see right away over the whole valley?"

"You would have to climb to the top of a high tower, a church tower, like that one over there with the gold ball above it. From there you can see right away ever so far."

Heidi climbed down quickly from her stool, ran to the door, down the steps and out into the street. Things were not, however, quite so easy as she thought. Looking from the window the tower had appeared so close that she imagined she had only to run over the road to reach it. But now, although she ran along the whole length of the street, she still did not get any nearer to it, and indeed soon lost sight of it altogether; she turned down another street, and went on and on, but still no tower. She passed a great many people, but they all seemed in such a hurry that Heidi thought they had not time to tell her which way to go. Then suddenly at one of the street corners she saw a boy standing, carrying a hand-organ on his back and a funny-looking animal on his arm. Heidi ran up to him and said, "Where is the tower with the gold ball on the top?"

"I don't know," was the answer.

"Who can I ask to show me?" she asked again.

"I don't know."

"Do you know any other church with a high tower?"

"Yes, I know one."

"Come then and show it me."

"Show me first what you will give me for it," and the boy held out his hand as he spoke. Heidi searched about in her pockets and presently drew out a card on which was painted a garland of beautiful red roses; she looked at it first for a moment or two, for she felt rather sorry to part with it; Clara had only that morning made her a present of it—but then, to look down into the valley and see all the lovely green slopes! "There," said Heidi, holding out the card, "would you like to have that?"

The boy drew back his hand and shook his head.

"What would you like then?" asked Heidi, not sorry to put the card back in her pocket.

"Money."

"I have none, but Clara has; I am sure she will give me some; how much do you want?"

"Twopence."

"Come along then."

They started off together along the street, and on the way Heidi asked her companion what he was carrying on his back; it was a hand-organ, he told her, which played beautiful music when he turned the handle. All at once they found themselves in front of an old church with a high tower; the boy stood still, and said, "There it is."

"But how shall I get inside?" asked Heidi, looking at the fast closed doors.

"I don't know," was the answer.

"Do you think that I can ring as they do for Sebastian?"

"I don't know."

Heidi had by this time caught sight of a bell in the wall which she now pulled with all her might. "If I go up you must stay down here, for I do not know the way back, and you will have to show me."

"What will you give me then for that?"

"What do you want me to give you?"

"Another twopence."

They heard the key turning inside, and then some one pulled open the heavy creaking door; an old man came out and at first looked with surprise and then in anger at the children, as he began scolding them: "What do you mean by ringing me down like this? Can't you read what is written over the bell, 'For those who wish to go up the tower'?"

The boy said nothing but pointed his finger at Heidi. The latter answered, "But I do want to go up the tower."

"What do you want up there?" said the old man. "Has somebody sent you?"

"No," replied Heidi, "I only wanted to go up that I might look down."

"Get along home with you and don't try this trick on me again, or you may not come off so easily a second time," and with that he turned and was about to shut the door. But Heidi took hold of his coat and said beseechingly, "Let me go up, just once."

He looked around, and his mood changed as he saw her pleading eyes; he took hold of her hand and said kindly, "Well, if you really wish it so much, I will take you."

The boy sat down on the church steps to show that he was content to wait where he was.

Hand in hand with the old man Heidi went up the many steps of the tower; they became smaller and smaller as they neared the top, and at last came one very narrow one, and there they were at the end of their climb. The old man lifted Heidi up that she might look out of the open window.

"There, now you can look down," he said.

Heidi saw beneath her a sea of roofs, towers, and chimney-pots; she quickly drew back her head and said in a sad, disappointed voice, "It is not at all what I thought."

"You see now, a child like you does not understand anything about a view! Come along down and don't go ringing at my bell again!"

He lifted her down and went on before her down the narrow stairway. To the left of the turn where it grew wider stood the door of the tower-keeper's room, and the landing ran out beside it to the edge of the steep slanting roof. At the far end of this was a large basket, in front of which sat a big grey cat, that snarled as it saw them, for she wished to warn the passersby that they were not to meddle with her family. Heidi stood still and looked at her in astonishment, for she had never seen such a monster cat before; there were whole armies of mice, however, in the old tower, so the cat had no difficulty in catching half a dozen for her dinner every day. The old man seeing Heidi so struck with admiration said, "She will not hurt you while I am near; come, you can have a peep at the kittens."

Heidi went up to the basket and broke out into expressions of delight.

"Oh, the sweet little things! the darling kittens," she kept on saying, as she jumped from side to side of the basket so as, not to lose any of the droll gambols of the seven or eight little kittens that were scrambling and rolling and falling over one another.

"Would you like to have one?" said the old man, who enjoyed watching the child's pleasure.

"For myself to keep?" said Heidi excitedly, who could hardly believe such happiness was to be hers.

"Yes, of course, more than one if you like—in short, you can take away the whole lot if you have room for them," for the old man was only too glad to think he could get rid of his kittens without more trouble.

Heidi could hardly contain herself for joy. There would be plenty of room for them in the large house, and then how astonished and delighted Clara would be when she saw the sweet little kittens.

"But how can I take them with me?" asked Heidi, and was going quickly to see how many she could carry away in her hands, when the old cat sprang at her so fiercely that she shrank back in fear.

"I will take them for you if you will tell me where," said the old man, stroking the cat to quiet her, for she was an old friend of his that had lived with him in the tower for many years.

"To Herr Sesemann's, the big house where there is a gold dog's head on the door, with a ring in its mouth," explained Heidi.

Such full directions as these were not really needed by the old man, who had had charge of the tower for many a long year and knew every house far and near, and moreover Sebastian was an acquaintance of his.

"I know the house," he said, "but when shall I bring them, and who shall I ask for?—You are not one of the family, I am sure."

"No, but Clara will be so delighted when I take her the kittens."

The old man wished now to go downstairs, but Heidi did not know how to tear herself away from the amusing spectacle.

"If I could just take one or two away with me! one for myself and one for Clara, may I?"

"Well, wait a moment," said the man, and he drew the cat cautiously away into his room, and leaving her by a bowl of food came out again and shut the door. "Now take two of them."

Heidi's eyes shone with delight. She picked up a white kitten and another striped white and yellow, and put one in the right, the other in the left pocket. Then she went downstairs. The boy was still sitting outside on the steps, and as the old man shut the door of the church behind them, she said, "Which is our way to Herr Sesemann's house?"

"I don't know," was the answer.

Heidi began a description of the front door and the steps and the windows, but the boy only shook his head, and was not any the wiser.

"Well, look here," continued Heidi, "from one window you can see a very, very large grey house, and the roof runs like this—" and Heidi drew a zigzag line in the air with her forefinger.

With this the boy jumped up, he was evidently in the habit of guiding himself by similar landmarks. He ran straight off with Heidi after him, and in a very short time they had reached the door with the large dog's head for the knocker. Heidi rang the bell. Sebastian opened it quickly, and when he saw it was Heidi, "Make haste! Make haste," he cried in a hurried voice.

Heidi sprang hastily in and Sebastian shut the door after her, leaving the boy, whom he had not noticed, standing in wonder on the steps.

"Make haste, little miss," said Sebastian again; "go straight into the dining-room, they are already at table; Fräulein Rottenmeier looks like a loaded cannon. What could make the little miss run off like that?"

Heidi walked into the room. The lady housekeeper did not look up, Clara did not speak; there was an uncomfortable silence. Sebastian pushed her chair up for her, and when she was seated Fräulein Rottenmeier, with a severe countenance, sternly and solemnly addressed her: "I will speak with you afterwards, Adelheid, only this much will I now say, that you behaved in a most unmannerly and reprehensible way by running out of the house as you did, without asking permission, without any one knowing a word about it; and then to go wandering about till this hour; I never heard of such behaviour before."

"Miau!" came the answer back.

This was too much for the lady's temper; with raised voice she exclaimed, "You dare, Adelheid, after your bad behaviour, to answer me as if it were a joke?"

"I did not—" began Heidi—"Miau! Miau!"

Sebastian almost dropped his dish and rushed out of the room.

"That will do," Fräulein Rottenmeier tried to say, but her voice was almost stifled with anger. "Get up and leave the room."

Heidi stood up frightened, and again made an attempt to explain. "I really did not—" "Miau! Miau! Miau!"

"But, Heidi," now put in Clara, "when you see that it makes Fräulein Rottenmeier angry, why do you keep on saying miau?"

"It isn't I, it's the kittens," Heidi was at last given time to say.

"How! What! Kittens!" shrieked Fräulein Rottenmeier. "Sebastian! Tinette! Find the horrid little things! Take them away!" And she rose and fled into the study and locked the door, so as to make sure that she was safe from the kittens, which to her were the most horrible things in creation.

Sebastian was obliged to wait a few minutes outside the door to get over his laughter before he went into the room again. He had, while serving Heidi, caught sight of a little kitten's head peeping out of her pocket, and guessing the scene that would follow, had been so overcome with amusement at the first miaus that he had hardly been able to finish handing the dishes. The lady's distressed cries for help had ceased before he had sufficiently regained his composure to go back into the dining-room. It was all peace and quietness there now, Clara had the kittens on her lap, and Heidi was kneeling beside her, both laughing and playing with the tiny, graceful little animals.

"Sebastian," exclaimed Clara as he came in, "you must help us; you must find a bed for the kittens where Fräulein Rottenmeier will not spy them out, for she is so afraid of them that she will send them away at once; but we want to keep them, and have them out whenever we are alone. Where can you put them?"

"I will see to that," answered Sebastian willingly. "I will make a bed in a basket and put it in some place where the lady is not likely to go; you leave it to me." He set about the work at once, sniggering to himself the while, for he guessed there would be a further rumpus about this some day, and Sebastian was not without a certain pleasure in the thought of Fräulein Rottenmeier being a little disturbed.

Not until some time had elapsed, and it was nearing the hour for going to bed, did Fräulein Rottenmeier venture to open the door a crack and call through, "Have you taken those dreadful little animals away, Sebastian?"

He assured her twice that he had done so; he had been hanging about the room in anticipation of this question, and now quickly and quietly caught up the kittens from Clara's lap and disappeared with them.

The castigatory sermon which Fräulein Rottenmeier had held in reserve for Heidi was put off till the following day, as she felt too exhausted now after all the emotions she had gone through of irritation, anger, and fright, of which Heidi had unconsciously been the cause. She retired without speaking, Clara and Heidi following, happy in their minds at knowing that the kittens were lying in a comfortable bed.

Chapter 8

There Is Great Commotion In The Large House

Sebastian had just shown the tutor into the study on the following morning when there came another and very loud ring at the bell, which Sebastian ran quickly to answer. "Only Herr Sesemann rings like that," he said to himself; "he must have returned home unexpectedly." He pulled open the door, and there in front of him he saw a ragged little boy carrying a hand-organ on his back.

"What's the meaning of this?" said Sebastian angrily. "I'll teach you to ring bells like that! What do you want here?"

"I want to see Clara," the boy answered.

"You dirty, good-for-nothing little rascal, can't you be polite enough to say 'Miss Clara'? What do you want with her?" continued Sebastian roughly. "She owes me fourpence," explained the boy.

"You must be out of your mind! And how do you know that any young lady of that name lives here?"

"She owes me twopence for showing her the way there, and twopence for showing her the way back."

"See what a pack of lies you are telling! The young lady never goes out, cannot even walk; be off and get back to where you came from, before I have to help you along."

But the boy was not to be frightened away; he remained standing, and said in a determined voice, "But I saw her in the street, and can describe her to you; she has short, curly black hair, and black eyes, and wears a brown dress, and does not talk quite like we do."

"Oho!" thought Sebastian, laughing to himself, "the little miss has evidently been up to more mischief." Then, drawing the boy inside he said aloud, "I understand now, come with me and wait outside the door till I tell you to go in. Be sure you begin playing your organ the instant you get inside the room; the lady is very fond of music."

Sebastian knocked at the study door, and a voice said, "Come in."

"There is a boy outside who says he must speak to Miss Clara herself," Sebastian announced.

Clara was delighted at such an extraordinary and unexpected message.

"Let him come in at once," replied Clara; "he must come in, must he not," she added, turning to her tutor, "if he wishes so particularly to see me?"

The boy was already inside the room, and according to Sebastian's directions immediately began to play his organ. Fräulein Rottenmeier, wishing to escape the A B C, had retired with her work to the dining-room. All at once she stopped and listened. Did those sounds come up from the street? And yet they seemed so near! But how could there be an organ playing in the study? And yet—it surely was so. She rushed to the other end of the long dining-room and tore open the door. She could hardly believe her eyes. There, in the middle of the study, stood a ragged boy turning away at his organ in the most energetic manner. The tutor appeared to be making efforts to speak, but his voice could not be heard. Both children were listening delightedly to the music.

"Leave off! Leave off at once!" screamed Fräulein Rottenmeier. But her voice was drowned by the music. She was making a dash for the boy, when she saw something on the ground crawling towards her feet—a dreadful dark object—a tortoise. At this sight she jumped higher than she had for many long years before, shrieking with all her might, "Sebastian! Sebastian!"

The organ-player suddenly stopped, for this time her voice had risen louder than the music. Sebastian was standing outside bent double with laughter, for he had been peeping to see what was going on. By the time he entered the room Fräulein Rottenmeier had sunk into a chair.

"Take them all out, boy and animal! Get them away at once!" she commanded him.

Sebastian pulled the boy away, the latter having quickly caught up the tortoise, and when he had got him outside he put something into his hand. "There is the fourpence from Miss Clara, and another fourpence for the music. You did it all quite right!" and with that he shut the front door upon him.

Quietness reigned again in the study, and lessons began once more; Fräulein Rottenmeier now took up her station in the study in order by her presence to prevent any further dreadful goings-on.

But soon another knock came to the door, and Sebastian again stepped in, this time to say that some one had brought a large basket with orders that it was to be given at once to Miss Clara.

"For me?" said Clara in astonishment, her curiosity very much excited, "bring it in at once that I may see what it is like."

Sebastian carried in a large covered basket and retired.

"I think the lessons had better be finished first before the basket is unpacked," said Fräulein Rottenmeier.

Clara could not conceive what was in it, and cast longing glances towards it. In the middle of one of her declensions she suddenly broke off and said to the tutor, "Mayn't I just give one peep inside to see what is in it before I go on?"

"On some considerations I am for it, on others against it," he began in answer; "for it, on the ground that if your whole attention is directed to the basket—" but the speech remained unfinished. The cover of the basket was loose, and at this moment one, two, three, and then two more, and again more kittens came suddenly tumbling on to the floor and racing about the room in every direction, and with such indescribable rapidity that it seemed as if the whole room was full of them. They jumped over the tutor's boots, bit at his trousers, climbed up Fräulein Rottenmeier's dress, rolled about her feet, sprang up on to Clara's couch, scratching, scrambling, and mewing: it was a sad scene of confusion. Clara, meanwhile, pleased with their gambols, kept on exclaiming, "Oh, the dear little things! How pretty they are! Look, Heidi, at this one; look, look, at that one over there!" And Heidi in her delight kept running after them first into one corner and then into the other. The tutor stood up by the table not knowing what to do, lifting first his right foot and then his left to get it away from the scrambling, scratching kittens. Fräulein Rottenmeier was unable at first to speak at all, so overcome was she with horror, and she did not dare rise from her chair for fear that all the dreadful little animals should jump upon her at once. At last she found voice to call loudly, "Tinette! Tinette! Sebastian! Sebastian!"

They came in answer to her summons and gathered up the kittens, by degrees they got them all inside the basket again and then carried them off to put with the other two.

Today again there had been no opportunity for gaping. Late that evening, when Fräulein Rottenmeier had somewhat recovered from the excitement of the morning, she sent for the two servants, and examined them closely concerning the events of the morning. And then it came out that Heidi was at the bottom of them, everything being the result of her excursion of the day before. Fräulein Rottenmeier sat pale with indignation and did not know at first how to express her anger. Then she made a sign to Tinette and Sebastian to withdraw, and turning to Heidi, who was standing by Clara's couch, quite unable to understand of what sin she had been guilty, began in a severe voice,—

"Adelaide, I know of only one punishment which will perhaps make you alive to your ill conduct, for you are an utter little barbarian, but we will see if we cannot tame you so that you shall not be guilty of such deeds again, by putting you in a dark cellar with the rats and black beetles."

Heidi listened in silence and surprise to her sentence, for she had never seen a cellar such as was now described; the place known at her grandfather's as the cellar, where the fresh made cheeses and the new milk were kept, was a pleasant and inviting place; neither did she know at all what rats and black beetles were like.

But now Clara interrupted in great distress. "No, no, Fräulein Rottenmeier, you must wait till papa comes; he has written to say that he will soon be home, and then I will tell him everything, and he will say what is to be done with Heidi."

Fräulein Rottenmeier could not do anything against this superior authority, especially as the father was really expected very shortly. She rose and said with some displeasure, "As you will, Clara, but I too shall have something to say to Herr Sesemann." And with that she left the room.

Two days now went by without further disturbance. Fräulein Rottenmeier, however, could not recover her equanimity; she was perpetually reminded by Heidi's presence of the deception that had been played upon her, and it seemed to her that ever since the child had come into the house everything had been topsy-turvy, and she could not bring things into proper order again. Clara had grown much more cheerful; she no longer found time hang heavy during the lesson hours, for Heidi was continually making a diversion of some kind or other. She jumbled all her letters up together and seemed quite unable to learn them, and when the tutor tried to draw her attention to their different shapes, and to help her by showing her that this was like a little horn, or that like a bird's bill, she would suddenly exclaim in a joyful voice, "That is a goat!" "That is a bird of prey!" For the tutor's descriptions suggested all kinds of pictures to her mind, but left her still incapable of the alphabet. In the later afternoons Heidi always sat with Clara, and then she would give the latter many and long descriptions of the mountain and of her life upon it, and the burning longing to return would become so overpowering that she always finished with the words, "Now I must go home! Tomorrow I must really go!" But Clara would try to quiet her, and tell Heidi that she must wait till her father returned, and then they would see what was to be done. And if Heidi gave in each time and seemed quickly to regain her good spirits, it was because of a secret delight she had in the thought that every day added two more white rolls to the number she was collecting for Grandmother; for she always pocketed the roll placed beside her plate at dinner and supper, feeling that she could not bear to eat them, knowing that Grandmother had no white bread and could hardly eat the black bread which was so hard. After dinner Heidi had to sit alone in her room for a couple of hours, for she understood now that she might not run about outside at Frankfurt as she did on the mountain, and so she did not attempt it. Any conversation with Sebastian in the dining room was also forbidden her, and as to Tinette, she kept out of her way, and never thought of speaking to her, for Heidi was quite aware that the maid looked scornfully at her and always spoke to her in a mocking voice. So Heidi had plenty of time from day to day to sit and picture how everything at home was now turning green, and how the yellow flowers were shining in the sun, and how all around lay bright in the warm sunshine, the snow and the rocks, and the whole wide valley, and Heidi at times could hardly contain herself for the longing to be back home again. And Dete had told her that she could go home whenever she liked. So it came about one day that Heidi felt she could not bear it any longer, and in haste she tied all the rolls up in her red shawl, put on her straw hat, and went downstairs. But just as she reached the hall-door she met Fräulein Rottenmeier herself, just returning from a walk, which put a stop to Heidi's journey.

Fräulein Rottenmeier stood still a moment, looking at her from top to toe in blank astonishment, her eye resting particularly on the red bundle. Then she broke out,—

"What have you dressed yourself like that for? What do you mean by this? Have I not strictly forbidden you to go running about in the streets? And here you are ready to start off again, and going out looking like a beggar."

"I was not going to run about, I was going home," said Heidi, frightened.

"What are you talking about! Going home! You want to go home?" exclaimed Fräulein Rottenmeier, her anger rising. "To run away like that! What would Herr Sesemann say if he knew! Take care that he never hears of this! And what is the matter with his house, I should like to know! Have you not been better treated than you deserved? Have you wanted for a thing? Have you ever in your life before had such a house to live in, such a table, or so many to wait upon you? Have you?"

"No," replied Heidi.

"I should think not indeed!" continued the exasperated lady. "You have everything you can possibly want here, and you are an ungrateful little thing; it's because you are too well off and comfortable that you have nothing to do but think what naughty thing you can do next!"

Then Heidi's feelings got the better of her, and she poured forth her trouble. "Indeed I only want to go home, for if I stay so long away Snowflake will begin crying again, and Grandmother is waiting for me, and Greenfinch will get beaten, because I am not there to give Peter any cheese, and

I can never see how the sun says good night to the mountains; and if the great bird were to fly over Frankfurt he would croak louder than ever about people huddling all together and teaching each other bad things, and not going to live up on the rocks, where it is so much better."

"Heaven have mercy on us, the child is out of her mind!" cried Fräulein Rottenmeier, and she turned in terror and went quickly up the steps, running violently against Sebastian in her hurry. "Go and bring that unhappy little creature in at once," she ordered him, putting her hand to her forehead which she had bumped against his.

Sebastian did as he was told, rubbing his own head as he went, for he had received a still harder blow.

Heidi had not moved, she stood with her eyes aflame and trembling all over with inward agitation.

"What, got into trouble again?" said Sebastian in a cheerful voice; but when he looked more closely at Heidi and saw that she did not move, he put his hand kindly on her shoulder, and said, trying to comfort her, "There, there, don't take it to heart so much; keep up your spirits, that is the great thing! She has nearly made a hole in my head, but don't you let her bully you." Then seeing that Heidi still did not stir, "We must go; she ordered me to take you in."

Heidi now began mounting the stairs, but with a slow, crawling step, very unlike her usual manner. Sebastian felt quite sad as he watched her, and as he followed her up he kept trying to encourage her. "Don't you give in! Don't let her make you unhappy! You keep up your courage! Why we've got such a sensible little miss that she has never cried once since she was here; many at that age cry a good dozen times a day. The kittens are enjoying themselves very much up in their home; they jump about all over the place and behave as if they were little mad things. Later we will go up and see them, when Fräulein is out of the way, shall we?"

Heidi gave a little nod of assent, but in such a joyless manner that it went to Sebastian's heart, and he followed her with sympathetic eyes as she crept away to her room.

At supper that evening Fräulein Rottenmeier did not speak, but she cast watchful looks towards Heidi as if expecting her at any minute to break out in some extraordinary way; but Heidi sat without moving or eating; all that she did was to hastily hide her roll in her pocket.

When the tutor arrived next morning, Fräulein Rottenmeier drew him privately aside, and confided her fear to him that the change of air and the new mode of life and unaccustomed surroundings had turned Heidi's head; then she told him of the incident of the day before, and of Heidi's strange speech. But the tutor assured her she need not be in alarm; he had already become aware that the child was somewhat eccentric, but otherwise quite right in her mind, and he was sure that, with careful treatment and education, the right balance would be restored, and it was this he was striving after. He was the more convinced of this by what he now heard, and by the fact that he had so far failed to teach her the alphabet, Heidi seeming unable to understand the letters.

Fräulein Rottenmeier was considerably relieved by his words, and released the tutor to his work. In the course of the afternoon the remembrance of Heidi's appearance the day before, as she was starting out on her travels, suddenly returned to the lady, and she made up her mind that she would supplement the child's clothing with various garments from Clara's wardrobe, so as to give her a decent appearance when Herr Sesemann returned. She confided her intention to Clara, who was quite willing to make over any number of dresses and hats to Heidi; so the lady went upstairs to overhaul the child's belongings and see what was to be kept and what thrown away. She returned, however, in the course of a few minutes with an expression of horror upon her face.

"What is this, Adelaide, that I find in your wardrobe!" she exclaimed. "I never heard of any one doing such a thing before! In a cupboard meant for clothes, Adelaide, what do I see at the bottom but a heap of rolls! Will you believe it, Clara, bread in a wardrobe! a whole pile of bread! Tinette," she called to that young woman, who was in the dining-room, "go upstairs and take away all those rolls out of Adelaide's cupboard and the old straw hat on the table."

"No! No!" screamed Heidi. "I must keep the hat, and the rolls are for Grandmother," and she was rushing to stop Tinette when Fräulein Rottenmeier took hold of her. "You will stop here, and all that bread and rubbish shall be taken to the place they belong to," she said in a determined tone as she kept her hand on the child to prevent her running forward.

Then Heidi in despair flung herself down on Clara's couch and broke into a wild fit of weeping, her crying becoming louder and more full of distress, every minute, while she kept on sobbing out at intervals, "Now Grandmother's' bread is all gone! They were all for Grandmother, and now they are taken away, and Grandmother won't have one," and she wept as if her heart would break. Fräulein Rottenmeier ran out of the room. Clara was distressed and alarmed at the child's crying. "Heidi, Heidi," she said imploringly, "pray do not cry so! listen to me; don't be so unhappy; look now, I promise you that you shall have just as many rolls, or more, all fresh and new to take to Grandmother when you go home; yours would have been hard and stale by then. Come, Heidi, do not cry any more!"

Heidi could not get over her sobs for a long time; she would never have been able to leave off crying at all if it had not been for Clara's promise, which comforted her. But to make sure that she could depend upon it she kept on saying to Clara, her voice broken with her gradually subsiding sobs, "Will you give me as many, quite as many, as I had, for Grandmother?"

And Clara assured her each time that she would give her as many, "or more," she added, "only be happy again."

Heidi appeared at supper with her eyes red with weeping, and when she saw her roll she could not suppress a sob. But she made an effort to control herself, for she knew she must sit quietly at table. Whenever Sebastian could catch her eye this evening he made all sorts of strange signs, pointing to his own head and then to hers, and giving little nods as much as to say, "Don't you be unhappy! I have got it all safe for you."

When Heidi was going to get into bed that night she found her old straw hat lying under the counterpane. She snatched it up with delight, made it more out of shape still in her joy, and then, after wrapping a handkerchief round it, she stuck it in a corner of the cupboard as far back as she could.

It was Sebastian who had hidden it there for her; he had been in the dining-room when Tinette was called, and had heard all that went on with the child and the latter's loud weeping. So he followed Tinette, and when she came out of Heidi's room carrying the rolls and the hat, he caught up the hat and said, "I will see to this old thing." He was genuinely glad to have been able to save it for Heidi, and that was the meaning of his encouraging signs to her at supper.

Chapter 9

Herr Sesemann Hears Of Things Which Are New To Him

A few days after these events there was great commotion and much running up and down stairs in Herr Sesemann's house. The master had just returned, and Sebastian and Tinette were busy carrying up one package after another from the carriage, for Herr Sesemann always brought back a lot of pretty things for his home. He himself had not waited to do anything before going in to see his daughter. Heidi was sitting beside her, for it was late afternoon, when the two were always together. Father and daughter greeted each other with warm affection, for they were deeply attached to one another. Then he held out his hand to Heidi, who had stolen away into the corner, and said kindly to her, "And this is our little Swiss girl; come and shake hands with me! That's right! Now, tell me, are Clara and you good friends with one another, or do you get angry and quarrel, and then cry and make it up, and then start quarreling again on the next occasion?"

"No, Clara is always kind to me," answered Heidi.

"And Heidi," put in Clara quickly, "has not once tried to quarrel."

"That's all right, I am glad to hear it," said her father, as he rose from his chair. "But you must excuse me, Clara, for I want my dinner; I have had nothing to eat all day. Afterwards I will show you all the things I have brought home with me."

He found Fräulein Rottenmeier in the dining-room superintending the preparation for his meal, and when he had taken his place she sat down opposite to him, looking the every embodiment of bad news, so that he turned to her and said, "What am I to expect, Fräulein Rottenmeier? You greet me with an expression of countenance that quite frightens me. What is the matter? Clara seems cheerful enough."

"Herr Sesemann," began the lady in a solemn voice, "it is a matter which concerns Clara; we have been frightfully imposed upon."

"Indeed, in what way?" asked Herr Sesemann as he went on calmly drinking his wine.

"We had decided, as you remember, to get a companion for Clara, and as I knew how anxious you were to have only those who were well-behaved and nicely brought up about her, I thought I would look for a little Swiss girl, as I hoped to find such a one as I have often read about, who, born as it were of the mountain air, lives and moves without touching the earth."

"Still I think even a Swiss child would have to touch the earth if she wanted to go anywhere," remarked Herr Sesemann, "otherwise they would have been given wings instead of feet."

"Ah, Herr Sesemann, you know what I mean," continued Fräulein Rottenmeier. "I mean one so at home among the living creatures of the high, pure mountain regions, that she would be like some idealistic being from another world among us."

"And what could Clara do with such an idealistic being as you describe, Fräulein Rottenmeier."

"I am not joking, Herr Sesemann, the matter is a more serious one than you think; I have been shockingly, disgracefully imposed upon."

"But how? what is there shocking and disgraceful? I see nothing shocking in the child," remarked Herr Sesemann quietly.

"If you only knew of one thing she has done, if you only knew of the kind of people and animals she has brought into the house during your absence! The tutor can tell you more about that."

"Animals? What am I to understand by animals, Fräulein Rottenmeier?"

"It is past understanding; the whole behaviour of the child would be past understanding, if it were not that at times she is evidently not in her right mind."

Herr Sesemann had attached very little importance to what was told him up till now—but not in her right mind! That was more serious and might be prejudicial to his own child. Herr Sesemann looked very narrowly at the lady opposite to assure himself that the mental aberration was not on her side. At that moment the door opened and the tutor was announced.

"Ah! Here is some one," exclaimed Herr Sesemann, "who will help to clear up matters for me. Take a seat," he continued, as he held out his hand to the tutor. "You will drink a cup of coffee with me—no ceremony, I pray! And now tell me, what is the matter with this child that has come to be a companion to my daughter? What is this strange thing I hear about her bringing animals into the house, and is she in her right senses?"

The tutor felt he must begin with expressing his pleasure at Herr Sesemann's return, and with explaining that he had come in on purpose to give him welcome, but Herr Sesemann begged him to explain without delay the meaning of all he had heard about Heidi. The tutor started in his usual style. "If I must give my opinion about this little girl, I should like first to state that, if on one side, there is a lack of development which has been caused by the more or less careless way in which she has been brought up, or rather, by the neglect of her education, when young, and by the solitary life she has led on the mountain, which is not wholly to be condemned; on the contrary, such a life has undoubtedly some advantages in it, if not allowed to overstep a certain limit of time—"

"My good friend," interrupted Herr Sesemann, "you are giving yourself more trouble than you need. I only want to know if the child has caused you alarm by any animals she has brought into the house, and what your opinion is altogether as to her being a fit companion or not for my daughter?"

"I should not like in any way to prejudice you against her," began the tutor once more; "for if on the one hand there is a certain inexperience of the ways of society, owing to the uncivilised life she led up to the time of her removal to Frankfurt, on the other hand she is endowed with certain good qualities, and, taken on the whole—"

"Excuse me, my dear sir, do not disturb yourself, but I must—I think my daughter will be wanting me," and with that Herr Sesemann quickly left the room and took care not to return. He sat himself down beside his daughter in the study, and then turning to Heidi, who had risen, "Little one, will you fetch me," he began, and then paused, for he could not think what to ask for, but he wanted to get the child out of the room for a little while, "fetch me a glass of water."

"Fresh water?" asked Heidi.

"Yes—yes—as fresh as you can get it," he answered. Heidi disappeared on the spot.

"And now, my dear little Clara," he said, drawing his chair nearer and laying her hand in his, "answer my questions clearly and intelligibly: what kind of animals has your little companion brought into the house, and why does Fräulein Rottenmeier think that she is not always in her right mind?"

Clara had no difficulty in answering. The alarmed lady had spoken to her also about Heidi's wild manner of talking, but Clara had not been able to put a meaning to it. She told her father everything about the tortoise and the kittens, and explained to him what Heidi had said the day Fräulein Rottenmeier had been put in such a fright. Herr Sesemann laughed heartily at her recital. "So you do not want me to send the child home again," he asked, "you are not tired of having her here?"

"Oh, no, no," Clara exclaimed, "please do not send her away. Time has passed much more quickly since Heidi was here, for something fresh happens every day, and it used to be so dull, and she has always so much to tell me."

"That's all right then—and here comes your little friend. Have you brought me some nice fresh water?" he asked as Heidi handed him a glass.

"Yes, fresh from the pump," answered Heidi.

"You did not go yourself to the pump?" said Clara.

"Yes I did; it is quite fresh. I had to go a long way, for there were such a lot of people at the first pump; so I went further down the street, but there were just as many at the second pump, but I was able to get some water at the one in the next street, and the gentleman with the white hair asked me to give his kind regards to Herr Sesemann."

"You have had quite a successful expedition," said Herr Sesemann laughing, "and who was the gentleman?"

"He was passing, and when he saw me he stood still and said, 'As you have a glass will you give me a drink; to whom are you taking the water?' and when I said, 'To Herr Sesemann,' he laughed very much, and then he gave me that message for you, and also said he hoped you would enjoy the water."

"Oh, and who was it, I wonder, who sent me such good wishes— tell me what he was like," said Herr Sesemann.

"He was kind and laughed, and he had a thick gold chain and a gold thing hanging from it with a large red stone, and a horse's head at the top of his stick."

"It's the doctor—my old friend the doctor," exclaimed Clara and her father at the same moment, and Herr Sesemann smiled to himself at the thought of what his friend's opinion must have been of this new way of satisfying his thirst for water.

That evening when Herr Sesemann and Fräulein Rottenmeier were alone, settling the household affairs, he informed her that he intended to keep Heidi; he found the child in a perfectly right state of mind, and his daughter liked her as a companion. "I desire, therefore," he continued, laying stress upon his words, "that the child shall be in every way kindly treated, and that her peculiarities shall not be looked upon as crimes. If you find her too much for you alone, I can hold out a prospect of help, for I am shortly expecting my mother here on a long visit, and she, as you know, can get on with anybody, whatever they may be like."

"O yes, I know," replied Fräulein Rottenmeier, but there was no tone of relief in her voice as she thought of the coming help.

Herr Sesemann was only home for a short time; he left for Paris again before the fortnight was over, comforting Clara, who could not bear that he should go from her again so soon, with the prospect of her grandmother's arrival, which was to take place in a few days' time. Herr Sesemann had indeed only just gone when a letter came from Frau Sesemann, announcing her arrival on the following day, and stating the hour when she might be expected, in order that a carriage should be sent to meet her at the station. Clara was overjoyed, and talked so much about her grandmother that evening, that Heidi began also to call her "Grandmamma," which brought down on her a look of displeasure from Fräulein Rottenmeier; this, however, had no particular effect on Heidi, for she was accustomed now to being continually in that lady's black books. But as she was going to her room that night, Fräulein Rottenmeier waylaid her, and drawing her into her own, gave her strict injunctions as to how she was to address Frau Sesemann when she arrived; on no account was she to call her "grandmamma," but always to say "Madam" to her. "Do you understand?" said the lady, as she saw a perplexed expression on Heidi's face. The latter had not understood, but seeing the severe expression of the lady's face she did not ask for more explanation.

Chapter 10

Another Grandmother

There was much expectation and preparation about the house on the following evening, and it was easy to see that the lady who was coming was one whose opinion was highly thought of, and for whom everybody had a great respect. Tinette had a new white cap on her head, and Sebastian collected all the footstools he could find and placed them in convenient spots, so that the lady might find one ready to her feet whenever she chose to sit. Fräulein Rottenmeier went about surveying everything, very upright and dignified, as if to show that though a rival power was expected, her own authority was not going to be extinguished.

And now the carriage came driving up to the door, and Tinette and Sebastian ran down the steps, followed with a slower and more stately step by the lady, who advanced to greet the guest. Heidi had been sent up to her room and ordered to remain there until called down, as the grandmother would certainly like to see Clara alone first. Heidi sat herself down in a corner and repeated her instructions over to herself. She had not to wait long before Tinette put her head in and said abruptly, "Go downstairs into the study."

Heidi had not dared to ask Fräulein Rottenmeier again how she was to address the grandmother: she thought the lady had perhaps made a mistake, for she had never heard any one called by other than their right name. As she opened the study door she heard a kind voice say, "Ah, here comes the child! Come along in and let me have a good look at you."

Heidi walked up to her and said very distinctly in her clear voice, "Good evening," and then wishing to follow her instructions called her what would be in English "Mrs. Madam."

"Well!" said the grandmother, laughing, "is that how they address people in your home on the mountain?"

"No," replied Heidi gravely, "I never knew any one with that name before."

"Nor I either," laughed the grandmother again as she patted Heidi's cheek. "Never mind! when I am with the children I am always Grandmamma; you won't forget that name, will you?"

"No, no," Heidi assured her, "I often used to say it at home."

"I understand," said the grandmother, with a cheerful little nod of the head. Then she looked more closely at Heidi, giving another nod from time to time, and the child looked back at her with steady, serious eyes, for there was something kind and warm-hearted about this new-comer that pleased Heidi, and indeed everything to do with the grandmother attracted her, so that she could not turn her eyes away. She had such beautiful white hair, and two long lace ends hung down from the cap on her head and waved gently about her face every time she moved, as if a soft breeze were blowing round her, which gave Heidi a peculiar feeling of pleasure.

"And what is your name, child?" the grandmother now asked.

"I am always called Heidi; but as I am now to be called Adelaide, I will try and take care—" Heidi stopped short, for she felt a little guilty; she had not yet grown accustomed to this name; she continued not to respond when Fräulein Rottenmeier suddenly addressed her by it, and the lady was at this moment entering the room.

"Frau Sesemann will no doubt agree with me," she interrupted, "that it was necessary to choose a name that could be pronounced easily, if only for the sake of the servants."

"My worthy Rottenmeier," replied Frau Sesemann, "if a person is called 'Heidi' and has grown accustomed to that name, I call her by the same, and so let it be."

Fräulein Rottenmeier was always very much annoyed that the old lady continually addressed her by her surname only; but it was no use minding, for the grandmother always went her own way, and so there was no help for it. Moreover the grandmother was a keen old lady, and had all her five wits about her, and she knew what was going on in the house as soon as she entered it.

When on the following day Clara lay down as usual on her couch after dinner, the grandmother sat down beside her for a few minutes and closed her eyes, then she got up again as lively as ever, and trotted off into the dining-room. No one was there. "She is asleep, I suppose," she said to herself, and then going up to Fräulein Rottenmeier's room she gave a loud knock at the door. She waited a few minutes and then Fräulein Rottenmeier opened the door and drew back in surprise at this unexpected visit.

"Where is the child, and what is she doing all this time? That is what I came to ask," said Frau Sesemann.

"She is sitting in her room, where she could well employ herself if she had the least idea of making herself useful; but you have no idea, Frau Sesemann, of the out-of-the-way things this child imagines and does, things which I could hardly repeat in good society."

"I should do the same if I had to sit in there like that child, I can tell you; I doubt if you would then like to repeat what I did, in good society! Go and fetch the child and bring her to my room; I have some pretty books with me that I should like to give her."

"That is just the misfortune," said Fräulein Rottenmeier with a despairing gesture, "what use are books to her? She has not been able to learn her A B C even, all the long time she has been here; it is quite impossible to get the least idea of it into her head, and that the tutor himself will tell you; if he had not the patience of an angel he would have given up teaching her long ago."

"That is very strange," said Frau Sesemann, "she does not look to me like a child who would be unable to learn her alphabet. However, bring her now to me, she can at least amuse herself with the pictures in the books."

Fräulein Rottenmeier was prepared with some further remarks, but the grandmother had turned away and gone quickly towards her own room. She was surprised at what she had been told about Heidi's incapacity for learning, and determined to find out more concerning this matter, not by inquiries from the tutor, however, although she esteemed him highly for his uprightness of character; she had always a friendly greeting for him, but always avoided being drawn into conversation with him, for she found his style of talk somewhat wearisome.

Heidi now appeared and gazed with open-eyed delight and wonder at the beautiful coloured pictures in the books which the grandmother gave her to look at. All of a sudden, as the latter turned over one of the pages to a fresh picture, the child gave a cry. For a moment or two she looked at it with brightening eyes, then the tears began to fall, and at last she burst into sobs. The grandmother looked at the picture—it represented a green pasture, full of young animals, some grazing and others nibbling at the shrubs. In the middle was a shepherd leaning upon his staff and looking on at his happy flock. The whole scene was bathed in golden light, for the sun was just sinking below the horizon.

The grandmother laid her hand kindly On Heidi's.

"Don't cry, dear child, don't cry," she said, "the picture has reminded you perhaps of something. But see, there is a beautiful tale to the picture which I will tell you this evening. And there are other nice tales of all kinds to read and to tell again. But now we must have a little talk together, so dry your tears and come and stand in front of me, so that I may see you well—there, now we are happy again."

But it was some little time before Heidi could overcome her sobs. The grandmother gave her time to recover herself, saying cheering words to her now and then, "There, it's all right now, and we are quite happy again."

When at last she saw that Heidi was growing calmer, she said, "Now I want you to tell me something. How are you getting on in your school-time; do you like your lessons, and have you learnt a great deal?"

"O no!" replied Heidi, sighing, "but I knew beforehand that it was not possible to learn."

"What is it you think impossible to learn?"

"Why, to read, it is too difficult."

"You don't say so! And who told you that?"

"Peter told me, and he knew all about it, for he had tried and tried and could not learn it."

"Peter must be a very odd boy then! But listen, Heidi, we must not always go by what Peter says, we must try for ourselves. I am certain that you did not give all your attention to the tutor when he was trying to teach you your letters."

"It's of no use," said Heidi in the tone of one who was ready to endure what could not be cured.

"Listen to what I have to say," continued the grandmother. "You have not been able to learn your alphabet because you believed what Peter said; but now you must believe what I tell you—and I tell you that you can learn to read in a very little while, as many other children do, who are made like you and not like Peter. And now hear what comes after—you see that picture with the shepherd and the animals—well, as soon as you are able to read you shall have that book for your own, and then you will know all about the sheep and the goats, and what the shepherd did, and the wonderful things that happened to him, just as if some one were telling you the whole tale. You will like to hear about all that, won't you?"

Heidi had listened with eager attention to the grandmother's words and now with a sigh exclaimed, "Oh, if only I could read now!"

"It won't take you long now to learn, that I can see; and now we must go down to Clara; bring the books with you." And hand in hand the two returned to the study.

Since the day when Heidi had so longed to go home, and Fräulein Rottenmeier had met her and scolded her on the steps, and told her how wicked and ungrateful she was to try and run away, and what a good thing it was that Herr Sesemann knew nothing about it, a change had come over the child. She had at last understood that day that she could not go home when she wished as Dete had told her, but that she would have to stay on in Frankfurt for a long, long time, perhaps for ever. She had also understood that Herr Sesemann would think it ungrateful of her if she wished to leave, and she believed that the grandmother and Clara would think the same. So there was nobody to whom she dared confide her longing to go home, for she would not for the world have given the grandmother, who was so kind to her, any reason for being as angry with her as Fräulein Rottenmeier had been. But the weight of trouble on the little heart grew heavier and heavier; she could no longer eat her food, and every day she grew a little paler. She lay awake for long hours at night, for as soon as she was alone and everything was still around her, the picture of the mountain with its sunshine and flowers rose vividly before her eyes; and when at last she fell asleep it was to dream of the rocks and the snow-field turning crimson in the evening light, and waking in the morning she would think herself back at the hut and prepare to run joyfully out into—the sun—and then—there was her large bed, and here she was in Frankfurt far, far away from home. And Heidi would often lay her face down on the pillow and weep long and quietly so that no one might hear her.

Heidi's unhappiness did not escape the grandmother's notice. She let some days go by to see if the child grew brighter and lost her down-cast appearance. But as matters did not mend, and she saw that many mornings Heidi had evidently been crying before she came downstairs, she took her again into her room one day, and drawing the child to her said, "Now tell me, Heidi, what is the matter; are you in trouble?"

But Heidi, afraid if she told the truth that the grandmother would think her ungrateful, and would then leave off being so kind to her, answered, "can't tell you."

"Well, could you tell Clara about it?"

"Oh, no, I cannot tell any one," said Heidi in so positive a tone, and with a look of such trouble on her face, that the grandmother felt full of pity for the child.

"Then, dear child, let me tell you what to do: you know that when we are in great trouble, and cannot speak about it to anybody, we must turn to God and pray Him to help, for He can deliver us from every care, that oppresses us. You understand that, do you not? You say your prayers every evening to the dear God in Heaven, and thank Him for all He has done for you, and pray Him to keep you from all evil, do you not?"

"No, I never say any prayers," answered Heidi.

"Have you never been taught to pray, Heidi; do you not know even what it means?"

"I used to say prayers with the first grandmother, but that is a long time ago, and I have forgotten them."

"That is the reason, Heidi, that you are so unhappy, because you know no one who can help you. Think what a comfort it is when the heart is heavy with grief to be able at any moment to go and tell everything to God, and pray Him for the help that no one else can give us. And He can help us and give us everything that will make us happy again."

A sudden gleam of joy came into Heidi's eyes. "May I tell Him everything, Everything?"

"Yes, everything, Heidi, everything."

Heidi drew her hand away, which the grandmother was holding affectionately between her own, and said quickly, "May I go?"

"Yes, of course," was the answer, and Heidi ran out of the room into her own, and sitting herself on a stool, folded her hands together and told God about everything that was making her so sad and unhappy, and begged Him earnestly to help her and to let her go home to her grandfather.

It was about a week after this that the tutor asked Frau Sesemann's permission for an interview with her, as he wished to inform her of a remarkable thing that had come to pass. So she invited him to her room, and as he entered she held out her hand in greeting, and pushing a chair towards him, "I am pleased to see you," she said, "pray sit down and tell me what brings you here; nothing bad, no complaints, I hope?"

"Quite the reverse," began the tutor. "Something has happened that I had given up hoping for, and which no one, knowing what has gone before, could have guessed, for, according to all expectations, that which has taken place could only be looked upon as a miracle, and yet it really has come to pass and in the most extraordinary manner, quite contrary to all that one could anticipate—"

"Has the child Heidi really learnt to read at last?" put in Frau Sesemann.

The tutor looked at the lady in speechless astonishment. At last he spoke again. "It is indeed truly marvellous, not only because she never seemed able to learn her A B C even after all my full explanations, and after spending unusual pains upon her, but because now she has learnt it so rapidly, just after I had made up my mind to make no further attempts at the impossible but to put the letters as they were before her without any dissertation on their origin and meaning, and now she has as you might say learnt her letters over night, and started at once to read correctly, quite unlike most beginners. And it is almost as astonishing to me that you should have guessed such an unlikely thing."

"Many unlikely things happen in life," said Frau Sesemann with a pleased smile. "Two things coming together may produce a happy result, as for instance, a fresh zeal for learning and a new method of teaching, and neither does any harm. We can but rejoice that the child has made such a good start and hope for her future progress."

After parting with the tutor she went down to the study to make sure of the good news. There sure enough was Heidi, sitting beside Clara and reading aloud to her, evidently herself very much surprised, and growing more and more delighted with the new world that was now open to her as the black letters grew alive and turned into men and things and exciting stories. That same evening Heidi found the large book with the beautiful pictures lying on her plate when she took her place at table, and when she looked questioningly at the grandmother, the latter nodded kindly to her and said, "Yes, it's yours now."

"Mine, to keep always? Even when I go home?" said, Heidi, blushing with pleasure.

"Yes, of course, yours for ever," the grandmother assured her. "Tomorrow we will begin to read it."

"But you are not going home yet, Heidi, not for years," put in Clara. "When Grandmother goes away, I shall want you to stay on with me."

When, Heidi went to her room that night she had another look at her book before going to bed, and from that day forth her chief pleasure was to read the tales which belonged to the beautiful pictures over and over again. If the grandmother said, as they were sitting together in the evening, "Now Heidi will read aloud to us," Heidi was delighted, for reading was no trouble to her now, and when she read the tales aloud the scenes seemed to grow more beautiful and distinct, and then Grandmother would explain and tell her more about them still.

Still the picture she liked best was the one of the shepherd leaning on his staff with his flock around him in the midst of the green pasture, for he was now at home and happy, following his father's sheep and goats. Then came the picture where he was seen far away from his father's house, obliged to look after the swine, and he had grown pale and thin from the husks which were all he had to eat. Even the sun seemed here to be less bright and everything looked grey and misty. But there was the third picture still to this tale: here was the old father with outstretched arms running to meet and embrace his returning and repentant son, who was advancing timidly, worn out and emaciated and clad in a ragged coat. That was Heidi's favourite tale, which she read over and over again, aloud and to herself, and she was never tired of hearing the grandmother explain it to her and Clara. But there were other tales in the book besides, and what with reading and looking at the pictures the days passed quickly away, and the time drew near for the grandmother to return home.

Chapter 11

Heidi Gains In One Way And Loses In Another

Every afternoon during her visit the grandmother went and sat down for a few minutes beside Clara after dinner, when the latter was resting, and Fräulein Rottenmeier, probably for the same reason, had disappeared inside her room; but five minutes sufficed her, and then she was up again, and Heidi was sent for to her room, and there she would talk to the child and employ and amuse her in all sorts of ways. The grandmother had a lot of pretty dolls, and she showed Heidi how to make dresses and pinafores for them, so that Heidi learnt how to sew and to make all sorts of beautiful clothes for the little people out of a wonderful collection of pieces that Grandmother had by her of every describable and lovely colour. And then Grandmother liked to hear her read aloud, and the oftener Heidi read her tales the fonder she grew of them. She entered into the lives of all the people she read about so that they became like dear friends to her, and it delighted her more and more to be with them. But still Heidi never looked really happy, and her bright eyes were no longer to be seen. It was the last week of the grandmother's visit. She called Heidi into her room as usual one day after dinner, and the child came with her book under her arm. The grandmother called her to come close, and then laying the book aside, said, "Now, child, tell me why you are not happy? Have you still the same trouble at heart?"

Heidi nodded in reply.

"Have you told God about it?"

"Yes."

"And do you pray every day that He will make things right and that you may be happy again?"

"No, I have left off praying."

"Do not tell me that, Heidi! Why have you left off praying?"

"It is of no use, God does not listen," Heidi went on in an agitated voice, "and I can understand that when there are so many, many people in Frankfurt praying to Him every evening that He cannot attend to them all, and He certainly has not heard what I said to Him."

"And why are you so sure of that, Heidi?"

"Because I have prayed for the same thing every day for weeks, and yet God has not done what I asked."

"You are wrong, Heidi; you must not think of Him like that. God is a good father to us all, and knows better than we do what is good for us. If we ask Him for something that is not good for us, He does not give it, but something better still, if only we will continue to pray earnestly and do not run away and lose our trust in Him. God did not think what you have been praying for was good for you just now; but be sure He heard you, for He can hear and see every one at the same time, because He is a God and not a human being like you and me. And because He thought it was better for you not to have at once what you wanted, He said to Himself: Yes, Heidi shall have what she asks for, but not until the right time comes, so that she may be quite happy. If I do what she wants now, and then one day she sees that it would have been better for her not to have had her own way, she will cry and say, 'If only God had not given me what I asked for! it is not so good as I expected!' And while God is watching over you, and looking to see if you will trust Him and go on praying to Him every day, and turn to Him for everything you want, you run away and leave off saying your prayers, and forget all about Him. And when God no longer hears the voice of one He knew among those who pray to Him, He lets that person go his own way, that he may learn how foolish he is. And then this one gets into trouble, and cries, 'Save me, God, for there is none other to help me,' and God says, 'Why did you go from Me; I could not help you when you ran away.' And you would not like to grieve God, would you Heidi, when He only wants to be kind to you? So will you not go and ask Him to forgive you, and continue to pray and to trust Him, for you may be sure that He will make everything right and happy for you, and then you will be glad and lighthearted again."

Heidi had perfect confidence in the grandmother, and every word she said sunk into her heart.

"I will go at once and ask God to forgive me, and I will never forget Him again," she replied repentantly.

"That is right, dear child," and anxious to cheer her, added, "Don't be unhappy, for He will do everything you wish in good time."

And Heidi ran away and prayed that she might always remember God, and that He would go on thinking about her.

The day came for Grandmother's departure—a sad one for Clara and Heidi. But the grandmother was determined to make it as much like a holiday as possible and not to let them mope, and she kept them so lively and amused that they had no time to think about their sorrow at her going until she really drove away. Then the house seemed so silent and empty that Heidi and Clara did not know what to do with themselves, and sat during the remainder of the day like two lost children.

The next day, when the hour came for Clara and Heidi to be together, the latter walked in with her book and proposed that she should go on reading aloud every afternoon to Clara, if the latter liked it. Clara agreed, and thought anyhow it would be nice for that day, so Heidi began with her usual enthusiasm. But the reading did not last long, for Heidi had hardly begun a tale about a dying grandmother before she cried out, "O! Then Grandmother is dead!" and burst into tears; for everything she read was so real to her that she quite thought it was the grandmother at home who had died, and she kept on exclaiming as her sobs increased, "She is dead, and I shall never see her again, and she never had one of the white rolls!"

Clara did all she could to explain to Heidi that the story was about quite a different grandmother; but even when at last she had been able to convince Heidi of this, the latter continued to weep inconsolably, for now she had awakened to the thought that perhaps the grandmother, and even the grandfather also, might die while she was so far away, and that if she did not go home for a long time she would find everything there all silent and dead, and there she would be all alone, and would never be able to see the dear ones she loved any more.

Fräulein Rottenmeier had meanwhile come into the room, and Clara explained to her what had happened. As Heidi continued her weeping, the lady, who was evidently getting impatient with her, went up to Heidi and said with decision, "Now, Adelaide, that is enough of all this causeless lamentation. I will tell you once for all, if there are any more scenes like this while you are reading, I shall take the book away from you and shall not let you have it again."

Her words had immediate effect on Heidi, who turned pale with fear. The book was her one great treasure. She quickly dried her tears and swallowed her sobs as best she could, so that no further sound of them should be heard. The threat did its work, for Heidi never cried aloud again whatever she might be reading, but she had often to struggle hard to keep back her tears, so that Clara would look at her and say,

"What faces you are making, Heidi, I never saw anything like it!" But the faces made no noise and did not offend Fräulein Rottenmeier, and Heidi, having overcome her fit of despairing misery, would go quietly on for a while, and no one perceived her sorrow. But she lost all her appetite, and looked so pale and thin that Sebastian was quite unhappy when he looked at her, and could not bear to see her refusing all the nice dishes he handed her. He would whisper to her sometimes, in quite a kind, fatherly manner, "Take a little; you don't know how nice it is! There, a good spoonful, now another." But it was of no use, Heidi hardly ate anything at all, and as soon as she laid her head down at night the picture of home would rise before her eyes, and she would weep, burying her face in the pillow that her crying might not be heard.

And so many weeks passed away. Heidi did not know it is was winter or summer, for the walls and windows she looked out upon showed no change, and she never went beyond the house except on rare occasions when Clara was well enough to drive out, and then they only went a very little way, as Clara could not bear the movement for long. So that on these occasions they generally only saw more fine streets and large houses and crowds of people; they seldom got anywhere beyond them, and grass and flowers, fir trees and mountains, were still far away. Heidi's longing for the old familiar and beautiful things grew daily stronger, so that now only to read a word that recalled them to her remembrance brought her to the verge of tears, which with difficulty she suppressed. So the autumn and winter passed, and again the sun came shining down on the white walls of the opposite houses, and Heidi would think to herself that now the time had come for Peter to go out again with the goats, to where the golden flowers of the cistus were glowing in the sunlight, and all the rocks around turned to fire at sunset. Heidi would go and sit in a corner of her lonely room and put her hands up to her eyes that she might not see the sun shining on the opposite wall; and then she would remain without moving, battling silently with her terrible homesickness until Clara sent for her again.

Chapter 12

A Ghost In The House

For some days past Fräulein Rottenmeier had gone about rather silently and as if lost in thought. As twilight fell, and she passed from room to room, or along the long corridors, she was seen to look cautiously behind her, and into the dark corners, as if she thought some one was coming silently behind her and might unexpectedly give her dress a pull. Nor would she now go alone into some parts of the house. If she visited the upper floor where the grand guest-chambers were, or had to go down into the large mysterious council-chamber, where every footstep echoed, and the old senators with their big white collars looked down so solemnly and immovably from their frames, she regularly called Tinette to accompany her, in case, as she said, there might be something to carry up or down. Tinette on her side did exactly the same; if she had business upstairs or down, she called Sebastian to accompany her, and there was always something he must help her with which she could not carry alone. More curious still, Sebastian, also, if sent into one of the more distant rooms, always called John to go with him in case he should want his assistance in bringing what was required. And John readily obeyed, although there was never anything to carry, and either might well have gone alone; but he did not know how soon he might want to ask Sebastian to do the same service for him. And while these things were going on upstairs, the cook, who had been in the house for years, would stand shaking her head over her pots and kettles, and sighing, "That ever I should live to know such a thing."

For something very strange and mysterious was going on in Herr Sesemann's house. Every morning, when the servants went downstairs, they found the front door wide open, although nobody could be seen far or near to account for it. During the first few days that this happened every room and corner was searched in great alarm, to see if anything had been stolen, for the general idea was that a thief had been hiding in the house and had gone off in the night with the stolen goods; but not a thing in the house had been touched, everything was safe in its place. The door was doubly locked at night, and for further security the wooden bar was fastened across it; but it was no good—next morning the door again stood open. The servants in their fear and excitement got up extra early, but not so early but what the door had been opened before they got downstairs, although everything and everybody around were still wrapped in slumber, and the doors and windows of the adjoining houses all fast shut. At last, after a great deal of persuasion from Fräulein Rottenmeier, Sebastian and John plucked up courage and agreed to sit up one night in the room next to the large council-chamber and to watch and see what would happen. Fräulein Rottenmeier looked up several weapons belonging to the master, and gave these and a bottle of spirits to Sebastian, so that their courage might not faint if it came to a fight.

On the appointed night the two sat down and began at once to take some of the strengthening cordial, which at first made them very talkative and then very sleepy, so that they leant back in their seats and became silent. As midnight struck, Sebastian roused himself and called to his companion, who, however, was not easy to wake, and kept rolling his head first to one side and then the other and continuing to sleep. Sebastian began to listen more attentively, for he was wide awake now. Everything was still as a mouse, all sound had died away from the streets even. He did not feel inclined to go to sleep again, for the stillness was ghostly to him, and he was afraid now to raise his voice to rouse John, so he shook him gently to make him stir. At last, as one struck, John work up, and came back to the consciousness of why he was sitting in a chair instead of lying in his bed. He now got up with a great show of courage and said, "Come, Sebastian, we must go outside and see what is going on; you need not be afraid, just follow me."

Whereupon he opened the door wide and stepped into the hall. Just as he did so a sudden gust of air blew through the open front door and put out the light which John held in his hand. He started back, almost overturning Sebastian, whom he clutched and pulled back into the room, and then shutting the door quickly he turned the key as far as he could make it go. Then he pulled out his matches and lighted his candle again. Sebastian, in the suddenness of the affair, did not know exactly what had happened, for he had not seen the open door or felt the breeze behind John's broad figure. But now, as he saw the latter in the light, he gave a cry of alarm, for John was trembling all over and as white as a ghost.

"What's the matter? What did you see, outside?" asked Sebastian sympathetically.

"The door partly open," gasped John, "and a white figure standing at the top of the steps—there it stood, and then all in a minute it disappeared."

Sebastian felt his blood run cold. The two sat down close to one another and did not dare move again till the morning broke and the streets began to be alive again. Then they left the room together, shut the front door, and went upstairs to tell Fräulein Rottenmeier of their experience. She was quite ready to receive them, for she had not been able to sleep at all in the anxiety of waiting to hear their report. They had no sooner given her details of the night's experience than she sat down and wrote straight off to Herr Sesemann, who had never received such a letter before in his life. She could hardly write, she told him, for her fingers were stiff with fear, and Herr Sesemann must please arrange to come back at once, for dreadful and unaccountable things were taking place at home. Then she entered into particulars of all that had happened, of how the door was found standing open every morning, and how nobody in the house now felt sure of their life in this unprotected state of things, and how it was impossible to tell what terrible results might follow on these mysterious doings.

Herr Sesemann answered that it was quite impossible for him to arrange to leave his business and return home at once. He was very much astonished at this ghost tale, but hoped by this time the ghost had disappeared. If, however, it still continued to disturb the household, would Fräulein Rottenmeier write to the grandmother and ask her if she could come and do something; she, he was sure, would soon find out a way to deal with the ghost so that it would not venture again to haunt his house. Fräulein Rottenmeier was not pleased with the tone of this letter; she did not think the matter was treated seriously enough. She wrote off without delay to

Frau Sesemann, but got no more satisfactory reply from that quarter, and some remarks in the letter she considered were quite offensive. Frau Sesemann wrote that she did not feel inclined to take the journey again from Holstein to Frankfurt because Rottenmeier fancied she saw ghosts. There had never been a ghost in the house since she had known it, and if there was one now it must be a live one, with which Rottenmeier ought to be able to deal; if not she had better send for the watchman to help her.

Fräulein Rottenmeier, however, was determined not to pass any more days in a state of fear, and she knew the right course to pursue. She had as yet said nothing to the children of the ghostly apparitions, for she knew if she did that the children would not remain alone for a single moment, and that might entail discomfort for herself. But now she walked straight off into the study, and there in a low mysterious voice told the two children everything that had taken place. Clara immediately screamed out that she could not remain another minute alone, her father must come home, and Fräulein Rottenmeier must sleep in her room at night, and Heidi too must not be left by herself, for the ghost might do something to her. She insisted that they should all sleep together in one room and keep a light burning all night, and Tinette had better be in the next room, and Sebastian and John come upstairs and spend the night in the hall, so that they might call out and frighten the ghost the instant they saw it appear on the steps. Clara, in short, grew very excited, and Fräulein Rottenmeier had great difficulty in quieting her. She promised to write at once to her father, and to have her bed put in her room and not to be left alone for a moment. They could not all sleep in the same room, but if Heidi was frightened, why Tinette must go into her room. But Heidi was far more frightened of Tinette than of ghosts, of which the child had never before heard, so she assured the others she did not mind the ghost, and would rather be alone at night.

Fräulein Rottenmeier now sat down to write another letter to Herr Sesemann, stating that these unaccountable things that were going on in the house had so affected his daughter's delicate constitution that the worst consequences might be expected. Epileptic fits and St. Vitus's dance often came on suddenly in cases like this, and Clara was liable to be attacked by either if the cause of the general alarm was not removed.

The letter was successful, and two days later Herr Sesemann stood at his front door and rang the bell in such a manner that everybody came rushing from all parts of the house and stood looking affrighted at everybody else, convinced that the ghost was impudently beginning its evil tricks in daylight. Sebastian peeped cautiously through a half-closed shutter; as he did so there came another violent ring at the bell, which it was impossible to mistake for anything but a very hard pull from a non-ghostly hand. And Sebastian recognised whose hand it was, and rushing pell-mell out of the room, fell heels over head downstairs, but picked himself up at the bottom and flung open the street door. Herr Sesemann greeted him abruptly and went up without a moment's delay into his daughter's room. Clara greeted him with a cry of joy, and seeing her so lively and apparently as well as ever, his face cleared, and the frown of anxiety passed gradually away from it as he heard from his daughter's own lips that she had nothing the matter with her, and moreover was so delighted to see him that she was quite glad about the ghost, as it was the cause of bringing him home again.

"And how is the ghost getting on?" he asked, turning to Fräulein Rottenmeier, with a twinkle of amusement in his eye.

"It is no joke, I assure you," replied that lady. "You will not laugh yourself tomorrow morning, Herr Sesemann; what is going on in the house points to some terrible thing that has taken place in the past and been concealed."

"Well, I know nothing about that," said the master of the house, "but I must beg you not to bring suspicion on my worthy ancestors. And now will you kindly call Sebastian into the dining room, as I wish to speak to him alone."

Herr Sesemann had been quite aware that Sebastian and Fräulein Rottenmeier were not on the best of terms, and he had his ideas about this scare.

"Come here, lad," he said as Sebastian appeared, "and tell me frankly—have you been playing at ghosts to amuse yourself at Fräulein Rottenmeier's expense?"

"No, on my honor, sir; pray, do not think it; I am very uncomfortable about the matter myself," answered Sebastian with unmistakable truthfulness.

"Well, if that is so, I will show you and John tomorrow morning how ghosts look in the daylight. You ought to be ashamed of yourself, Sebastian, a great strong lad like you, to run away from a ghost! But now go and take a message to my old friend the doctor; give him my kind regards, and ask him if he will come to me tonight at nine o'clock without fail; I have come by express from Paris to consult him. I shall want him to spend the night here, so bad a case is it; so he will arrange accordingly. You understand?"

"Yes, sir," replied Sebastian, "I will see to the matter as you wish." Then Herr Sesemann returned to Clara, and begged her to have no more fear, as he would soon find out all about the ghost and put an end to it.

Punctually at nine o'clock, after the children had gone to bed and Fräulein Rottenmeier had retired, the doctor arrived. He was a grey-haired man with a fresh face, and two bright, kindly eyes. He looked anxious as he walked in, but, on catching sight of his patient, burst out laughing and clapped him on the shoulder. "Well," he said, "you look pretty bad for a person that I am to sit up with all night."

"Patience, friend," answered Herr Sesemann, "the one you have to sit up for will look a good deal worse when we have once caught him."

"So there is a sick person in the house, and one that has first to be caught?"

"Much worse than that, doctor! a ghost in the house! My house is haunted!"

The doctor laughed aloud.

"That's a nice way of showing sympathy, doctor!" continued Herr, Sesemann. "It's a pity my friend Rottenmeier cannot hear you. She is firmly convinced that some old member of the family is wandering about the house doing penance for some awful crime he committed."

"How did she become acquainted with him?" asked the doctor, still very much amused.

So Herr Sesemann recounted to him how the front door was nightly opened by somebody, according to the testimony of the combined household, and he had therefore provided two loaded revolvers, so as to be prepared for anything that happened; for either the whole thing was a joke got up by some friend of the servants, just to alarm the household while he was away—and in that case a pistol fired into the air would procure him a wholesome fright—or else it was a thief, who, by leading everybody at first to think there was a ghost, made it safe for himself when he came later to steal, as no one would venture to run out if they heard him, and in that case too a good weapon would not be amiss.

The two took up their quarters for the night in the same room in which Sebastian and John had kept watch. A bottle of wine was placed on the table, for a little refreshment would be welcome from time to time if the night was to be passed sitting up. Beside it lay the two revolvers, and two good-sized candles had also been lighted, for Herr Sesemann was determined not to wait for ghosts in any half light.

The door was shut close to prevent the light being seen in the hall outside, which might frighten away the ghost. And now the two gentlemen sat comfortably back in the arm-chairs and began talking of all sorts of things, now and then pausing to take a good draught of wine, and so twelve o'clock struck before they were aware.

"The ghost has got scent of us and is keeping away tonight," said the doctor.

"Wait a bit, it does not generally appear before one o'clock," answered his friend.

They started talking again. One o'clock struck. There was not a sound about the house, nor in the street outside. Suddenly the doctor lifted his finger.

"Hush! Sesemann, don't you hear something?"

They both listened, and they distinctly heard the bar softly pushed aside and then the key turned in the lock and the door opened. Herr Sesemann put out his hand for his revolver.

"You are not afraid, are you?" said the doctor as he stood up.

"It is better to take precautions," whispered Herr Sesemann, and seizing one of the lights in his other hand, he followed the doctor, who, armed in like manner with a light and a revolver, went softly on in front. They stepped into the hall. The moonlight was shining in through the open door and fell on a white figure standing motionless in the doorway.

"Who is there?" thundered the doctor in a voice that echoed through the hall, as the two men advanced with lights and weapons towards the figure.

It turned and gave a low cry. There in her little white nightgown stood Heidi, with bare feet, staring with wild eyes at the lights and the revolvers, and trembling from head to foot like a leaf in the wind. The two men looked as one another in surprise.

"Why, I believe it is your little water-carrier, Sesemann," said the doctor.

"Child, what does this mean?" said Herr Sesemann. "What did you want? Why did you come down here?"

White with terror, and hardly able to make her voice heard, Heidi answered, "I don't know."

But now the doctor stepped forward. "This is a matter for me to see to, Sesemann; go back to your chair. I must take the child upstairs to her bed."

And with that he put down his revolver and gently taking the child by the hand led her upstairs. "Don't be frightened," he said as they went up side by side, "it's nothing to be frightened about; it's all right, only just go quietly."

On reaching Heidi's room the doctor put the candle down on the table, and taking Heidi up in his arms laid her on the bed and carefully covered her over. Then he sat down beside her and waited until Heidi had grown quieter and no longer trembled so violently. He took her hand and said in a kind, soothing voice, "There, now you feel better, and now tell me where you were wanting to go to?"

"I did not want to go anywhere," said Heidi. "I did not know I went downstairs, but all at once I was there."

"I see, and had you been dreaming, so that you seemed to see and hear something very distinctly?"

"Yes, I dream every night, and always about the same things. I think I am back with the grandfather and I hear the sound in the fir trees outside, and I see the stars shining so brightly, and then I open the door quickly and run out, and it is all so beautiful! But when I wake I am still in Frankfurt." And Heidi struggled as she spoke to keep back the sobs which seemed to choke her.

"And have you no pain anywhere? No pain in your head or back?"

"No, only a feeling as if there were a great stone weighing on me here."

"As if you had eaten something that would not go down."

"No, not like that; something heavy as if I wanted to cry very much."

"I see, and then do you have a good cry?"

"Oh, no, I mustn't; Fräulein Rottenmeier forbade me to cry."

"So you swallow it all down, I suppose? Are you happy here in Frankfurt?"

"Yes," was the low answer; but it sounded more like "No."

"And where did you live with your grandfather?"

"Up on the mountain."

"That wasn't very amusing; rather dull at times, eh?"

"No, no, it was beautiful, beautiful!" Heidi could go no further; the remembrance of the past, the excitement she had just gone through, the long suppressed weeping, were too much for the child's strength; the tears began to fall fast, and she broke into violent weeping.

The doctor stood up and laid her head kindly down on the pillow. "There, there, go on crying, it will do you good, and then go to sleep; it will be all right tomorrow."

Then he left the room and went downstairs to Herr Sesemann; when he was once more sitting in the armchair opposite his friend, "Sesemann," he said, "let me first tell you that your little charge is a sleepwalker; she is the ghost who has nightly opened the front door and put your household into this fever of alarm. Secondly, the child is consumed with homesickness, to such an extent that she is nearly a skeleton already, and soon will be quite one; something must be done at once. For the first trouble, due to her over-excited nerves, there is but one remedy, to send her back to her native mountain air; and for the second trouble there is also but one cure, and that the same. So tomorrow the child must start for home; there you have my prescription."

Herr Sesemann had arisen and now paced up and down the room in the greatest state of concern.

"What!" he exclaimed, "the child a sleepwalker and ill! Homesick, and grown emaciated in my house! All this has taken place in my house and no one seen or known anything about it! And you mean, doctor, that the child who came here happy and healthy, I am to send back to her grandfather a miserable little skeleton? I can't do it; you cannot dream of my doing such a thing! Take the child in hand, do with her what you will, and make her whole and sound, and then she shall go home; but you must do something first."

"Sesemann," replied the doctor, "consider what you are doing! This illness of the child's is not one to be cured with pills and powders. The child has not a tough constitution, but if you send her back at once she may recover in the mountain air, if not—you would rather she went back ill than not at all?"

Herr Sesemann stood still; the doctor's words were a shock to him.

"If you put it so, doctor, there is assuredly only one way—and the thing must be seen to at once." And then he and the doctor walked up and down for a while arranging what to do, after which the doctor said goodbye, for some time had passed since they first sat down together, and as the master himself opened the hall door this time the morning light shone down through it into the house.

Chapter 13

A Summer Evening On The Mountain

Herr Sesemann, a good deal irritated and excited, went quickly upstairs and along the passage to Fräulein Rottenmeier's room, and there gave such an unusually loud knock at the door that the lady awoke from sleep with a cry of alarm. She heard the master of the house calling to her from the other side of the door, "Please make haste and come down to me in the dining-room; we must make ready for a journey at once." Fräulein Rottenmeier looked at her clock: it was just half-past four; she had never got up so early before in her life. What could have happened? What with her curiosity and excitement she took hold of everything the wrong way, and it was a case with her of more haste less speed, for she kept on searching everywhere for garments which she had already put on.

Meanwhile Herr Sesemann had gone on farther and rung the bells in turn which communicated with the several servants' rooms, causing frightened figures to leap out of bed, convinced that the ghost had attacked the master and that he was calling for help. One by one they made their appearance in the dining-room, each with a more terrified face than the last, and were astonished to see their master walking up and down, looking well and cheerful, and with no appearance of having had an encounter with a ghost. John was sent off without delay to get the horses and carriage ready; Tinette was ordered to wake Heidi and get her dressed for a journey; Sebastian was hurried off to the house where Dete was in service to bring the latter round. Then Fräulein Rottenmeier, having at last accomplished her toilet, came down, with everything well adjusted about her except her cap, which was put on hind side before. Herr Sesemann put down her flurried appearance to the early awakening he had caused her, and began without delay to give her directions. She was to get out a trunk at once and pack up all the things belonging to the Swiss child— for so he usually spoke of Heidi, being unaccustomed to her name—and a good part of Clara's clothes as well, so that the child might take home proper apparel; but everything was to be done immediately, as there was no time for consideration.

Fräulein Rottenmeier stood as if rooted to the spot and stared in astonishment at Herr Sesemann. She had quite expected a long and private account of some terrible ghostly experience of his during the night, which she would have enjoyed hearing about in the broad daylight. Instead of this there were these prosaic and troublesome directions, which were so unexpected that she took some time to get over her surprise and disappointment, and continued standing awaiting further explanation.

But Herr Sesemann had no thought or time for explanations and left her standing there while he went to speak to Clara. As he anticipated, the unusual commotion in the house had disturbed her, and she was lying and listening and wondering what had happened. So he sat down and told her everything that had occurred during the past night, and explained that the doctor had given his verdict and pronounced Heidi to be in a very highly strung state, so that her nightly wanderings might gradually lead her farther and farther, perhaps even on to the roof, which of course would be very dangerous for her. And so they had decided to send her home at once, as he did not like to take the responsibility of her remaining, and Clara would see for herself that it was the only thing to do. Clara was very much distressed, and at first made all kinds of suggestions for keeping Heidi with her; but her father was firm, and promised her, if she would be reasonable and make no further fuss, that he would take her to Switzerland next summer. So Clara gave in to the inevitable, only stipulating that the box might be brought into her room to be packed, so that she might add whatever she liked, and her father was only too pleased to let her provide a nice outfit for the child. Meanwhile Dete had arrived and was waiting in the hall, wondering what extraordinary event had come to pass for her to be sent for at such an unusual hour. Herr Sesemann informed her of the state Heidi was in, and that he wished her that very day to take her home. Dete was greatly disappointed, for she had not expected such a piece of news. She remembered Uncle's last words, that he never wished to set eyes on her again, and it seemed to her that to take back the child to him, after having left it with him once and then taken it away again, was not a safe or wise thing for her to do. So she excused herself to Herr Sesemann with her usual flow of words; today and tomorrow it would be quite impossible for her to take the journey, and there was so much to do that she doubted if she could get off on any of the following days. Herr Sesemann understood that she was unwilling to go at all, and so dismissed her. Then he sent for Sebastian and told him to make ready to start: he was to travel with the child as far as Basle that day, and the next day take her home. He would give him a letter to carry to the grandfather, which would explain everything, and he himself could come back by return.

"But there is one thing in particular which I wish you to look after," said Herr Sesemann in conclusion, "and be sure you attend to what I say. I know the people of this hotel in Basle, the name of which I give you on this card. They will see to providing rooms for the child and you. When there, go at once into the child's room and see that the windows are all firmly fastened so that they cannot be easily opened. After the child is in bed, lock the door of her room on the outside, for the child walks in her sleep and might run into danger in a strange house if she went wandering downstairs and tried to open the front door; so you understand?"

"Oh! Then that was it?" exclaimed Sebastian, for now a light was thrown on the ghostly visitations.

"Yes, that was it! And you are a coward, and you may tell John he is the same, and the whole household a pack of idiots." And with this Herr Sesemann went off to his study to write a letter to Alm-Uncle. Sebastian remained standing, feeling rather foolish.

"If only I had not let that fool of a John drag me back into the room, and had gone after the little white figure, which I should do certainly if I saw it now!" he kept on saying to himself; but just now every corner of the room was clearly visible in the daylight.

Meanwhile Heidi was standing expectantly dressed in her Sunday frock waiting to see what would happen next, for Tinette had only woke her up with a shake and put on her clothes without a word of explanation. The little uneducated child was far too much beneath her for Tinette to speak to.

Herr Sesemann went back to the dining-room with the letter; breakfast was now ready, and he asked, "Where is the child?"

Heidi was fetched, and as she walked up to him to say "Good morning," he looked inquiringly into her face and said, "Well, what do you say to this, little one?"

Heidi looked at him in perplexity.

"Why, you don't know anything about it, I see," laughed Herr Sesemann. "You are going home today, going at once."

"Home," murmured Heidi in a low voice, turning pale; she was so overcome that for a moment or two she could hardly breathe.

"Don't you want to hear more about it?"

"Oh, yes, yes!" exclaimed Heidi, her face now rosy with delight.

"All right, then," said Herr Sesemann as he sat down and made her a sign to do the same, "but now make a good breakfast, and then off you go in the carriage."

But Heidi could not swallow a morsel though she tried to do what she was told; she was in such a state of excitement that she hardly knew if she was awake or dreaming, or if she would again open her eyes to find herself in her nightgown at the front door.

"Tell Sebastian to take plenty of provisions with him," Herr Sesemann called out to Fräulein Rottenmeier, who just then came into the room; "the child can't eat anything now, which is quite natural. Now run up to Clara and stay with her till the carriage comes round," he added kindly, turning to Heidi.

Heidi had been longing for this, and ran quickly upstairs. An immense trunk was standing open in the middle of the room.

"Come along, Heidi," cried Clara, as she entered; "see all the things I have had put in for you—aren't you pleased?"

And she ran over a list of things, dresses and aprons and handkerchiefs, and all kinds of working materials. "And look here," she added, as she triumphantly held up a basket. Heidi peeped in and jumped for joy, for inside it were twelve beautiful round white rolls, all for Grandmother. In their delight the children forgot that the time had come for them to separate, and when some one called out, "The carriage is here," there was no time for grieving.

Heidi ran to her room to fetch her darling book; she knew no one could have packed that, as it lay under her pillow, for Heidi had kept it by her night and day. This was put in the basket with the rolls. Then she opened her wardrobe to look for another treasure, which perhaps no one would have thought of packing—and she was right—the old red shawl had been left behind, Fräulein Rottenmeier not considering it worth putting in with the other things. Heidi wrapped it round something else which she laid on the top of the basket, so that the red package was quite conspicuous. Then she put on her pretty hat and left the room. The children could not spend much time over their farewells, for Herr Sesemann was waiting to put Heidi in the carriage. Fräulein Rottenmeier was waiting at the top of the stairs to say goodbye to her. When she caught sight of the strange little red bundle, she took it out of the basket and threw it on the ground. "No, no, Adelaide," she exclaimed, "you cannot leave the house with that thing. What can you possibly want with it!" And then she said goodbye to the child. Heidi did not dare take up her little bundle, but she gave the master of the house an imploring look, as if her greatest treasure had been taken from her.

"No, no," said Herr Sesemann in a very decided voice, "the child shall take home with her whatever she likes, kittens and tortoises, if it pleases her; we need not put ourselves out about that, Fräulein Rottenmeier."

Heidi quickly picked up her bundle, with a look of joy and gratitude. As she stood by the carriage door, Herr Sesemann gave her his hand and said he hoped she would remember him and Clara. He wished her a happy journey, and Heidi thanked him for all his kindness, and added, "And please say goodbye to the doctor for me and give him many, many thanks." For she had not forgotten that he had said to her the night before, 'It will be all right tomorrow,' and she rightly divined that he had helped to make it so for her. Heidi was now lifted into the carriage, and then the basket and the provisions were put in, and finally Sebastian took his place. Then Herr Sesemann called out once more, "A pleasant journey to you," and the carriage rolled away.

Heidi was soon sitting in the railway carriage, holding her basket tightly on her lap; she would not let it out of her hands for a moment, for it contained the delicious rolls for Grandmother; so she must keep it carefully, and even peep inside it from time to time to enjoy the sight of them. For many hours she sat as still as a mouse; only now was she beginning to realise that she was going home to the grandfather, the mountain, the grandmother, and Peter, and pictures of all she was going to see again rose one by one before her eyes; she thought of how everything would look at home, but this brought other thoughts to her mind, and all of a sudden she said anxiously, "Sebastian, are you sure that Grandmother on the mountain is not dead?"

"No, no," said Sebastian, wishing to soothe her, "we will hope not; she is sure to be alive still."

Then Heidi fell back on her own thoughts again. Now and then she looked inside the basket, for the thing she looked forward to most was laying all the rolls out on Grandmother's table. After a long silence she spoke again, "If only we could know for certain that Grandmother is alive!"

"Yes, yes," said Sebastian, half asleep; "she is sure to be alive, there is no reason why she should be dead."

After a while sleep fell on Heidi too, and after her disturbed night and early rising she slept so soundly that she did not wake till Sebastian shook her by the arm and called to her, "Wake up, wake up! We shall have to get out directly; we are just in Basle!"

There was a further railway journey of many hours the next day. Heidi again sat with her basket on her knee, for she would not have given it up to Sebastian on any consideration; today she never even opened her mouth, for her excitement, which increased with every mile of the journey, kept her speechless. All of a sudden, before Heidi expected it, a voice called out, "Mayenfeld." She and Sebastian both jumped up, the latter also taken by surprise. In another minute they were both standing on the platform with Heidi's trunk, and the train was steaming away down the valley. Sebastian looked after it regretfully, for he preferred the easier mode of travelling to a wearisome climb on foot, especially as there was danger no doubt as well as fatigue in a country like this, where, according to Sebastian's idea, everything and everybody were half savage. He therefore looked cautiously to either side to see who was a likely person to ask the safest way to Dörfli.

Just outside the station he saw a shabby-looking little cart and horse which a broad-shouldered man was loading with heavy sacks that had been brought by the train, so he went up to him and asked which was the safest way to get to Dörfli.

"All the roads about here are safe," was the curt reply.

So Sebastian altered his question and asked which was the best way to avoid falling over the precipice, and also how a box could be conveyed to Dörfli. The man looked at the box, weighing it with his eye, and then volunteered if it was not too heavy to take it on his own cart, as he was driving to Dörfli. After some little interchange of words it was finally agreed that the man should take both the child and the box to Dörfli, and there find some one who could be sent on with Heidi up the mountain.

"I can go by myself, I know the way well from Dörfli," put in Heidi, who had been listening attentively to the conversation. Sebastian was greatly relieved at not having to do any mountain climbing. He drew Heidi aside and gave her a thick rolled parcel, and a letter for her grandfather; the parcel, he told her, was a present from Herr Sesemann, and she must put it at the bottom of her basket under the rolls and be very careful not to lose it, as Herr Sesemann would be very vexed if she did, and never be the same to her again; so little miss was to think well of what he said.

"I shall be sure not to lose it," said Heidi confidently, and she at once put the roll and the letter at the bottom of her basket. The trunk meanwhile had been hoisted into the cart, and now Sebastian lifted Heidi and her basket on to the high seat and shook hands with her; he then made signs to her to keep her eye on the basket, for the driver was standing near and Sebastian thought it better to be careful, especially as he knew that he ought himself to have seen the child safely to her journey's end. The driver now swung himself up beside Heidi, and the cart rolled away in the direction of the mountains, while Sebastian, glad of having no tiring and dangerous journey on foot before him, sat down in the station and awaited the return train.

The driver of the car was the miller at Dörfli and was taking home his sacks of flour. He had never seen Heidi, but like everybody in Dörfli knew all about her. He had known her parents, and felt sure at once that this was the child of whom he had heard so much. He began to wonder why she had come back, and as they drove along he entered into conversation with her. "You are the child who lived with your grandfather, Alm-Uncle, are you not?"

"Yes."

"Didn't they treat you well down there that you have come back so soon?"

"Yes, it was not that; everything in Frankfurt is as nice as it could be."

"Then why are you running home again?"

"Only because Herr Sesemann gave me leave, or else I should not have come."

"If they were willing to let you stay, why did you not remain where you were better off than at home?"

"Because I would a thousand times rather be with Grandfather on the mountain than anywhere else in the world."

"You will think differently perhaps when you get back there," grumbled the miller; and then to himself, "It's strange of her, for she must know what it's like."

He began whistling and said no more, while Heidi looked around her and began to tremble with excitement, for she knew every tree along the way, and there overhead were the high jagged peaks of the mountain looking down on her like old friends. And Heidi nodded back to them, and grew every moment more wild with her joy and longing, feeling as if she must jump down from the cart and run with all her might till she reached the top. But she sat quite still and did not move, although inwardly in such agitation. The clock was striking five as they drove into Dörfli. A crowd of women and children immediately surrounded the cart, for the box and the child arriving with the miller had excited the curiosity of everybody in the neighbourhood, inquisitive to know whence they came and whither they were going and to whom they belonged. As the miller lifted Heidi down, she said hastily, "Thank you, Grandfather will send for the trunk," and was just going to run off, when first one and then another of the bystanders caught hold of her, each one having a different question to put to her. But Heidi pushed her way through them with such an expression of distress on her face that they were forced to let her go. "You see," they said to one another, "how frightened she is, and no wonder," and then they went on to talk of Alm-Uncle, how much worse he had grown that last year, never speaking a word and looking as if he would like to kill everybody he met, and if the child had anywhere else to go to she certainly would not run back to the old dragon's den. But here the miller interrupted them, saying he knew more about it than they did, and began telling them how a kind gentleman had brought her to Mayenfeld and seen her off, and had given him his fare without any bargaining, and extra money for himself; what was more, the child had assured him that she had had everything she wanted where she had been, and that it was her own wish to return to her grandfather. This information caused great surprise and was soon repeated all over Dörfli, and that evening there was not a house in the place in which the astounding news was not discussed, of how Heidi had of her own accord given up a luxurious home to return to her grandfather.

Heidi climbed up the steep path from Dörfli as quickly as she could; she was obliged, however, to pause now and again to take breath, for the basket she carried was rather heavy, and the way got steeper as she drew nearer the top. One thought alone filled Heidi's mind, "Would she find the grandmother sitting in her usual corner by the spinning-wheel, was she still alive?" At last Heidi caught sight of the grandmother's house in the hollow of the mountain and her heart began to beat; she ran faster and faster and her heart beat louder and louder—and now she had reached the house, but she trembled so she could hardly open the door—and then she was standing inside, unable in her breathlessness to utter a sound.

"Ah, my God!" cried a voice from the corner, "that was how Heidi used to run in; if only I could have her with me once again! Who is there?"

"It's I, I, Grandmother," cried Heidi as she ran and flung herself on her knees beside the old woman, and seizing her hands, clung to her, unable to speak for joy. And the grandmother herself could not say a word for some time, so unexpected was this happiness; but at last she put out her hand and stroked Heidi's curly hair, and said, "Yes, yes, that is her hair, and her voice; thank God that He has granted my prayer!" And tears of joy fell from the blind eyes on to Heidi's hand. "Is it really you, Heidi; have you really come back to me?"

"Yes, Grandmother, I am really here," answered Heidi in a reassuring voice. "Do not cry, for I have really come back and I am never going away again, and I shall come every day to see you, and you won't have any more hard bread to eat for some days, for look, look!"

And Heidi took the rolls from the basket and piled the whole twelve up on Grandmother's lap.

"Ah, child! Child! What a blessing you bring with you!" the old woman exclaimed, as she felt and seemed never to come to the end of the rolls. "But you yourself are the greatest blessing, Heidi," and again she touched the child's hair and passed her hand over her hot cheeks, and said, "Say something, child, that I may hear your voice."

Then Heidi told her how unhappy she had been, thinking that the grandmother might die while she was away and would never have her white rolls, and that then she would never, never see her again.

Peter's mother now came in and stood for a moment overcome with astonishment. "Why, it's Heidi," she exclaimed, "and yet can it be?"

Heidi stood up, and Brigitta now could not say enough in her admiration of the child's dress and appearance; she walked round her, exclaiming all the while, "Grandmother, if you could only see her, and see what a pretty frock she has on; you would hardly know her again. And the hat with the feather in it is yours too, I suppose? Put it on that I may see how you look in it?"

"No, I would rather not," replied Heidi firmly. "You can have it if you like; I do not want it; I have my own still." And Heidi so saying undid her red bundle and took out her own old hat, which had become a little more battered still during the journey. But this was no trouble to Heidi; she had not forgotten how her grandfather had called out to Dete that he never wished to see her and her hat and feathers again, and this was the reason she had so anxiously preserved her old hat, for she had never ceased to think about going home to her grandfather. But Brigitta told her not to be so foolish as to give it away; she would not think of taking such a beautiful hat; if Heidi did not want to wear it she might sell it to the schoolmaster's daughter in Dörfli and get a good deal of money for it. But Heidi stuck to her intention and hid the hat quietly in a corner behind the grandmother's chair. Then she took off her pretty dress and put her red shawl on over her under-petticoat, which left her arms bare; and now she clasped the old woman's hand. "I must go home to Grandfather," she said, "but tomorrow I shall come again. Good night, Grandmother."

"Yes, come again, be sure you come again tomorrow," begged the grandmother, as she pressed Heidi's hands in hers, unwilling to let her go.

"Why have you taken off that pretty dress?" asked Brigitta.

"Because I would rather go home to Grandfather as I am or else perhaps he would not know me; you hardly did at first."

Brigitta went with her to the door, and there said in rather a mysterious voice, "You might have kept on your dress, he would have known you all right; but you must be careful, for Peter tells me that Alm-Uncle is always now in a bad temper and never speaks."

Heidi bid her good night and continued her way up the mountain, her basket on her arm. All around her the steep green slopes shone bright in the evening sun, and soon the great gleaming snowfield up above came in sight. Heidi was obliged to keep on pausing to look behind her, for the higher peaks were behind her as she climbed. Suddenly a warm red glow fell on the grass at her feet; she looked back again—she had not remembered how splendid it was, nor seen anything to compare to it in her dreams— for there the two high mountain peeks rose into the air like two great flames, the whole snow-field had turned crimson, and rosy-coloured clouds floated in the sky above. The grass upon the mountain sides had turned to gold, the rocks were all aglow, and the whole valley was bathed in golden mist. And as Heidi stood gazing around her at all this splendor the tears ran down her cheeks for very delight and happiness, and impulsively she put her hands together, and lifting her eyes to heaven, thanked God aloud for having brought her home, thanked Him that everything was as beautiful as ever, more beautiful even than she had thought, and that it was all hers again once more. And she was so overflowing with joy and thankfulness that she could not find words to thank Him enough. Not until the glory began to fade could she tear herself away. Then she ran on so quickly that in a very little while she caught sight of the tops of the fir trees above the hut roof, then the roof itself, and at last the whole hut, and there was Grandfather sitting as in old days smoking his pipe, and she could see the fir trees waving in the wind. Quicker and quicker went her little feet, and before Alm-Uncle had time to see who was coming, Heidi had rushed up to him, thrown down her basket and flung her arms round his neck, unable in the excitement of seeing him again to say more than "Grandfather! Grandfather! Grandfather!" over and over again.

And the old man himself said nothing. For the first time for many years his eyes were wet, and he had to pass his hand across them. Then he unloosed Heidi's arms, put her on his knee, and after looking at her for a moment, "So you have come back to me, Heidi," he said, "how is that? You don't look much of a grand lady. Did they send you away?"

"Oh, no, Grandfather," said Heidi eagerly, "you must not think that; they were all so kind—Clara, and Grandmamma, and Herr Sesemann. But you see, Grandfather, I did not know how to bear myself till I got home again to you. I used to think I should die, for I felt as if I could not breathe; but I never said anything because it would have been ungrateful. And then suddenly one morning quite early Herr Sesemann said to me—but I think it was partly the doctor's doing—but perhaps it's all in the letter—" and Heidi jumped down and fetched the roll and the letter and handed them both to her grandfather.

"That belongs to you," said the latter, laying the roll down on the bench beside him. Then he opened the letter, read it through and without a word put it in his pocket.

"Do you think you can still drink milk with me, Heidi?" he asked, taking the child by the hand to go into the hut. "But bring your money with you; you can buy a bed and bedclothes and dresses for a couple of years with it."

"I am sure I do not want it," replied Heidi. "I have got a bed already, and Clara has put such a lot of clothes in my box that I shall never want any more."

"Take it and put it in the cupboard; you will want it some day I have no doubt."

Heidi obeyed and skipped happily after her grandfather into the house; she ran into all the corners, delighted to see everything again, and then went up the ladder—but there she came to a pause and called down in a tone of surprise and distress, "Oh, Grandfather, my bed's gone."

"We can soon make it up again," he answered her from below. "I did not know that you were coming back; come along now and have your milk."

Heidi came down, sat herself on her high stool in the old place, and then taking up her bowl drank her milk eagerly, as if she had never come across anything so delicious, and as she put down her bowl, she exclaimed, "Our milk tastes nicer than anything else in the world, Grandfather."

A shrill whistle was heard outside. Heidi darted out like a flash of lightning. There were the goats leaping and springing among the rocks, with Peter in their midst. When he caught sight of Heidi he stood still with astonishment and gazed speechlessly at her. Heidi called out, "Good evening, Peter," and then ran in among the goats. "Little Swan! Little Bear! Do you know me again?" And the animals evidently recognised her voice at once, for they began rubbing their heads against her and bleating loudly as if for joy, and as she called the other goats by name one after the other, they all came scampering towards her helter-skelter and crowding round her. The impatient Greenfinch sprang into the air and over two of her companions in order to get nearer, and even the shy little Snowflake butted the Great Turk out of her way in quite a determined manner, which left him standing taken aback by her boldness, and lifting his beard in the air as much as to say, You see who I am.

Heidi was out of her mind with delight at being among all her old friends again; she flung her arms round the pretty little Snowflake, stroked the obstreperous Greenfinch, while she herself was thrust at from all sides by the affectionate and confiding goats; and so at last she got near to where Peter was still standing, not having yet got over his surprise.

"Come down, Peter," cried Heidi, "and say good evening to me."

"So you are back again?" he found words to say at last, and now ran down and took Heidi's hand which she was holding out in greeting, and immediately put the same question to her which he had been in the habit of doing in the old days when they returned home in the evening, "Will you come out with me again tomorrow?"

"Not tomorrow, but the day after perhaps, for tomorrow I must go down to Grandmother."

"I am glad you are back," said Peter, while his whole face beamed with pleasure, and then he prepared to go on with his goats; but he never had had so much trouble with them before, for when at last, by coaxing and threats, he had got them all together, and Heidi had gone off with an arm over either head of her grandfather's two, the whole flock suddenly turned and ran after her. Heidi had to go inside the stall with her two and shut the door, or Peter would never have got home that night. When Heidi went indoors after this she found her bed already made up for her; the hay had been piled high for it and smelt deliciously, for it had only just been got in, and the grandfather had carefully spread and tucked in the clean sheets. It was with a happy heart that Heidi lay down in it that night, and her sleep was sounder than it had been for a whole year past. The grandfather got up at least ten times during the night and mounted the ladder to see if Heidi was all right and showing no signs of restlessness, and to feel that the hay he had stuffed into the round window was keeping the moon from shining too brightly upon her. But Heidi did not stir; she had no need now to wander about, for the great burning longing of her heart was satisfied; she had seen the high mountains and rocks alight in the evening glow, she had heard the wind in the fir trees, she was at home again on the mountain.

Chapter 14

Sunday Bells

Heidi was standing under the waving fir trees waiting for her grandfather, who was going down with her to Grandmother's, and then on to Dörfli to fetch her box. She was longing to know how Grandmother had enjoyed her white bread and impatient to see and hear her again; but no time seemed weary to her now, for she could not listen long enough to the familiar voice of the trees, or drink in too much of the fragrance wafted to her from the green pastures where the golden-headed flowers were glowing in the sun, a very feast to her eyes. The grandfather came out, gave a look round, and then called to her in a cheerful voice, "Well, now we can be off."

It was Saturday, a day when Alm-Uncle made everything clean and tidy inside and outside the house; he had devoted his morning to this work so as to be able to accompany Heidi in the afternoon, and the whole place was now as spick and span as he liked to see it. They parted at the grandmother's cottage and Heidi ran in. The grandmother had heard her steps approaching and greeted her as she crossed the threshold, "Is it you, child? Have you come again?"

Then she took hold of Heidi's hand and held it fast in her own, for she still seemed to fear that the child might be torn from her again. And now she had to tell Heidi how much she had enjoyed the white bread, and how much stronger she felt already for having been able to eat it, and then Peter's mother went on and said she was sure that if her mother could eat like that for a week she would get back some of her strength, but she was so afraid of coming to the end of the rolls, that she had only eaten one as yet. Heidi listened to all Brigitta said, and sat thinking for a while. Then she suddenly thought of a way.

"I know, Grandmother, what I will do," she said eagerly, "I will write to Clara, and she will send me as many rolls again, if not twice as many as you have already, for I had ever such a large heap in the wardrobe, and when they were all taken away she promised to give me as many back, and she would do so I am sure."

"That is a good idea," said Brigitta; "but then, they would get hard and stale. The baker in Dörfli makes the white rolls, and if we could get some of those he has over now and then—but I can only just manage to pay for the black bread."

A further bright thought came to Heidi, and with a look of joy, "Oh, I have lots of money, Grandmother," she cried gleefully, skipping about the room in her delight, "and I know now what I will do with it. You must have a fresh white roll every day, and two on Sunday, and Peter can bring them up from Dörfli."

"No, no, child!" answered the grandmother, "I cannot let you do that; the money was not given to you for that purpose; you must give it to your grandfather, and he will tell you how you are to spend it."

But Heidi was not to be hindered in her kind intentions, and she continued to jump about, saying over and over again in a tone of exultation, "Now, Grandmother can have a roll every day and will grow quite strong again—and, Oh, Grandmother," she suddenly exclaimed with an increase of jubilation in her voice, "if you get strong everything will grow light again for you; perhaps it's only because you are weak that it is dark." The grandmother said nothing, she did not wish to spoil the child's pleasure. As she went jumping about Heidi suddenly caught sight of the grandmother's song book, and another happy idea struck her, "Grandmother, I can also read now, would you like me to read you one of your hymns from your old book?"

"Oh, yes," said the grandmother, surprised and delighted; "but can you really read, child, really?"

Heidi had climbed on to a chair and had already lifted down the book, bringing a cloud of dust with it, for it had lain untouched on the shelf for a long time. Heidi wiped it, sat herself down on a stool beside the old woman, and asked her which hymn she should read.

"What you like, child, what you like," and the grandmother pushed her spinning-wheel aside and sat in eager expectation waiting for Heidi to begin. Heidi turned over the leaves and read a line out softly to herself here and there. At last she said,

"Here is one about the sun, Grandmother, I will read you that." And Heidi began, reading with more and more warmth of expression as she went on,—

The morning breaks,
And warm and bright
The earth lies still
In the golden light—
For Dawn has scattered the clouds of night.

God's handiwork
Is seen around,
Things great and small
To His praise abound—
Where are the signs of His love not found?

All things must pass,
But God shall still

With steadfast power
His will fulfil—
Sure and unshaken is His will.

His saving grace
Will never fail,
Though grief and fear
The heart assail—
O'er life's wild seas He will prevail.

Joy shall be ours
In that garden blest,
Where after storm
We find our rest—
I wait in peace—God's time is best.

The grandmother sat with folded hands and a look of indescribable joy on her face, such as Heidi had never seen there before, although at the same time the tears were running down her cheeks. As Heidi finished, she implored her, saying, "Read it once again, child, just once again."

And the child began again, with as much pleasure in the verses as the grandmother,—

Joy shall be ours
In that garden blest,
Where after storm
We find our rest—
I wait in peace—God's time is best.

"Ah, Heidi, that brings light to the heart! What comfort you have brought me!"

And the old woman kept on repeating the glad words, while Heidi beamed with happiness, and she could not take her eyes away from the grandmother's face, which had never looked like that before. It had no longer the old troubled expression, but was alight with peace and joy as if she were already looking with clear new eyes into the garden or Paradise.

Some one now knocked at the window and Heidi looked up and saw her grandfather beckoning her to come home with him. She promised the grandmother before leaving her that she would be with her the next day, and even if she went out with Peter she would only spend half the day with him, for the thought that she might make it light and happy again for the grandmother gave her the greatest pleasure, greater even than being out on the sunny mountain with the flowers and goats. As she was going out Brigitta ran to her with the frock and hat she had left. Heidi put the dress over her arm, for, as she thought to herself, the grandfather had seen that before, but she obstinately refused to take back the hat; Brigitta could keep it, for she should never put it on her head again. Heidi was so full of her morning's doings that she began at once to tell her grandfather all about them: how the white bread could be fetched every day from Dörfli if there was money for it, and how the grandmother had all at once grown stronger and happier, and light had come to her. Then she returned to the subject of the rolls. "If the grandmother won't take the money, Grandfather, will you give it all to me, and I can then give Peter enough every day to buy a roll and two on Sunday?"

"But how about the bed?" said her grandfather. "It would be nice for you to have a proper bed, and there would then be plenty for the bread."

But Heidi gave her grandfather no peace till he consented to do what she wanted; she slept a great deal better, she said, on her bed of hay than on her fine pillowed bed in Frankfurt. So at last he said, "The money is yours, do what you like with it; you can buy bread for Grandmother for years to come with it."

Heidi shouted for joy at the thought that Grandmother would never need any more to eat hard black bread, and "Oh, Grandfather!" she said, "everything is happier now than it has ever been in our lives before!" and she sang and skipped along, holding her grandfather's hand as light-hearted as a bird. But all at once she grew quiet and said, "If God had let me come at once, as I prayed, then everything would have been different, I should only have had a little bread to bring to Grandmother, and I should not have been able to read, which is such a comfort to her; but God has arranged it all so much better than I knew how to; everything has happened just as the other grandmother said it would. Oh, how glad I am that God did not let me have at once all I prayed and wept for! And now I shall always pray to God as she told me, and always thank Him, and when He does not do anything I ask for I shall think to myself, It's just like it was in Frankfurt: God, I am sure, is going to do something better still. So we will pray every day, won't we, Grandfather, and never forget Him again, or else He may forget us."

"And supposing one does forget Him?" said the grandfather in a low voice.

"Then everything goes wrong, for God lets us then go where we like, and when we get poor and miserable and begin to cry about it no one pities us, but they say, You ran away from God, and so God, who could have helped you, left you to yourself."

"That is true, Heidi; where did you learn that?"

"From Grandmamma; she explained it all to me."

The grandfather walked on for a little while without speaking, then he said, as if following his own train of thought: "And if it once is so, it is so always; no one can go back, and he whom God has forgotten, is forgotten for ever."

"Oh, no, Grandfather, we can go back, for Grandmamma told me so, and so it was in the beautiful tale in my book—

but you have not heard that yet; but we shall be home directly now, and then I will read it you, and you will see how beautiful it is." And in her eagerness Heidi struggled faster and faster up the steep ascent, and they were no sooner at the top than she let go her grandfather's hand and ran into the hut. The grandfather slung the basket off his shoulders in which he had brought up a part of the contents of the trunk which was too heavy to carry up as it was. Then he sat down on his seat and began thinking.

Heidi soon came running out with her book under her arm. "That's right, Grandfather," she exclaimed as she saw he had already taken his seat, and in a second she was beside him and had her book open at the particular tale, for she had read it so often that the leaves fell open at it of their own accord. And now in a sympathetic voice Heidi began to read of the son when he was happily at home, and went out into the fields with his father's flocks, and was dressed in a fine cloak, and stood leaning on his shepherd's staff watching as the sun went down, just as he was to be seen in the picture. But then all at once he wanted to have his own goods and money and to be his own master, and so he asked his father to give him his portion, and he left his home and went and wasted all his substance. And when he had nothing left he hired himself out to a master who had no flocks and fields like his father, but only swine to keep; and so he was obliged to watch these, and he only had rags to wear and a few husks to eat such as the swine fed upon. And then he thought of his old happy life at home and of how kindly his father had treated him and how ungrateful he had been, and he wept for sorrow and longing. And he thought to himself, "I will arise and go to my father, and will say to him, 'Father, I am not worthy to be called thy son; make me as one of thy hired servants.'" And when he was yet a great way off his father saw him . . . Here Heidi paused in her reading. "What do you think happens now, Grandfather?" she said. "Do you think the father is still angry and will say to him, 'I told you so!' Well, listen now to what comes next." His father saw him, and had compassion, and ran, and fell on his neck and kissed him. And the son said to him, "Father, I have sinned against heaven and in thy sight, and am no more worthy to be called thy son." But the father said to his servants, "Bring forth the best robe, and put it on him; and put a ring on his hand and shoes on his feet: and bring hither the fatted calf and kill it; and let us eat and be merry, for this my son was dead and is alive again; he was lost and is found." And they began to be merry.

"Isn't that a beautiful tale, Grandfather," said Heidi, as the latter continued to sit without speaking, for she had expected him to express pleasure and astonishment.

"You are right, Heidi; it is a beautiful tale," he replied, but he looked so grave as he said it that Heidi grew silent herself and sat looking quietly at her pictures. Presently she pushed her book gently in front of him and said, "See how happy he is there," and she pointed with her finger to the figure of the returned prodigal, who was standing by his father clad in fresh raiment as one of his own sons again.

A few hours later, as Heidi lay fast asleep in her bed, the grandfather went up the ladder and put his lamp down near her bed so that the light fell on the sleeping child. Her hands were still folded as if she had fallen asleep saying her prayers, an expression of peace and trust lay on the little face, and something in it seemed to appeal to the grandfather, for he stood a long time gazing down at her without speaking. At last he too folded his hands, and with bowed head said in a low voice, "Father, I have sinned against heaven and before thee and am not worthy to be called thy son." And two large tears rolled down the old man's cheeks.

Early the next morning he stood in front of his hut and gazed quietly around him. The fresh bright morning sun lay on mountain and valley. The sound of a few early bells rang up from the valley, and the birds were singing their morning song in the fir trees. He stepped back into the hut and called up, "Come along, Heidi! The sun is up! Put on your best frock, for we are going to church together!"

Heidi was not long getting ready; it was such an unusual summons from her grandfather that she must make haste. She put on her smart Frankfurt dress and soon went down, but when she saw her grandfather she stood still, gazing at him in astonishment. "Why, Grandfather!" she exclaimed, "I never saw you look like that before! And the coat with the silver buttons! Oh, you do look nice in your Sunday coat!"

The old man smiled and replied, "And you too; now come along!" He took Heidi's hand in his and together they walked down the mountain side. The bells were ringing in every direction now, sounding louder and fuller as they neared the valley, and Heidi listened to them with delight. "Hark at them, Grandfather! It's like a great festival!"

The congregation had already assembled and the singing had begun when Heidi and her grandfather entered the church at Dörfli and sat down at the back. But before the hymn was over every one was nudging his neighbour and whispering, "Do you see? Alm-Uncle is in church!"

Soon everybody in the church knew of Alm-Uncle's presence, and the women kept on turning round to look and quite lost their place in the singing. But everybody became more attentive when the sermon began, for the preacher spoke with such warmth and thankfulness that those present felt the effect of his words, as if some great joy had come to them all. At the close of the service Alm-Uncle took Heidi by the hand, and on leaving the church made his way towards the pastor's house; the rest of the congregation looked curiously after him, some even following to see whether he went inside the pastor's house, which he did. Then they collected in groups and talked over this strange event, keeping their eyes on the pastor's door, watching to see whether Alm-Uncle came out looking angry and quarrelsome, or as if the interview had been a peaceful one, for they could not imagine what had brought the old man down, and what it all meant. Some, however, adopted a new tone and expressed their opinion that Alm-Uncle was not so bad after all as they thought, "for see how carefully he took the little one by the hand." And others responded and said they had always thought people had exaggerated about him, that if he was so downright bad he would be afraid to go inside the pastor's house. Then the miller put in his word, "Did I not tell you so from the first? What child is there who would run away from where she had plenty to eat and drink and everything of the best, home to a grandfather who was cruel and unkind, and of whom she was afraid?"

And so everybody began to feel quite friendly towards Alm-Uncle, and the women now came up and related all they had been told by Peter and his grandmother, and finally they all stood there like people waiting for an old friend whom they had long missed from among their number.

Meanwhile Alm-Uncle had gone into the pastor's house and knocked at the study door. The latter came out and greeted him, not as if he was surprised to see him, but as if he had quite expected to see him there; he probably had caught sight of the old man in church. He shook hands warmly with him, and Alm-Uncle was unable at first to speak, for he had not expected such a friendly reception. At last he collected himself and said, "I have come to ask you, pastor, to forget the words I spoke to you when you called on me, and to beg you not to owe me ill-will for having been so obstinately set against your well-meant advice. You were right, and I was wrong, but I have now made up my mind to follow your advice and to find a place for myself at Dörfli for the winter, for the child is not strong enough to stand the bitter cold up on the mountain.

And if the people down here look askance at me, as at a person not to be trusted, I know it is my own fault, and you will, I am sure, not do so."

The pastor's kindly eyes shone with pleasure. He pressed the old man's hand in his, and said with emotion, "Neighbour, you went into the right church before you came to mine; I am greatly rejoiced. You will not repent coming to live with us again; as for myself you will always be welcome as a dear friend and neighbour, and I look forward to our spending many a pleasant winter evening together, for I shall prize your companionship, and we will find some nice friends too for the little one." And the pastor laid his hand kindly on the child's curly head and took her by the hand as he walked to the door with the old man. He did not say goodbye to him till they were standing outside, so that all the people standing about saw him shake hands as if parting reluctantly from his best friend. The door had hardly shut behind him before the whole congregation now came forward to greet Alm-Uncle; every one striving to be the first to shake hands with him, and so many were held out that Alm-Uncle did not know with which to begin; and some said, "We are so pleased to see you among us again," and another, "I have long been wishing we could have a talk together again," and greetings of all kinds echoed from every side, and when Alm-Uncle told them he was thinking of returning to his old quarters in Dörfli for the winter, there was such a general chorus of pleasure that any one would have thought he was the most beloved person in all Dörfli, and that they had hardly known how to live without him. Most of his friends accompanied him and Heidi some way up the mountain, and each as they bid him goodbye made him promise that when he next came down he would without fail come and call. As the old man at last stood alone with the child, watching their retreating figures, there was a light upon his face as if reflected from some inner sunshine of heart. Heidi, looking up at him with her clear steady eyes, said, "Grandfather, you look nicer and nicer today, I never saw you quite like that before."

"Do you think so?" he answered with a smile. "Well, yes, Heidi, I am happier today than I deserve, happier than I had thought possible; it is good to be at peace with God and man! God was good to me when He sent you to my hut."

When they reached Peter's home the grandfather opened the door and walked straight in. "Good morning, Grandmother," he said. "I think we shall have to do some more patching, up before the autumn winds come."

"Dear God, if it is not Uncle!" cried the grandmother in pleased surprise. "That I should live to see such a thing! And now I can thank you for all that you have done for me. May God reward you! May God reward you!" She stretched out a trembling hand to him, and when the grandfather shook it warmly, she went on, still holding his, "And I have something on my heart I want to say, a prayer to make to you! If I have injured you in any way, do not punish me by sending the child away again before I lie under the grass. Oh, you do not know what that child is to me!" and she clasped the child to her, for Heidi had already taken her usual stand close to the grandmother.

"Have no fear, Grandmother," said Uncle in a reassuring voice, "I shall not punish either you or myself by doing so. We are all together now, and pray God we may continue so for long."

Brigitta now drew the Uncle aside towards a corner of the room and showed him the hat with the feathers, explaining to him how it came there, and adding that of course she could not take such a thing from a child.

But the grandfather looked towards Heidi without any displeasure of countenance and said, "The hat is hers, and if she does not wish to wear it any more she has a right to say so and to give it to you, so take it, pray."

Brigitta was highly delighted at this. "It is well worth more than ten shillings!" she said as she held it up for further admiration. "And what a blessing Heidi has brought home with her from Frankfurt! I have thought sometimes that it might be good to send Peter there for a little while; what do you think, Uncle?"

A merry look came into the grandfather's eye. He thought it would do Peter no harm, but he had better wait for a good opportunity before starting. At this moment the subject of their conversation himself rushed in, evidently in a great hurry, knocking his head violently against the door in his haste, so that everything in the room rattled. Gasping and breathless he stood still after this and held out a letter. This was another great event, for such a thing had never happened before; the letter was addressed to Heidi and had been delivered at the post-office in Dörfli. They all sat down round the table to hear what was in it, for Heidi opened it at once and read it without hesitation. The letter was from Clara. The latter wrote that the house had been so dull since Heidi left that she did not know how to bear herself, and she had at last persuaded her father to take her to the baths at Ragatz in the coming autumn; Grandmamma had arranged to join them there, and they both were looking forward to paying her and her grandfather a visit. And Grandmamma sent a further message to Heidi which was that the latter had done quite right to take the rolls to the grandmother, and so that she might not have to eat them dry, she was sending some coffee, which was already on its way, and Grandmamma hoped when she came to the Alm in the autumn that Heidi would take her to see her old friend.

There were exclamations of pleasure and astonishment on hearing all this news, and so much to talk and ask about that even the grandfather did not notice how the time was passing; there was general delight at the thought of the coming days, and even more at the meeting which had taken place on this one, and the grandmother spoke and said, "The happiest of all things is when an old friend comes and greets us as in former times; the heart is comforted with the assurance that some day everything that we have loved will be given back to us. —You will come soon again, uncle, and you child, tomorrow?"

The old man and Heidi promised her faithfully to do so; then it was time to break up the party, and these two went back up the mountain. As they had been greeted with bells when they made their journey down in the morning, so now they were accompanied by the peaceful evening chimes as they climbed to the hut, which had quite a Sunday-like appearance as it stood bathed in the light of the low evening sun.

But when Grandmamma comes next autumn there will be many fresh joys and surprises both for Heidi and Grandmother; without doubt a proper bed will be put up in the hay-loft, for wherever Grandmamma steps in, there everything is soon in right order, outside and in.

Chapter 15

Preparations For A Journey

The kind doctor who had given the order that Heidi was to be sent home was walking along one of the broad streets towards Herr Sesemann's house. It was a sunny September morning, so full of light and sweetness that it seemed as if everybody must rejoice. But the doctor walked with his eyes fastened to the ground and did not once lift them to the blue sky above him. There was an expression of sadness on his face, formerly so cheerful, and his hair had grown greyer since the spring. The doctor had had an only daughter, who, after his wife's death, had been his sole and constant companion, but only a few months previously death had deprived him of his dear child, and he had never been the same bright and cheery man since.

Sebastian opened the door to him, greeting him with every mark of respectful civility, for the doctor was not only the most cherished friend of the master and his daughter, but had by his kindness won the hearts of the whole household.

"Everything as usual, Sebastian?" asked the doctor in his pleasant voice as he preceded Sebastian up the stairs.

"I am glad you have come, doctor," exclaimed Herr Sesemann as the latter entered. "We must really have another talk over this Swiss journey; do you still adhere to your decision, even though Clara is decidedly improving in health?"

"My dear Sesemann, I never knew such a man as you!" said the doctor as he sat down beside his friend. "I really wish your mother was here; everything would be clear and straightforward then and she would soon put things in right train. You sent for me three times yesterday only to ask me the same question, though you know what I think."

"Yes, I know, it's enough to make you out of patience with me; but you must understand, dear friend"—and Herr Sesemann laid his hand imploringly on the doctor's shoulder—"that I feel I have not the courage to refuse the child what I have been promising her all along, and for months now she has been living on the thought of it day and night. She bore this last bad attack so patiently because she was buoyed up with the hope that she should soon start on her Swiss journey, and see her friend Heidi again; and now must I tell the poor child, who has to give up so many pleasures, that this visit she has so long looked forward to must also be cancelled? I really have not the courage to do it."

"You must make up your mind to it, Sesemann," said the doctor with authority, and as his friend continued silent and dejected he went on after a pause, "Consider yourself how the matter stands. Clara has not had such a bad summer as this last one for years. Only the worst results would follow from the fatigue of such a journey, and it is out of the question for her. And then we are already in September, and although it may still be warm and fine up there, it may just as likely be already very cold. The days too are growing short, and as Clara cannot spend the night up there she would only have a two hours' visit at the outside. The journey from Ragatz would take hours, for she would have to be carried up the mountain in a chair. In short, Sesemann, it is impossible. But I will go in with you and talk to Clara; she is a reasonable child, and I will tell her what my plans are. Next May she shall be taken to the baths and stay there for the cure until it is quite hot weather. Then she can be carried up the mountain from time to time, and when she is stronger she will enjoy these excursions far more than she would now. Understand, Sesemann, that if we want to give the child a chance of recovery we must use the utmost care and watchfulness."

Herr Sesemann, who had listened to the doctor in sad and submissive silence, now suddenly jumped up. "Doctor," he said, "tell me truly: have you really any hope of her final recovery?"

The doctor shrugged his shoulders. "Very little," he replied quietly. "But, friend, think of my trouble. You have still a beloved child to look for you and greet you on your return home. You do not come back to an empty house and sit down to a solitary meal. And the child is happy and comfortable at home too. If there is much that she has to give up, she has on the other hand many advantages. No, Sesemann, you are not so greatly to be pitied—you have still the happiness of being together. Think of my lonely house!"

Herr Sesemann was now striding up and down the room as was his habit when deeply engaged in thought. Suddenly he came to a pause beside his friend and laid his hand on his shoulder. "Doctor, I have an idea; I cannot bear to see you look as you do; you are no longer the same man. You must be taken out of yourself for a while, and what do you think I propose? That you shall take the journey and go and pay Heidi a visit in our name."

The doctor was taken aback at this sudden proposal and wanted to make objections, but his friend gave him no time to say anything. He was so delighted with his idea, that he seized the doctor by the arm and drew him into Clara's room. The kind doctor was always a welcome visitor to Clara, for he generally had something amusing to tell her. Lately, it is true, he had been graver, but Clara knew the reason why and would have given much to see him his old lively self again. She held out her hand to him as he came up to her; he took a seat beside her, and her father also drew up his chair, and taking Clara's hand in his began to talk to her of the Swiss journey and how he himself had looked forward to it. He passed as quickly as he could over the main point that it was now impossible for her to undertake it, for he dreaded the tears that would follow; but he went on without pause to tell her of his new plan, and dwelt on the great benefit it would be to his friend if he could be persuaded to take this holiday.

The tears were indeed swimming in the blue eyes, although Clara struggled to keep them down for her father's sake, but it was a bitter disappointment to give up the journey, the thought of which had been her only joy and solace during the lonely hours of her long illness. She knew, however, that her father would never refuse her a thing unless he was certain that it would be harmful for her. So she swallowed her tears as well as she could and turned her thoughts to the one hope still left her. Taking the doctor's hand and stroking it, she said pleadingly,—

"Dear doctor, you will go and see Heidi, won't you? and then you can come and tell me all about it, what it is like up there, and what Heidi and the grandfather, and Peter and the goats do all day. I know them all so well! And then you can take what I want to send to Heidi; I have thought about it all, and also something for the grandmother. Do pray go, dear doctor, and I will take as much cod liver oil as you like."

Whether this promise finally decided the doctor it is impossible to say, but it is certain that he smiled and said,—

"Then I must certainly go, Clara, for you will then get as plump and strong as your father and I wish to see you. And have you decided when I am to start?"

"Tomorrow morning—early if possible," replied Clara.

"Yes, she is right," put in Herr Sesemann; "the sun is shining and the sky is blue, and there is no time to be lost; it is a pity to miss a single one of these days on the mountain."

The doctor could not help laughing. "You will be reproaching me next for not being there already; well, I must go and make arrangements for getting off."

But Clara would not let him go until she had given him endless messages for Heidi, and had explained all he was to look at so as to give her an exact description on his return. Her presents she would send round later, as Fräulein Rottenmeier must first help her to pack them up; at that moment she was out on one of her excursions into the town which always kept her engaged for some time. The doctor promised to obey Clara's directions in every particular; he would start some time during the following day if not the first thing in the morning, and would bring back a faithful account of his experiences and of all he saw and heard.

The servants of a household have a curious faculty of divining what is going on before they are actually told about anything. Sebastian and Tinette must have possessed this faculty in a high degree, for even as the doctor was going downstairs, Tinette, who had been rung for, entered Clara's room.

"Take that box and bring it back filled with the soft cakes which we have with coffee," said Clara, pointing to a box which had been brought long before in preparation for this. Tinette took it up, and carried it out, dangling it contemptuously in her hand.

"Hardly worth the trouble I should have thought," she said pertly as she left the room.

As Sebastian opened the door for the doctor he said with a bow, "Will the Herr Doctor be so kind as to give the little miss my greetings?"

"I see," said the doctor, "you know then already that I am off on a journey."

Sebastian hesitated and gave an awkward little cough. "I am—I have—I hardly know myself. O yes, I remember; I happened to pass through the dining-room and caught little miss's name, and I put two and two together—and so I thought—"

"I see, I see," smiled the doctor, "one can find out a great many thinks by thinking. Goodbye till I see you again, Sebastian, I will be sure and give your message."

The doctor was hastening off when he met with a sudden obstacle; the violent wind had prevented Fräulein Rottenmeier prosecuting her walk any farther, and she was just returning and had reached the door as he was coming out. The white shawl she wore was so blown out by the wind that she looked like a ship in full sail. The doctor drew back, but Fräulein Rottenmeier had always evinced peculiar appreciation and respect for this man, and she also drew back with exaggerated politeness to let him pass. The two stood for a few seconds, each anxious to make way for the other, but a sudden gust of wind sent Fräulein Rottenmeier flying with all her sails almost into the doctor's arms, and she had to pause and recover herself before she could shake hands with the doctor with becoming decorum. She was put out at having been forced to enter in so undignified a manner, but the doctor had a way of smoothing people's ruffled feathers, and she was soon listening with her usual composure while he informed her of his intended journey, begging her in his most conciliatory voice to pack up the parcels for Heidi as she alone knew how to pack. And then he took his leave.

Clara quite expected to have a long tussle with Fräulein Rottenmeier before she would get the latter to consent to sending all the things that she had collected as presents for Heidi. But this time she was mistaken, for Fräulein Rottenmeier was in a more than usually good temper. She cleared the large table so that all the things for Heidi could be spread out upon it and packed under Clara's own eyes. It was no light job, for the presents were of all shapes and sizes. First there was the little warm cloak with a hood, which had been designed by Clara herself, in order that Heidi during the coming winter might be able to go and see Grandmother when she liked, and not have to wait till her grandfather could take her wrapped up in a sack to keep her from freezing. Then came a thick warm shawl for the grandmother, in which she could wrap herself well up and not feel the cold when the wind came sweeping in such terrible gusts round the house. The next object was the large box full of cakes; these were also for the grandmother, that she might have something to eat with her coffee besides bread. An immense sausage was the next article; this had been originally intended for Peter, who never had anything but bread and cheese, but Clara had altered her mind, fearing that in his delight he might eat it all up at once and make himself ill. So she arranged to send it to Brigitta, who could take some for herself and the grandmother and give Peter his portion out by degrees. A packet of tobacco was a present for Grandfather, who was fond of his pipe as he sat resting in the evening. Finally there was a whole lot of mysterious little bags, and parcels, and boxes, which Clara had had especial pleasure in collecting, as each was to be a joyful surprise for Heidi as she opened it. The work came to an end at last, and an imposing-looking package lay on the floor ready for transport. Fräulein Rottenmeier looked at it with satisfaction, lost in the consideration of the art of packing. Clara eyed it too with pleasure, picturing Heidi's exclamations and jumps of joy and surprise when the huge parcel arrived at the hut.

And now Sebastian came in, and lifting the package on to his shoulder, carried it off to be forwarded at once to the doctor's house.

Chapter 16

A Visitor

The early light of morning lay rosy red upon the mountains, and a fresh breeze rustled through the fir trees and set their ancient branches waving to and fro. The sound awoke Heidi and she opened her eyes. The roaring in the trees always stirred a strong emotion within her and seemed to drew her irresistibly to them. So she jumped out of bed and dressed herself as quickly as she could, but it took her some time even then, for she was careful now to be always clean and tidy.

When she went down her ladder she found her grandfather had already left the hut. He was standing outside looking at the sky and examining the landscape as he did every morning, to see what sort of weather it was going to be.

Little pink clouds were floating over the sky, that was growing brighter and bluer with every minute, while the heights and the meadow lands were turning gold under the rising sun, which was just appearing above the topmost peaks.

"O how beautiful! How beautiful! Good morning, Grandfather!" cried Heidi, running out.

"What, you are awake already, are you?" he answered, giving her a morning greeting.

Then Heidi ran round to the fir trees to enjoy the sound she loved so well, and with every fresh gust of wind which came roaring through their branches she gave a fresh jump and cry of delight.

Meanwhile the grandfather had gone to milk the goats; this done he brushed and washed them, ready for their mountain excursion, and brought them out of their shed. As soon as Heidi caught sight of her two friends she ran and embraced them, and they bleated in return, while they vied with each other in showing their affection by poking their heads against her and trying which could get nearest her, so that she was almost crushed between them. But Heidi was not afraid of them, and when the lively Little Bear gave rather too violent a thrust, she only said, "No, Little Bear, you are pushing like the Great Turk," and Little Bear immediately drew back his head and left off his rough attentions, while Little Swan lifted her head and put on an expression as much as to say, "No one shall ever accuse me of behaving like the Great Turk." For White Swan was a rather more distinguished person than Brown Bear.

And now Peter's whistle was heard and all the goats came along, leaping and springing, and Heidi soon found herself surrounded by the whole flock, pushed this way and that by their obstreperous greetings, but at last she managed to get through them to where Snowflake was standing, for the young goat had in vain striven to reach her.

Peter now gave a last tremendous whistle, in order to startle the goats and drive them off, for he wanted to get near himself to say something to Heidi. The goats sprang aside and he came up to her.

"Can you come out with me today?" he asked, evidently unwilling to hear her refuse.

"I am afraid I cannot, Peter," she answered. "I am expecting them every minute from Frankfurt, and I must be at home when they come."

"You have said the same thing for days now," grumbled Peter.

"I must continue to say it till they come," replied Heidi. "How can you think, Peter, that I would be away when they came? As if I could do such a thing?"

"They would find Uncle at home," he answered with a snarling voice.

But at this moment the grandfather's stentorian voice was heard. "Why is the army not marching forward? Is it the field-marshal who is missing or some of the troops?"

Whereupon Peter turned and went off, swinging his stick round so that it whistled through the air, and the goats, who understood the signal, started at full trot for their mountain pasture, Peter following in their wake.

Since Heidi had been back with her grandfather things came now and then into her mind of which she had never thought in former days. So now, with great exertion, she put her bed in order every morning, patting and stroking it till she had got it perfectly smooth and flat. Then she went about the room downstairs, put each chair back in its place, and if she found anything lying about she put it in the cupboard. After that she fetched a duster, climbed on a chair, and rubbed the table till it shone again. When the grandfather came in later he would look round well pleased and say to himself, "We look like Sunday every day now; Heidi did not go abroad for nothing."

After Peter had departed and she and her grandfather had breakfasted, Heidi began her daily work as usual, but she did not get on with it very fast. It was so lovely out of doors today, and every minute something happened to interrupt her in her work. Now it was a bright beam of sun shining cheerfully through the open window, and seeming to say, "Come out, Heidi, come out!" Heidi felt she could not stay indoors, and she ran out in answer to the call. The sunlight lay sparkling on everything around the hut and on all the mountains and far away along the valley, and the grass slope looked so golden and inviting that she was obliged to sit down for a few minutes and look about her. Then she suddenly remembered that her stool was left standing in the middle of the floor and that the table had not been rubbed, and she jumped up and ran inside again. But it was not long before the fir trees began their old song; Heidi felt it in all her limbs, and again the desire to run outside was irresistible, and she was off to play and leap to the tune of the waving branches. The grandfather, who was busy in his work-shed, stepped out from time to time smiling to watch her at her gambols. He had just gone back to his work on one of these occasions when Heidi called out, "Grandfather! Grandfather! Come, come!"

He stepped quickly out, almost afraid something had happened to the child, but he saw her running towards where the mountain path descended, crying, "They are coming! They are coming! And the doctor is in front of them!"

Heidi rushed forward to welcome her old friend, who held out his hands in greeting to her. When she came up to him she clung to his outstretched arm, and exclaimed in the joy of her heart, "Good-morning, doctor, and thank you ever so many times."

"God bless you, child! What have you got to thank me for?" asked the doctor, smiling.

"For being at home again with Grandfather," the child explained.

The doctor's face brightened as if a sudden ray of sunshine had passed across it; he had not expected such a reception as this. Lost in the sense of his loneliness he had climbed the mountain without heeding how beautiful it was on every side, and how more and more beautiful it became the higher he got. He had quite thought that Heidi would have forgotten him; she had seen so little of him, and he had felt rather like one bearing a message of disappointment, anticipating no great show of favor, coming as he did without the expected friends. But instead, here was Heidi, her eyes dancing for joy, and full of gratitude and affection, clinging to the arm of her kind friend.

He took her by the hand with fatherly tenderness.

"Take me now to your grandfather, Heidi, and show me where you live."

But Heidi still remained standing, looking down the path with a questioning gaze. "Where are Clara and Grandmother?" she asked.

"Ah, now I have to tell you something which you will be as sorry about as I am," answered the doctor. "You see, Heidi, I have come alone. Clara was very ill and could not travel, and so the grandmother stayed behind too. But next spring, when the days grow warm and long again, they are coming here for certain."

Heidi was greatly concerned; she could not at first bring herself to believe that what she had for so long been picturing to herself was not going to happen after all. She stood motionless for a second or two, overcome by the unexpected disappointment. The doctor said nothing further; all around lay the silence, only the sighing of the fir trees could be heard from where they stood. Then Heidi suddenly remembered why she had run down there, and that the doctor had really come. She lifted her eyes and saw the sad expression in his as he looked down at her; she had never seen him with that look on his face when she was in Frankfurt. It went to Heidi's heart; she could not bear to see anybody unhappy, especially her dear doctor. No doubt it was because Clara and

Grandmother could not come, and so she began to think how best she might console him.

"Oh, it won't be very long to wait for spring, and then they will be sure to come," she said in a reassuring voice. "Time passes very quickly with us, and then they will be able to stay longer when they are here, and Clara will be pleased at that. Now let us go and find Grandfather."

Hand in hand with her friend she climbed up to the hut. She was so anxious to make the doctor happy again that she began once more assuring him that the winter passed so quickly on the mountain that it was hardly to be taken account of, and that summer would be back again before they knew it, and she became so convinced of the truth of her own words that she called out quite cheerfully to her grandfather as they approached, "They have not come today, but they will be here in a very short time."

The doctor was no stranger to the grandfather, for the child had talked to him so much about her friend. The old man held out his hand to his guest in friendly greeting. Then the two men sat down in front of the hut, and Heidi had her little place too, for the doctor beckoned her to come and sit beside him. The doctor told Uncle how Herr Sesemann had insisted on his taking this journey, and he felt himself it would do him good as he had not been quite the thing for a long time. Then he whispered to Heidi that there was something being brought up the mountain which had travelled with him from Frankfurt, and which would give her even more pleasure than seeing the old doctor. Heidi got into a great state of excitement on hearing this, wondering what it could be, The old man urged the doctor to spend as many of the beautiful autumn days on the mountain as he could, and at least to come up whenever it was fine; he could not offer him a lodging, as he had no place to put him; he advised the doctor, however, not to go back to Ragatz, but to stay at Dörfli, where there was a clean tidy little inn. Then the doctor could come up every morning, which would do him no end of good, and if he liked, he, the grandfather, would act as his guide to any part of the mountains he would like to see. The doctor was delighted with this proposal, and it was settled that it should be as the grandfather suggested.

Meanwhile the sun had been climbing up the sky, and it was now noon. The wind had sunk and the fir trees stood motionless. The air was still wonderfully warm and mild for that height, while a delicious freshness was mingled with the warmth of the sun.

Alm-Uncle now rose and went indoors, returning in a few minutes with a table which he placed in front of the seat.

"There, Heidi, now run in and bring us what we want for the table," he said. "The doctor must take us as he finds us; if the food is plain, he will acknowledge that the dining-room is pleasant."

"I should think so indeed," replied the doctor as he looked down over the sun-lit valley, "and I accept the kind invitation; everything must taste good up here."

Heidi ran backwards and forwards as busy as a bee and brought out everything she could find in the cupboard, for she did not know how to be pleased enough that she could help to entertain the doctor. The grandfather meanwhile had been preparing the meal, and now appeared with a steaming jug of milk and golden-brown toasted cheese. Then he cut some thin slices from the meat he had cured himself in the pure air, and the doctor enjoyed his dinner better than he had for a whole year past.

"Our Clara must certainly come up here," he said, "it would make her quite a different person, and if she ate for any length of time as I have today, she would grow plumper than any one has ever known her before."

As he spoke a man was seen coming up the path carrying a large package on his back. When he reached the hut he threw it on the ground and drew in two or three good breaths of the mountain air.

"Ah, here's what travelled with me from Frankfurt," said the doctor, rising, and he went up to the package and began undoing it, Heidi looking on in great expectation. After he had released it from its heavy outer covering, "There, child," he said, "now you can go on unpacking your treasures yourself."

Heidi undid her presents one by one until they were all displayed; she could not speak the while for wonder and delight. Not till the doctor went up to her again and opened the large box to show Heidi the cakes that were for the grandmother to eat with her coffee, did she at last give a cry of joy, exclaiming, "Now Grandmother will have nice things to eat," and she wanted to pack everything up again and start at once to give them to her. But the grandfather said he should walk down with the doctor that evening and she could go with them and take the things. Heidi now found the packet of tobacco which she ran and gave to her grandfather; he was so pleased with it that he immediately filled his pipe with some, and the two men then sat down together again, the smoke curling up from their pipes as they talked of all kinds of things, while Heidi continued to examine first one and then another of her presents. Suddenly she ran up to them, and standing in front of the doctor waited till there was a pause in the conversation, and then said, "No, the other thing has not given me more pleasure than seeing you, doctor."

The two men could not help laughing, and the doctor answered that he should never have thought it.

As the sun began to sink behind the mountains the doctor rose, thinking it was time to return to Dörfli and seek for quarters. The grandfather carried the cakes and the shawl and the large sausage, and the doctor took Heidi's hand, so they all three started down the mountain. Arrived at Peter's home Heidi bid the others goodbye; she was to wait at Grandmother's till her grandfather, who was going on to Dörfli with his guest, returned to fetch her. As the doctor shook hands with her she asked, "Would you like to come out with the goats tomorrow morning?" for she could think of no greater treat to offer him.

"Agreed!" answered the doctor, "we will go together,"

Heidi now ran in to the grandmother; she first, with some effort, managed to carry in the box of cakes; then she ran out again and brought in the sausage—for her grandfather had put the presents down by the door—and then a third time for the shawl. She had placed them as close as she could to the grandmother, so that the latter might be able to feel them and understand what was there. The shawl she laid over the old woman's knees.

"They are all from Frankfurt, from Clara and Grandmamma," she explained to the astonished Grandmother and Brigitta, the latter having watched her dragging in all the heavy things, unable to imagine what was happening.

"And you are very pleased with the cakes, aren't you, Grandmother? Taste how soft they are!" said Heidi over and over again, to which the grandmother continued to answer, "Yes, yes, Heidi, I should think so! What kind people they must be!" And then she would pass her hand over the warm thick shawl and add, "This will be beautiful for the cold winter! I never thought I should ever have such a splendid thing as this to put on."

Heidi could not help feeling some surprise at the grandmother seeming to take more pleasure in the shawl than the cakes. Meanwhile Brigitta stood gazing at the sausage with almost an expression of awe. She had hardly in her life seen such a monster sausage, much less owned one, and she could scarcely believe her eyes. She shook her head and said doubtfully, "I must ask Uncle what it is meant for."

But Heidi answered without hesitation, "It is meant for eating, not for anything else."

Peter came tumbling in at this minute. "Uncle is just behind me, he is coming—" he began, and then stopped short, for his eye had caught sight of the sausage, and he was too much taken aback to say more. But Heidi understood that her grandfather was near and so said goodbye to Grandmother. The old man now never passed the door without going in to wish the old woman good day, and she liked to hear his footstep approaching, for he always had a cheery word for her. But today it was growing late for Heidi, who was always up with the lark, and the grandfather would never let her go to bed after hours; so this evening he only called good night through the open door and started home at once with the child, and the two climbed under the starlit sky back to their peaceful dwelling.

Chapter 17

A Compensation

The next morning the doctor climbed up from Dörfli with Peter and the goats. The kindly gentleman tried now and then to enter into conversation with the boy, but his attempts failed, for he could hardly get a word out of Peter in answer to his questions. Peter was not easily persuaded to talk. So the party silently made their way up to the hut, where they found Heidi awaiting them with her two goats, all three as fresh and lively as the morning sun among the mountains.

"Are you coming today?" said Peter, repeating the words with which he daily greeted her, either in question or in summons.

"Of course I am, if the doctor is coming too," replied Heidi.

Peter cast a sidelong glance at the doctor. The grandfather now came out with the dinner bag, and after bidding good day to the doctor he went up to Peter and slung it over his neck. It was heavier than usual, for Alm-Uncle had added some meat today, as he thought the doctor might like to have his lunch out and eat it when the children did. Peter gave a grin, for he felt sure there was something more than ordinary in it.

And so the ascent began. The goats as usual came thronging around Heidi, each trying to be nearest her, until at last she stood still and said, "Now you must go on in front and behave properly, and not keep on turning back and pushing and poking me, for I want to talk to the doctor," and she gave Snowflake a little pat on the back and told her to be good and obedient. By degrees she managed to make her way out from among them and joined the doctor, who took her by the hand. He had no difficulty now in conversing with his companion, for Heidi had a great deal to say about the goats and their peculiarities, and about the flowers and the rocks and the birds, and so they clambered on and reached their resting-place before they were aware. Peter had sent a good many unfriendly glances towards the doctor on the way up, which might have quite alarmed the latter if he had happened to notice them, which, fortunately, he did not.

Heidi now led her friend to her favourite spot where she was accustomed to sit and enjoy the beauty around her; the doctor followed her example and took his seat beside her on the warm grass. Over the heights and over the far green valley hung the golden glory of the autumn day. The great snow-field sparkled in the bright sunlight, and the two grey rocky peaks rose in their ancient majesty against the dark blue sky. A soft, light morning breeze blew deliciously across the mountain, gently stirring the bluebells that still remained of the summer's wealth of flowers, their slender heads nodding cheerfully in the sunshine. Overhead the great bird was flying round and round in wide circles, but today he made no sound; poised on his large wings he floated contentedly in the blue ether. Heidi looked about her first at one thing and then at another. The waving flowers, the blue sky, the bright sunshine, the happy bird—everything was so beautiful! So beautiful! Her eyes were alight with joy. And now she turned to her friend to see if he too were enjoying the beauty. The doctor had been sitting thoughtfully gazing around him. As he met her glad bright eyes, "Yes, Heidi," he responded, "I see how lovely it all is, but tell me—if one brings a sad heart up here, how may it be healed so that it can rejoice in all this beauty?"

"Oh, but," exclaimed Heidi, "no one is sad up here, only in Frankfurt."

The doctor smiled and then growing serious again he continued, "But supposing one is not able to leave all the sadness behind at Frankfurt; can you tell me anything that will help then?"

"When you do not know what more to do you must go and tell everything to God," answered Heidi with decision.

"Ah, that is a good thought of yours, Heidi," said the doctor. "But if it is God Himself who has sent the trouble, what can we say to Him then?"

Heidi sat pondering for a while; she was sure in her heart that God could help out of every trouble. She thought over her own experiences and then found her answer.

"Then you must wait," she said, "and keep on saying to yourself: God certainly knows of some happiness for us which He is going to bring out of the trouble, only we must have patience and not run away. And then all at once something happens and we see clearly ourselves that God has had some good thought in His mind all along; but because we cannot see things beforehand, and only know how dreadfully miserable we are, we think it is always going to be so."

"That is a beautiful faith, child, and be sure you hold it fast," replied the doctor. Then he sat on a while in silence, looking at the great overshadowing mountains and the green, sunlit valley below before he spoke again,—

"Can you understand, Heidi, that a man may sit here with such a shadow over his eyes that he cannot feel and enjoy the beauty around him, while the heart grows doubly sad knowing how beautiful it could be? Can you understand that?"

A pain shot through the child's young happy heart. The shadow over the eyes brought to her remembrance the grandmother, who would never again be able to see the sunlight and the beauty up here. This was Heidi's great sorrow, which re-awoke each time she thought about the darkness. She did not speak for a few minutes, for her happiness was interrupted by this sudden pang. Then in a grave voice she said,—

"Yes, I can understand it. And I know this, that then one must say one of Grandmother's hymns, which bring the light back a little, and often make it so bright for her that she is quite happy again. Grandmother herself told me this."

"Which hymns are they, Heidi?" asked the doctor.

"I only know the one about the sun and the beautiful garden, and some of the verses of the long one, which are favourites with her, and she always likes me to read them to her two or three times over," replied Heidi.

"Well, say the verses to me then, I should like to hear them too," and the doctor sat up in order to listen better.

Heidi put her hands together and sat collecting her thoughts for a second or two: "Shall I begin at the verse that Grandmother says gives her a feeling of hope and confidence?"

The doctor nodded his assent, and Heidi began,—

> Let not your heart be troubled
> Nor fear your soul dismay,

There is a wise Defender
And He will be your stay.
Where you have failed, He conquers,
See, how the foeman flies!
And all your tribulation
Is turned to glad surprise.

If for a while it seemeth
His mercy is withdrawn,
That He no longer careth
For His wandering child forlorn,
Doubt not His great compassion,
His love can never tire,
To those who wait in patience
He gives their heart's desire.

Heidi suddenly paused; she was not sure if the doctor was still listening. He was sitting motionless with his hand before his eyes. She thought he had fallen asleep; when he awoke, if he wanted to hear more verses, she would go on. There was no sound anywhere. The doctor sat in silence, but he was certainly not asleep. His thoughts had carried him back to a long past time: he saw himself as a little boy standing by his dear mother's chair; she had her arm round his neck and was saying the very verses to him that Heidi had just recited—words which he had not heard now for years. He could hear his mother's voice and see her loving eyes resting upon him, and as Heidi ceased the old dear voice seemed to be saying other things to him; and the words he heard again must have carried him far, far away, for it was a long time before he stirred or took his hand from his eyes. When at last he roused himself he met Heidi's eyes looking wonderingly at him.

"Heidi," he said, taking the child's hand in his, "that was a beautiful hymn of yours," and there was a happier ring in his voice as he spoke. "We will come out here together another day, and you will let me hear it again."

Peter meanwhile had had enough to do in giving vent to his anger. It was now some days since Heidi had been out with him, and when at last she did come, there she sat the whole time beside the old gentleman, and Peter could not get a word with her. He got into a terrible temper, and at last went and stood some way back behind the doctor, where the latter could not see him, and doubling his fist made imaginary hits at the enemy. Presently he doubled both fists, and the longer Heidi stayed beside the gentleman, the more fiercely did he threaten with them.

Meanwhile the sun had risen to the height which Peter knew pointed to the dinner hour. All of a sudden he called at the top of his voice, "It's dinner time."

Heidi was rising to fetch the dinner bag so that the doctor might eat his where he sat. But he stopped her, telling her he was not hungry at all, and only cared for a glass of milk, as he wanted to climb up a little higher. Then Heidi found that she also was not hungry and only wanted milk, and she should like, she said, to take the doctor up to the large moss-covered rock where Greenfinch had nearly jumped down and killed herself. So she ran and explained matters to Peter, telling him to go and get milk for the two. Peter seemed hardly to understand. "Who is going to eat what is in the bag then?" he asked.

"You can have it," she answered, "only first make haste and get the milk."

Peter had seldom performed any task more promptly, for he thought of the bag and its contents, which now belonged to him. As soon as the other two were sitting quietly drinking their milk, he opened it, and quite trembled for joy at the sight of the meat, and he was just putting his hand in to draw it out when something seemed to hold him back. His conscience smote him at the remembrance of how he had stood with his doubled fists behind the doctor, who was now giving up to him his whole good dinner. He felt as if he could not now enjoy it. But all at once he jumped up and ran back to the spot where he had stood before, and there held up his open hands as a sign that he had no longer any wish to use them as fists, and kept them up until he felt he had made amends for his past conduct. Then he rushed back and sat down to the double enjoyment of a clear conscience and an unusually satisfying meal.

Heidi and the doctor climbed and talked for a long while, until the latter said it was time for him to be going back, and no doubt Heidi would like to go and be with her goats. But Heidi would not hear of this, as then the doctor would have to go the whole way down the mountain alone. She insisted on accompanying him as far as the grandfather's hut, or even a little further. She kept hold of her friend's hand all the time, and the whole way she entertained him with accounts of this thing and that, showing him the spots where the goats loved best to feed, and others where in summer the flowers of all colours grew in greatest abundance. She could give them all their right names, for her grandfather had taught her these during the summer months. But at last the doctor insisted on her going back; so they bid each other good night and the doctor continued his descent, turning now and again to look back, and each time he saw Heidi standing on the same spot and waving her hand to him. Even so in the old days had his own dear little daughter watched him when he went from home.

It was a bright sunny autumn month. The doctor came up to the hut every morning, and thence made excursions over the mountain. Alm-Uncle accompanied him on some of his higher ascents, when they climbed up to the ancient storm-beaten fir trees and often disturbed the great bird which rose startled from its nest, with the whirl of wings and croakings, very near their heads. The doctor found great pleasure in his companion's conversation, and was astonished at his knowledge of the plants that grew on the mountain: he knew the uses of them all, from the aromatic fir trees and the dark pines with their scented needles, to the curly moss that sprang up everywhere about the roots of the trees and the smallest plant and tiniest flower. He was as well versed also in the ways of the animals, great and small, and had many amusing anecdotes to tell of these dwellers in caves and holes and in the tops of the fir trees. And so the time passed pleasantly and quickly for the doctor, who seldom said goodbye to the old man at the end of the day without adding, "I never leave you, friend, without having learnt something new from you."

On some of the very finest days, however, the doctor would wander out again with Heidi, and then the two would sit together as on the first day, and the child would repeat her hymns and tell the doctor things which she alone knew. Peter sat at a little distance from them, but he was now quite reconciled in spirit and gave vent to no angry pantomime.

September had drawn to its close, and now one morning the doctor appeared looking less cheerful than usual. It was his last day, he said, as he must return to Frankfurt, but he was grieved at having to say goodbye to the mountain, which he had begun to feel quite like home. Alm-Uncle, on his side, greatly regretted the departure of his guest, and Heidi had been now accustomed for so long to see her good friend every day that she could hardly believe the time had suddenly come to separate. She looked up at him in doubt, taken by surprise, but there was no help, he must go. So he bid farewell to the old man and asked that Heidi might go with him part of the return way, and Heidi took his hand and went down the mountain with him, still unable to grasp the idea that he was going for good. After some distance the doctor stood still, and passing his hand over the child's curly head said, "Now, Heidi, you must go back, and I must say goodbye! If only I could take you with me to Frankfurt and keep you there!"

The picture of Frankfurt rose before the child's eyes, its rows of endless houses, its hard streets, and even the vision of Fräulein Rottenmeier and Tinette, and she answered hesitatingly, "I would rather that you came back to us."

"Yes, you are right, that would be better. But now goodbye, Heidi." The child put her hand in his and looked up at him; the kind eyes looking down on her had tears in them. Then the doctor tore himself away and quickly continued his descent.

Heidi remained standing without moving. The friendly eyes with the tears in them had gone to her heart. All at once she burst into tears and started running as fast as she could after the departing figure, calling out in broken tones: "Doctor! Doctor!"

He turned round and waited till the child reached him. The tears were streaming down her face and she sobbed out: "I will come to Frankfurt with you, now at once, and I will stay with you as long as you like, only I must just run back and tell Grandfather."

The doctor laid his hand on her and tried to calm her excitement. "No, no, dear child," he said kindly, "not now; you must stay for the present under the fir trees, or I should have you ill again. But hear now what I have to ask you. If I am ever ill and alone, will you come then and stay with me? May I know that there would then be some one to look after me and care for me?"

"Yes, yes, I will come the very day you send for me, and I love you nearly as much as Grandfather," replied Heidi, who had not yet got over her distress.

And so the doctor again bid her goodbye and started on his way, while Heidi remained looking after him and waving her hand as long as a speck of him could be seen. As the doctor turned for the last time and looked back at the waving Heidi and the sunny mountain, he said to himself, "It is good to be up there, good for body and soul, and a man might learn how to be happy once more."

Chapter 18

Winter In Dörfli

The snow was lying so high around the hut that the windows looked level with the ground, and the door had entirely disappeared from view. If Alm-Uncle had been up there he would have had to do what Peter did daily, for fresh snow fell every night. Peter had to get out of the window of the sitting-room every morning, and if the frost had not been very hard during the night, he immediately sank up to his shoulders almost in the snow and had to struggle with hands, feet, and head to extricate himself. Then his mother handed him the large broom, and with this he worked hard to make a way to the door. He had to be careful to dig the snow well away, or else as soon as the door was opened the whole soft mass would fall inside, or, if the frost was severe enough, it would have made such a wall of ice in front of the house that no one could have gone in or out, for the window was only big enough for Peter to creep through. The fresh snow froze like this in the night sometimes, and this was an enjoyable time for Peter, for he would get through the window on to the hard, smooth, frozen ground, and his mother would hand him out the little sleigh, and he could then make his descent to Dörfli along any route he chose, for the whole mountain was nothing but one wide, unbroken sleigh road.

Alm-Uncle had kept his word and was not spending the winter in his old home. As soon as the first snow began to fall, he had shut up the hut and the outside buildings and gone down to Dörfli with Heidi and the goats. Near the church was a straggling half-ruined building, which had once been the house of a person of consequence. A distinguished soldier had lived there at one time; he had taken service in Spain and had there performed many brave deeds and gathered much treasure. When he returned home to Dörfli he spent part of his booty in building a fine house, with the intention of living in it. But he had been too long accustomed to the noise and bustle of arms and the world to care for a quiet country life, and he soon went off again, and this time did not return. When after many long years it seemed certain that he was dead, a distant relative took possession of the house, but it had already fallen into disrepair, and he had no wish to rebuild it. So it was let to poor people, who paid but a small rent, and when any part of the building fell it was allowed to remain. This had now gone on for many years. As long ago as when his son Tobias was a child Alm-Uncle had rented the tumbledown old place. Since then it had stood empty, for no one could stay in it who had not some idea of how to stop up the holes and gaps and make it habitable. Otherwise the wind and rain and snow blew into the rooms, so that it was impossible even to keep a candle alight, and the indwellers would have been frozen to death during the long cold winters. Alm-Uncle, however, knew how to mend matters. As soon as he made up his mind to spend the winter in Dörfli, he rented the old place and worked during the autumn to get it sound and tight. In the middle of October he and Heidi took up their residence there.

On approaching the house from the back one came first into an open space with a wall on either side, of which one was half in ruins. Above this rose the arch of an old window thickly overgrown with ivy, which spread over the remains of a domed roof that had evidently been part of a chapel. A large hall came next, which lay open, without doors, to the square outside. Here also walls and roof only partially remained, and indeed what was left of the roof looked as if it might fall at any minute had it not been for two stout pillars that supported it. Alm-Uncle had here put up a wooden partition and covered the floor with straw, for this was to be the goats' house. Endless passages led from this, through the rents of which the sky as well as the fields and the road outside could be seen at intervals; but at last one came to a stout oak door that led into a room that still stood intact. Here the walls and the dark wainscoting remained as good as ever, and in the corner was an immense stove reaching nearly to the ceiling, on the white tiles of which were painted large pictures in blue. These represented old castles surrounded with trees, and huntsmen riding out with their hounds; or else a quiet lake scene, with broad oak trees and a man fishing. A seat ran all round the stove so that one could sit at one's ease and study the pictures. These attracted Heidi's attention at once, and she had no sooner arrived with her grandfather than she ran and seated herself and began to examine them. But when she had gradually worked herself round to the back, something else diverted her attention. In the large space between the stove and the wall four planks had been put together as if to make a large receptacle for apples; there were no apples, however, inside, but something Heidi had no difficulty in recognising, for it was her very own bed, with its hay mattress and sheets, and sack for a coverlid, just as she had it up at the hut. Heidi clapped her hands for joy and exclaimed, "O Grandfather, this is my room, how nice! But where are you going to sleep?"

"Your room must be near the stove or you will freeze," he replied, "but you can come and see mine too."

Heidi got down and skipped across the large room after her grandfather, who opened a door at the farther end leading into a smaller one which was to be his bedroom. Then came another door. Heidi pushed it open and stood amazed, for here was an immense room like a kitchen, larger than anything of the kind that Heidi had seen before. There was still plenty of work for the grandfather before this room could be finished, for there were holes and cracks in the walls through which the wind whistled, and yet he had already nailed up so many new planks that it looked as if a lot of small cupboards had been set up round the room. He had, however, made the large old door safe with many screws and nails, as a protection against the outside air, and this was very necessary, for just beyond was a mass of ruined buildings overgrown with tall weeds, which made a dwelling-place for endless beetles and lizards.

Heidi was very delighted with her new home, and by the morning after their arrival she knew every nook and corner so thoroughly that she could take Peter over it and show him all that was to be seen; indeed she would not let him go till he had examined every single wonderful thing contained in it.

Heidi slept soundly in her corner by the stove; but every morning when she first awoke she still thought she was on the mountain, and that she must run outside at once to see if the fir trees were so quiet because their branches were weighed down with the thick snow. She had to look about her for some minutes before she felt quite sure where she was, and a certain sensation of trouble and oppression would come over her as she grew aware that she was not at home in the hut. But then she would hear her grandfather's voice outside, attending to the goats, and these would give one or two loud bleats, as if calling to her to make haste and go to them, and then Heidi was happy again, for she knew she was still at home, and she would jump gladly out of bed and run out to the animals as quickly as she could. On the fourth morning, as soon as she saw her grandfather, she said, "I must go up to see Grandmother today; she ought not to be alone so long."

But the grandfather would not agree to this. "Neither today nor tomorrow can you go," he said; "the mountain is covered fathom-deep in snow, and the snow is still falling; the sturdy Peter can hardly get along. A little creature like you would soon be smothered by it, and we should not be able to find you again. Wait a bit till it freezes, then you will be able to walk over the hard snow."

Heidi did not like the thought of having to wait, but the days were so busy that she hardly knew how they went by.

Heidi now went to school in Dörfli every morning and afternoon, and eagerly set to work to learn all that was taught her. She hardly ever saw Peter there, for as a rule he was absent. The teacher was an easy-going man who merely remarked now and then, "Peter is not turning up today again, it seems, but there is a lot of snow up on the mountain and I daresay he cannot get along." Peter, however, always seemed able to make his way through the snow in the evening when school was over, and he then generally paid Heidi a visit.

At last, after some days, the sun again appeared and shone brightly over the white ground, but he went to bed again behind the mountains at a very early hour, as if he did not find such pleasure in looking down on the earth as when everything was green and flowery. But then the moon came out clear and large and lit up the great white snowfield all through the night, and the next morning the whole mountain glistened and sparkled like a huge crystal. When Peter got out of his window as usual, he was taken by surprise, for instead of sinking into the soft snow he fell on the hard ground and went sliding some way down the mountain side like a sleigh before he could stop himself. He picked himself up and tested the hardness of the ground by stamping on it and trying with all his might to dig his heels into it, but even then he could not break off a single little splinter of ice; the Alm was frozen hard as iron. This was just what Peter had been hoping for, as he knew now that Heidi would be able to come up to them. He quickly got back into the house, swallowed the milk which his mother had put ready for him, thrust a piece of bread in his pocket, and said, "I must be off to school." "That's right, go and learn all you can," said the grandmother encouragingly. Peter crept through the window again— the door was quite blocked by the frozen snow outside—pulling his little sleigh after him, and in another minute was shooting down the mountain.

He went like lightning, and when he reached Dörfli, which stood on the direct road to Mayenfeld, he made up his mind to go on further, for he was sure he could not stop his rapid descent without hurting himself and the sleigh too. So down he still went till he reached the level ground, where the sleigh came to a pause of its own accord. Then he got out and looked round. The impetus with which he had made his journey down had carried him some little way beyond Mayenfeld. He bethought himself that it was too late to get to school now, as lessons would already have begun, and it would take him a good hour to walk back to Dörfli. So he might take his time about returning, which he did, and reached Dörfli just as Heidi had got home from school and was sitting at dinner with her grandfather. Peter walked in, and as on this occasion he had something particular to communicate, he began without a pause, exclaiming as he stood still in the middle of the room, "She's got it now."

"Got it? What?" asked the Uncle. "Your words sound quite warlike, general."

"The frost," explained Peter.

"Oh! Then now I can go and see Grandmother!" said Heidi joyfully, for she had understood Peter's words at once. "But why were you not at school then? You could have come down in the sleigh," she added reproachfully, for it did not agree with Heidi's ideas of good behaviour to stay away when it was possible to be there.

"It carried me on too far and I was too late," Peter replied.

"I call that being a deserter," said the Uncle, "and deserters get their ears pulled, as you know."

Peter gave a tug to his cap in alarm, for there was no one of whom he stood in so much awe as Alm-Uncle.

"And an army leader like yourself ought to be doubly ashamed of running away," continued Alm-Uncle. "What would you think of your goats if one went off this way and another that, and refused to follow and do what was good for them? What would you do then?"

"I should beat them," said Peter promptly.

"And if a boy behaved like these unruly goats, and he got a beating for it, what would you say then?"

"Serve him right," was the answer.

"Good, then understand this: next time you let your sleigh carry you past the school when you ought to be inside at your lessons, come on to me afterwards and receive what you deserve."

Peter now understood the drift of the old man's questions and that he was the boy who behaved like the unruly goats, and he looked somewhat fearfully towards the corner to see if anything happened to be there such as he used himself on such occasions for the punishment of his animals.

But now the grandfather suddenly said in a cheerful voice, "Come and sit down and have something, and afterwards Heidi shall go with you. Bring her back this evening and you will find supper waiting for you here."

This unexpected turn of conversation set Peter grinning all over with delight. He obeyed without hesitation and took his seat beside Heidi. But the child could not eat any more in her excitement at the thought of going to see Grandmother. She pushed the potatoes and toasted cheese which still stood on her plate towards him while Uncle was filling his plate from the other side, so that he had quite a pile of food in front of him, but he attacked it without any lack of courage.

Heidi ran to the cupboard and brought out the warm cloak Clara had sent her; with this on and the hood drawn over her head, she was all ready for her journey. She stood waiting beside Peter, and as soon as his last mouthful had disappeared she said, "Come along now." As the two walked together Heidi had much to tell Peter of her two goats that had been so unhappy the first day in their new stall that they would not eat anything, but stood hanging their heads, not even rousing themselves to bleat. And when she asked her grandfather the reason of this, he told her it was with them as with her in Frankfurt, for it was the first time in their lives they had come down from the mountain. "And you don't know what that is, Peter, unless you have felt it yourself," added Heidi.

The children had nearly reached their destination before Peter opened his mouth; he appeared to be so sunk in thought that he hardly heard what was said to him. As they neared home, however, he stood still and said in a somewhat sullen voice, "I had rather go to school even than get what Uncle threatened."

Heidi was of the same mind, and encouraged him in his good intention. They found Brigitta sitting alone knitting, for the grandmother was not very well and had to stay the day in bed on account of the cold. Heidi had never before missed the old figure in her place in the corner, and she ran quickly into the next room. There lay Grandmother on her little poorly covered bed, wrapped up in her warm grey shawl.

"Thank God," she exclaimed as Heidi came running in; the poor old woman had had a secret fear at heart all through the autumn, especially if Heidi was absent for any length of time, for Peter had told her of a strange gentleman who had come from Frankfurt, and who had gone out with them and always talked to Heidi, and she had felt sure he had come to take her away again. Even when she heard he had gone off alone, she still had an idea that a messenger would be sent over from Frankfurt to fetch the child. Heidi went up to the side of the bed and said, "Are you very ill, Grandmother?"

"No, no, child," answered the old woman reassuringly, passing her hand lovingly over the child's head, "It's only the frost that has got into my bones a bit."

"Shall you be quite well then directly it turns warm again?"

"Yes, God willing, or even before that, for I want to get back to my spinning; I thought perhaps I should do a little today, but tomorrow I am sure to be all right again." The old woman had detected that Heidi was frightened and was anxious to set her mind at ease.

Her words comforted Heidi, who had in truth been greatly distressed, for she had never before seen the grandmother ill in bed. She now looked at the old woman seriously for a minute or two, and then said, "In Frankfurt everybody puts on a shawl to go out walking; did you think it was to be worn in bed, Grandmother?"

"I put it on, dear child, to keep myself from freezing, and I am so pleased with it, for my bedclothes are not very thick," she answered.

"But, Grandmother," continued Heidi, "your bed is not right, because it goes downhill at your head instead of uphill."

"I know it, child, I can feel it," and the grandmother put up her hand to the thin flat pillow, which was little more than a board under her head, to make herself more comfortable; "the pillow was never very thick, and I have lain on it now for so many years that it has grown quite flat."

"Oh, if only I had asked Clara to let me take away my Frankfurt bed," said Heidi. "I had three large pillows, one above the other, so that I could hardly sleep, and I used to slip down to try and find a flat place, and then I had to pull myself up again, because it was proper to sleep there like that. Could you sleep like that, Grandmother?"

"Oh, yes! The pillows keep one warm, and it is easier to breathe when the head is high," answered the grandmother, wearily raising her head as she spoke as if trying to find a higher resting-place. "But we will not talk about that, for I have so much that other old sick people are without for which I thank God; there is the nice bread I get every day, and this warm wrap, and your visits, Heidi. Will you read me something today?"

Heidi ran into the next room to fetch the hymn book. Then she picked out the favourite hymns one after another, for she knew them all by heart now, as pleased as the grandmother to hear them again after so many days. The grandmother lay with folded hands, while a smile of peace stole over the worn, troubled face, like one to whom good news has been brought.

Suddenly Heidi paused. "Grandmother, are you feeling quite well again already?"

"Yes, child, I have grown better while listening to you; read it to the end."

The child read on, and when she came to the last words:—

> As the eyes grow dim, and darkness
> Closes round, the soul grows clearer,
> Sees the goal to which it travels,
> Gladly feels its home is nearer.

the grandmother repeated them once or twice to herself, with a look of happy expectation on her face. And Heidi took equal pleasure in them, for the picture of the beautiful sunny day of her return home rose before her eyes, and she exclaimed joyfully, "Grandmother, I know exactly what it is like to go home." The old woman did not answer, but she had heard Heidi's words, and the expression that had made the child think she was better remained on her face.

A little later Heidi said, "It is growing dark and I must go home; I am glad to think, that you are quite well again."

The grandmother took the child's hand in hers and held it closely. "Yes," she said, "I feel quite happy again; even if I have to go on lying here, I am content. No one knows what it is to lie here alone day after day, in silence and darkness, without hearing a voice or seeing a ray of light. Sad thoughts come over me, and I do not feel sometimes as if I could bear it any longer or as if it could ever be light again. But when you come and read those words to me, then I am comforted and my heart rejoices once more."

Then she let the child go, and Heidi ran into the next room, and bid Peter come quickly, for it had now grown quite dark. But when they got outside they found the moon shining down on the white snow and everything as clear as in the daylight. Peter got his sleigh, put Heidi at the back, he himself sitting in front to guide, and down the mountain they shot like two birds darting through the air.

When Heidi was lying that night on her high bed of hay she thought of the grandmother on her low pillow, and of all she had said about the light and comfort that awoke in her when she heard the hymns, and she thought: if I could read to her every day, then I should go on making her better. But she knew that it would be a week, if not two, before she would be able to go up the mountain again. This was a thought of great trouble to Heidi, and she tried hard to think of some way which would enable the grandmother to hear the words she loved every day. Suddenly an idea struck her, and she was so delighted with it that she could hardly bear to wait for morning, so eager was she to begin carrying out her plan. All at once she sat upright in her bed, for she had been so busy with her thoughts that she had forgotten to say her prayers, and she never now finished her day without saying them.

When she had prayed with all her heart for herself, her grandfather and grandmother, she lay back again on the warm soft hay and slept soundly and peacefully till morning broke.

Chapter 19

The Winter Continues

Peter arrived punctually at school the following day. He had brought his dinner with him, for all the children who lived at a distance regularly seated themselves at mid-day on the tables, and resting their feet firmly on the benches, spread out their meal on their knees and so ate their dinner, while those living in Dörfli went home for theirs. Till one o'clock they might all do as they liked, and then school began again. When Peter had finished his lessons on the days he attended school, he went over to Uncle's to see Heidi.

When he walked into the large room at Uncle's today, Heidi immediately rushed forward and took hold of him, for it was for Peter she had been waiting. "I've thought of something, Peter," she said hastily.

"What is it?" he asked.

"You must learn to read," she informed him.

"I have learnt," was the answer.

"Yes, yes, but I mean so that you can really make use of it," continued Heidi eagerly.

"I never shall," was the prompt reply.

"Nobody believes that you cannot learn, nor I either now," said Heidi in a very decided tone of voice. "Grandmamma in Frankfurt said long ago that it was not true, and she told me not to believe you."

Peter looked rather taken aback at this piece of intelligence.

"I will soon teach you to read, for I know how," continued Heidi. "You must learn at once, and then you can read one or two hymns every day to Grandmother."

"Oh, I don't care about that," he grumbled in reply.

This hard-hearted way of refusing to agree to what was right and kind, and to what Heidi had so much at heart, aroused her anger. With flashing eyes she stood facing the boy and said threateningly, "If you won't learn as I want you to, I will tell you what will happen; you know your mother has often spoken of sending you to Frankfurt, that you may learn a lot of things, and I know where the boys there have to go to school; Clara pointed out the great house to me when we were driving together. And they don't only go when they are boys, but have more lessons still when they are grown men. I have seen them myself, and you mustn't think they have only one kind teacher like we have. There are ever so many of them, all in the school at the same time, and they are all dressed in black, as if they were going to church, and have black hats on their heads as high as that—" and Heidi held out her hand to show their height from the floor.

Peter felt a cold shudder run down his back.

"And you will have to go in among all those gentlemen," continued Heidi with increasing animation, "and when it comes to your turn you won't be able to read and will make mistakes in your spelling. Then you'll see how they'll make fun of you; even worse than Tinette, and you ought to have seen what she was like when she was scornful."

"Well, I'll learn then," said Peter, half sorrowfully and half angrily.

Heidi was instantly mollified. "That's right, then we'll begin at once," she said cheerfully, and went busily to work on the spot, dragging Peter to the table and fetching her books.

Among other presents Clara had sent Heidi a book which the latter had decided, in bed the night before, would serve capitally for teaching Peter, for it was an A B C book with rhyming lines. And now the two sat together at the table with their heads bent over the book, for the lesson had begun.

Peter was made to spell out the first sentence two or three times over, for Heidi wished him to get it correct and fluent. At last she said, "You don't seem able to get it right, but I will read it aloud to you once; when you know what it ought to be you will find it easier." And she read out:—

A B C must be learnt today
Or the judge will call you up to pay.

"I shan't go," said Peter obstinately.

"Go where?" asked Heidi.

"Before the judge," he answered.

"Well then make haste and learn these three letters, then you won't have to go."

Peter went at his task again and repeated the three letters so many times and with such determination that she said at last,—

"You must know those three now."

Seeing what an effect the first two lines of verse had had upon him, she thought she would prepare the ground a little for the following lessons.

"Wait, and I will read you some of the next sentences," she continued, "then you will see what else there is to expect."

And she began in a clear slow voice:—

D E F G must run with ease
Or something will follow that does not please.

Should H I J K be now forgot
Disgrace is yours upon the spot.

And then L M must follow at once
Or punished you'll be for a sorry dunce.

If you knew what next awaited you
You'd haste to learn N O P Q.

Now R S T be quick about
Or worse will follow there's little doubt.

Heidi paused, for Peter was so quiet that she looked to see what he was doing. These many secret threats and hints of dreadful punishments had so affected him that he sat as if petrified and stared at Heidi with horror-stricken eyes. Her kind heart was moved at once, and she said, wishing to reassure him, "You need not be afraid, Peter; come here to me every evening, and if you learn as you have today you will at last know all your letters, and the other things won't come. But you must come regularly, not now and then as you do to school; even if it snows it won't hurt you."

Peter promised, for the trepidation he had been in had made him quite tame and docile. Lessons being finished for this day he now went home.

Peter obeyed Heidi's instructions punctually, and every evening went diligently to work to learn the following letters, taking the sentences thoroughly to heart. The grandfather was frequently in the room smoking his pipe comfortably while the lesson was going on, and his face twitched occasionally as if he was overtaken with a sudden fit of merriment. Peter was often invited to stay to supper after the great exertion he had gone through, which richly compensated him for the anguish of mind he had suffered with the sentence for the day.

So the winter went by, and Peter really made progress with his letters; but he went through a terrible fight each day with the sentences.

He had got at last to U. Heidi read out:—

And if you put the U for V,
You'll go where you would not like to be.

Peter growled, "Yes, but I shan't go!" But he was very diligent that day, as if under the impression that some one would seize him suddenly by the collar and drag him where he would rather not go. The next evening Heidi read:—

> If you falter at W, worst of all,
> Look at the stick against the wall.

Peter looked at the wall and said scornfully, "There isn't one."

"Yes, but do you know what Grandfather has in his box?" asked Heidi. "A stick as thick almost as your arm, and if he took that out, you might well say, look at the stick on the wall."

Peter knew that thick hazel stick, and immediately bent his head over the W and struggled to master it. Another day the lines ran:—

> Then comes the X for you to say
> Or be sure you'll get no food today.

Peter looked towards the cupboard where the bread and cheese were kept and said crossly, "I never said that I should forget the X."

"That's all right; if you don't forget it we can go on to learn the next, and then you will only have one more," replied Heidi, anxious to encourage him.

Peter did not quite understand, but when Heidi went on and read:—

> And should you make a stop at Y,
> They'll point at you and cry, Fie, fie.

All the gentlemen in Frankfurt with tall black hats on their heads, and scorn and mockery in their faces rose up before his mind's eye, and he threw himself with energy on the Y, not letting it go till at last he knew it so thoroughly that he could see what it was like even when he shut his eyes.

He arrived on the following day in a somewhat lofty frame of mind, for there was now only one letter to struggle over, and when Heidi began the lesson with reading aloud:—

> Make haste with Z, if you›re too slow
> Off to the Hottentots you'll go.

Peter remarked scornfully, "I dare say, when no one knows even where such people live."

"I assure you, Peter," replied Heidi, "grandfather knows all about them. Wait a second and I will run and ask him, for he is only over the way with the pastor." And she rose and ran to the door to put her words into action, but Peter cried out in a voice of agony,—

"Stop!" for he already saw himself being carried off by Alm-Uncle and the pastor and sent straight away to the Hottentots, since as yet he did not know his last letter. His cry of fear brought Heidi back.

"What is the matter?" she asked in astonishment.

"Nothing! Come back! I am going to learn my letter," he said, stammering with fear. Heidi, however, herself wished to know where the Hottentots lived and persisted that she should ask her grandfather, but she gave in at last to Peter's despairing entreaties. She insisted on his doing something in return, and so not only had he to repeat his Z until it was so fixed in his memory that he could never forget it again, but she began teaching him to spell, and Peter really made a good start that evening. So it went on from day to day.

The frost had gone and the snow was soft again, and moreover fresh snow continually fell, so that it was quite three weeks before Heidi could go to the grandmother again. So much the more eagerly did she pursue her teaching so that Peter might compensate for her absence by reading hymns to the old woman. One evening he walked in home after leaving Heidi, and as he entered he said, "I can do it now."

"Do what, Peter?" asked his mother.

"Read," he answered.

"Do you really mean it? Did you hear that, Grandmother?" she called out.

The grandmother had heard, and was already wondering how such a thing could have come to pass.

"I must read one of the hymns now; Heidi told me to," he went on to inform them. His mother hastily fetched the book, and the grandmother lay in joyful expectation, for it was so long since she had heard the good words. Peter sat down to the table and began to read. His mother sat beside him listening with surprise and exclaiming at the close of each verse, "Who would have thought it possible!"

The grandmother did not speak though she followed the words he read with strained attention.

It happened on the day following this that there was a reading lesson in Peter's class. When it came to his turn, the teacher said,—

"We must pass over Peter as usual, or will you try again once more—I will not say to read, but to stammer through a sentence."

Peter took the book and read off three lines without the slightest hesitation.

The teacher put down his book and stared at Peter as at some out-of-the-way and marvellous thing unseen before. At last he spoke,—

"Peter, some miracle has been performed upon you! Here have I been striving with unheard-of patience to teach you and you have not hitherto been able to say your letters even. And now, just as I had made up my mind not to waste any more trouble upon you, you suddenly are able to read a consecutive sentence properly and distinctly. How has such a miracle come to pass in our days?"

"It was Heidi," answered Peter.

The teacher looked in astonishment towards Heidi, who was sitting innocently on her bench with no appearance of anything supernatural about her. He continued, "I have noticed a change in you altogether, Peter. Whereas formerly you often missed coming to school for a week, or even weeks at a time, you have lately not stayed away a single day. Who has wrought this change for good in you?"

"It was Uncle," answered Peter.

With increasing surprise the teacher looked from Peter to Heidi and back again at Peter.

"We will try once more," he said cautiously, and Peter had again to show off his accomplishment by reading another three lines. There was no mistake about it—Peter could read. As soon as school was over the teacher went over to the pastor to tell him this piece of news, and to inform him of the happy result of Heidi's and the grandfather's combined efforts.

Every evening Peter read one hymn aloud; so far he obeyed Heidi. Nothing would induce him to read a second, and indeed the grandmother never asked for it. His mother Brigitta could not get over her surprise at her son's attainment, and when the reader was in bed would often express her pleasure at it. "Now he has learnt to read there is no knowing what may be made of him yet."

On one of these occasions the grandmother answered, "Yes, it is good for him to have learnt something, but I shall indeed be thankful when spring is here again and Heidi can come; they are not like the same hymns when Peter reads them. So many words seem missing, and I try to think what they ought to be and then I lose the sense, and so the hymns do not come home to my heart as when Heidi reads them."

The truth was that Peter arranged to make his reading as little troublesome for himself as possible. When he came upon a word that he thought was too long or difficult in any other way, he left it out, for he decided that a word or two less in a verse, where there were so many of them, could make no difference to his grandmother. And so it came about that most of the principal words were missing in the hymns that Peter read aloud.

Chapter 20

News From Distant Friends

It was the month of May. From every height the full fresh streams of spring were flowing down into the valley. The clear warm sunshine lay upon the mountain, which had turned green again. The last snows had disappeared and the sun had already coaxed many of the flowers to show their bright heads above the grass. Up above the gay young wind of spring was singing through the fir trees, and shaking down the old dark needles to make room for the new bright green ones that were soon to deck out the trees in their spring finery. Higher up still the great bird went circling round in the blue ether as of old, while the golden sunshine lit up the grandfather's hut, and all the ground about it was warm and dry again so that one might sit out where one liked. Heidi was at home again on the mountain, running backwards and forwards in her accustomed way, not knowing which spot was most delightful. Now she stood still to listen to the deep, mysterious voice of the wind, as it blew down to her from the mountain summits, coming nearer and nearer and gathering strength as it came, till it broke with force against the fir trees, bending and shaking them, and seeming to shout for joy, so that she too, though blown about like a feather, felt she must join in the chorus of exulting sounds. Then she would run round again to the sunny space in front of the hut, and seating herself on the ground would peer closely into the short grass to see how many little flower cups were open or thinking of opening. She rejoiced with all the myriad little beetles and winged insects that jumped and crawled and danced in the sun, and drew in deep draughts of the spring scents that rose from the newly-awakened earth, and thought the mountain was more beautiful than ever. All the tiny living creatures must be as happy as she, for it seemed to her there were little voices all round her singing and humming in joyful tones, "On the mountain! On the mountain!"

From the shed at the back came the sound of sawing and chopping, and Heidi listened to it with pleasure, for it was the old familiar sound she had known from the beginning of her life up here. Suddenly she jumped up and ran round, for she must know what her grandfather was doing. In front of the shed door already stood a finished new chair, and a second was in course of construction under the grandfather's skilful hand.

"Oh, I know what these are for," exclaimed Heidi in great glee. "We shall want them when they all come from Frankfurt. This one is for Grandmamma, and the one you are now making is for Clara, and then—then, there will, I suppose, have to be another," continued Heidi with more hesitation in her voice, "or do you think, Grandfather, that perhaps Fräulein Rottenmeier will not come with them?"

"Well, I cannot say just yet," replied her grandfather, "but it will be safer to make one so that we can offer her a seat if she does."

Heidi looked thoughtfully at the plain wooden chair without arms as if trying to imagine how Fräulein Rottenmeier and a chair of this sort would suit one another. After a few minutes' contemplation, "Grandfather," she said, shaking her head doubtfully, "I don't think she would be able to sit on that."

"Then we will invite her on the couch with the beautiful green turf feather-bed," was her grandfather's quiet rejoinder.

While Heidi was pausing to consider what this might be there approached from above a whistling, calling, and other sounds which Heidi immediately recognised. She ran out and found herself surrounded by her four-footed friends. They were apparently as pleased as she was to be among the heights again, for they leaped about and bleated for joy, pushing Heidi this way and that, each anxious to express his delight with some sign of affection. But Peter sent them flying to right and left, for he had something to give to Heidi. When he at last got up to her he handed her a letter.

"There!" he exclaimed, leaving the further explanation of the matter to Heidi herself.

"Did some one give you this while you were out with the goats," she asked, in her surprise.

"No," was the answer.

"Where did you get it from then?

"I found it in the dinner bag."

Which was true to a certain extent. The letter to Heidi had been given him the evening before by the postman at Dörfli, and Peter had put it into his empty bag. That morning he had stuffed his bread and cheese on the top of it, and had forgotten it when he fetched Alm-Uncle's two goats; only when he had finished his bread and cheese at mid-day and was searching in the bag for any last crumbs did he remember the letter which lay at the bottom.

Heidi read the address carefully; then she ran back to the shed holding out her letter to her grandfather in high glee. "From Frankfurt! From Clara! Would you like to hear it?"

The grandfather was ready and pleased to do so, as also Peter, who had followed Heidi into the shed. He leant his back against the door post, as he felt he could follow Heidi's reading better if firmly supported from behind, and so stood prepared to listen.

"Dearest Heidi,— Everything is packed and we shall start now in two or three days, as soon as papa himself is ready to leave; he is not coming with us as he has first to go to Paris. The doctor comes every day, and as soon as he is inside the door, he cries, 'Off now as quickly as you can, off to the mountain.' He is most impatient about our going. You cannot think how much he enjoyed himself when he was with you! He has called nearly every day this winter, and each time he has come in to my room and said he must tell me about everything again. And then he sits down and describes all he did with you and the grandfather, and talks of the mountains and the flowers and of the great silence up there far above all towns and the villages, and of the fresh delicious air, and often adds, 'No one can help getting well up there.' He himself is quite a different man since his visit, and looks quite young again and happy, which he had not been for a long time before. Oh, how I am looking forward to seeing everything and to being with you on the mountain, and to making the acquaintance of Peter and the goats.

"I shall have first to go through a six weeks' cure at Ragatz; this the doctor has ordered, and then we shall move up to Dörfli, and every fine day I shall be carried up the mountain in my chair and spend the day with you. Grandmamma is travelling with me and will remain with me; she also is delighted at the thought of paying you a visit. But just imagine, Fräulein Rottenmeier refuses to come with us. Almost every day grandmamma says to her, 'Well, how about this Swiss journey, my worthy Rottenmeier? Pray say if you really would like to come with us.' But she always thanks Grandmamma very politely and says she has quite made up her mind. I think I know what has done it: Sebastian gave such a frightful description of the mountain, of how the rocks were so overhanging and dangerous that at any minute you might fall into a crevasse, and how it was such steep climbing that you feared at every step to go slipping to the bottom, and that goats alone could make their way up without fear of being killed. She shuddered when she heard him tell of all this, and since then she has not been so enthusiastic about Switzerland as she was before. Fear has also taken possession of Tinette, and she also refuses to come. So Grandmamma and I will be alone; Sebastian will go with us as far as Ragatz and then return here.

"I can hardly bear waiting till I see you again. Goodbye, dearest Heidi; Grandmamma sends you her best love and all good wishes.—Your affectionate friend, Clara."

Peter, as soon as the conclusion of the letter had been reached, left his reclining position and rushed out, twirling his stick in the air in such a reckless fashion that the frightened goats fled down the mountain before him with higher and wider leaps than usual. Peter followed at full speed, his stick still raised in air in a menacing manner as if he was longing to vent his fury on some invisible foe. This foe was indeed the prospect of the arrival of the Frankfurt visitors, the thought of whom filled him with exasperation.

Heidi was so full of joyful anticipation that she determined to seize the first possible moment next day to go down and tell Grandmother who was coming, and also particularly who was not coming. These details would be of great interest to her, for Grandmother knew well all the persons named from Heidi's description, and had entered with deep sympathy into all that the child had told her of her life and surroundings in Frankfurt. Heidi paid her visit in the early afternoon, for she could now go alone again; the sun was bright in the heavens and the days were growing longer, and it was delightful to go racing down the mountain over the dry ground, with the brisk May wind blowing from behind, and speeding Heidi on her way a little more quickly than her legs alone would have carried her.

The grandmother was no longer confined to her bed. She was back in her corner at her spinning-wheel, but there was an expression on her face of mournful anxiety. Peter had come in the evening before brimful of anger and had told about the large party who were coming up from Frankfurt, and he did not know what other things might happen after that; and the old woman had not slept all night, pursued by the old thought of Heidi being taken from her. Heidi ran in, and taking her little stool immediately sat down by Grandmother and began eagerly pouring out all her news, growing more excited with her pleasure as she went on. But all of a sudden she stopped short and said anxiously, "What is the matter, Grandmother, aren't you a bit pleased with what I am telling you?"

"Yes, yes, of course, child, since it gives you so much pleasure," she answered, trying to look more cheerful.

"But I can see all the same that something troubles you. Is it because you think after all that Fräulein Rottenmeier may come?" asked Heidi, beginning to feel anxious herself.

"No, no! It is nothing, child," said the grandmother, wishing to reassure her. "Just give me your hand that I may feel sure you are there. No doubt it would be the best thing for you, although I feel I could scarcely survive it."

"I do not want anything of the best if you could scarcely survive it," said Heidi, in such a determined tone of voice that the grandmother's fears increased as she felt sure the people from Frankfurt were coming to take Heidi back with them, since now she was well again they naturally wished to have her with them once more. But she was anxious to hide her trouble from Heidi if possible, as the latter was so sympathetic that she might refuse perhaps to go away, and that would not be right. She sought for help, but not for long, for she knew of only one.

"Heidi," she said, "there is something that would comfort me and calm my thoughts; read me the hymn beginning: 'All things will work for good.'"

Heidi found the place at once and read out in her clear young voice:—

All things will work for good
To those who trust in Me;
I come with healing on my wings,
To save and set thee free.

"Yes, yes, that is just what I wanted to hear," said the grandmother, and the deep expression of trouble passed from her face. Heidi looked at her thoughtfully for a minute or two and then said, "Healing means that which cures everything and makes everybody well, doesn't it, Grandmother?"

"Yes, that is it," replied the old woman with a nod of assent, "and we may be sure everything will come to pass according to God's good purpose. Read the verse again, that we may remember it well and not forget it again."

And Heidi read the words over two or three times, for she also found pleasure in this assurance of all things being arranged for the best.

When the evening came, Heidi returned home up the mountain. The stars came out overhead one by one, so bright and sparkling that each seemed to send a fresh ray of joy into her heart; she was obliged to pause continually to look up, and as the whole sky at last grew spangled with them she spoke aloud, "Yes, I understand now why we feel so happy, and are not afraid about anything, because God knows what is good and beautiful for us." And the stars with their glistening eyes continued to nod to her till she reached home, where she found her grandfather also standing and looking up at them, for they had seldom been more glorious than they were this night.

Not only were the nights of this month of May so clear and bright, but the days as well; the sun rose every morning into the cloudless sky, as undimmed in its splendor as when it sank the evening before, and the grandfather would look out early and exclaim with astonishment, "This is indeed a wonderful year of sun; it will make all the shrubs and plants grow apace;

you will have to see, general, that your army does not get out of hand from overfeeding." And Peter would swing his stick with an air of assurance and an expression on his face as much as to say, "see to that."

So May passed, everything growing greener and greener, and then came the month of June, with a hotter sun and long light days, that brought the flowers out all over the mountain, so that every spot was bright with them and the air full of their sweet scents. This month too was drawing to its close when one day Heidi, having finished her domestic duties, ran out with the intention of paying first a visit to the fir trees, and then going up higher to see if the bush of rock roses was yet in bloom, for its flowers were so lovely when standing open in the sun. But just as she was turning the corner of the hut, she gave such a loud cry that her grandfather came running out of the shed to see what had happened.

"Grandfather, Grandfather!" she cried, beside herself with excitement. "Come here! Look! Look!"

The old man was by her side by this time and looked in the direction of her outstretched hand.

A strange looking procession was making its way up the mountain; in front were two men carrying a sedan chair, in which sat a girl well wrapped up in shawls; then followed a horse, mounted by a stately-looking lady who was looking about her with great interest and talking to the guide who walked beside her; then a reclining chair, which was being pushed up by another man, it having evidently been thought safer to send the invalid to whom it belonged up the steep path in a sedan chair. The procession wound up with a porter, with such a bundle of cloaks, shawls, and furs on his back that it rose well above his head.

"Here they come! Here they come!" shouted Heidi, jumping with joy. And sure enough it was the party from Frankfurt; the figures came nearer and nearer, and at last they had actually arrived. The men in front put down their burden, Heidi rushed forward and the two children embraced each other with mutual delight. Grandmamma having also reached the top, dismounted, and gave Heidi an affectionate greeting, before turning to the grandfather, who had meanwhile come up to welcome his guests. There was no constraint about the meeting, for they both knew each other perfectly well from hearsay and felt like old acquaintances.

After the first words of greeting had been exchanged Grandmamma broke out into lively expressions of admiration. "What a magnificent residence you have, Uncle! I could hardly have believed it was so beautiful! A king might well envy you! And how well my little Heidi looks—like a wild rose!" she continued, drawing the child towards her and stroking her fresh pink cheeks. "I don't know which way to look first, it is all so lovely! What do you say to it, Clara, what do you say?"

Clara was gazing round entranced; she had never imagined, much less seen, anything so beautiful. She gave vent to her delight in cries of joy. "O Grandmamma," she said, "I should like to remain here for ever."

The grandfather had meanwhile drawn up the invalid chair and spread some of the wraps over it; he now went up to Clara.

"Supposing we carry the little daughter now to her accustomed chair; I think she will be more comfortable, the travelling sedan is rather hard," he said, and without waiting for any one to help him he lifted the child in his strong arms and laid her gently down on her own couch. He then covered her over carefully and arranged her feet on the soft cushion, as if he had never done anything all his life but attend on cripples. The grandmamma looked on with surprise.

"My dear Uncle," she exclaimed, "if I knew where you had learned to nurse I would at once send all the nurses I know to the same place that they might handle their patients in like manner. How do you come to know so much?"

Uncle smiled. "I know more from experience than training," he answered, but as he spoke the smile died away and a look of sadness passed over his face. The vision rose before him of a face of suffering that he had known long years before, the face of a man lying crippled on his couch of pain, and unable to move a limb. The man had been his Captain during the fierce fighting in Sicily; he had found him lying wounded and had carried him away, and after that the captain would suffer no one else near him, and Uncle had stayed and nursed him till his sufferings ended in death. It all came back to Uncle now, and it seemed natural to him to attend on the sick Clara and to show her all those kindly attentions with which he had been once so familiar.

The sky spread blue and cloudless over the hut and the fir trees and far above over the high rocks, the grey summits of which glistened in the sun. Clara could not feast her eyes enough on all the beauty around her.

"O Heidi, if only I could walk about with you," she said longingly, "if I could but go and look at the fir trees and at everything I know so well from your description, although I have never been here before."

Heidi in response put out all her strength, and after a slight effort, managed to wheel Clara's chair quite easily round the hut to the fir trees. There they paused. Clara had never seen such trees before, with their tall, straight stems, and long thick branches growing thicker and thicker till they touched the ground. Even the grandmamma, who had followed the children, was astonished at the sight of them. She hardly knew what to admire most in these ancient trees: the lofty tops rising in their full green splendor towards the sky, or the pillar-like stems, with their straight and gigantic boughs, that spoke of such antiquity of age, of such long years during which they had looked down upon the valley below, where men came and went, and all things were continually changing, while they stood undisturbed and changeless.

Heidi had now wheeled Clara on to the goat shed, and had flung open the door, so that Clara might have a full view of all that was inside. There was not much to see just now as its indwellers were absent. Clara lamented to her grandmother that they would have to leave early before the goats came home. "I should so like to have seen Peter and his whole flock."

"Dear child, let us enjoy all the beautiful things that we can see, and not think about those that we cannot," Grandmamma replied as she followed the chair which Heidi was pushing further on.

"Oh, the flowers!" exclaimed Clara. "Look at the bushes of red flowers, and all the nodding blue bells! Oh, if I could but get up and pick some!"

Heidi ran off at once and picked her a large nosegay of them.

"But these are nothing, Clara," she said, laying the flowers on her lap. "If you could come up higher to where the goats are feeding, then you would indeed see something! Bushes on bushes of the red centaury, and ever so many more of the blue bell-flowers; and then the bright yellow rock roses, that gleam like pure gold, and all crowding together in the one spot. And then there are others with the large leaves that grandfather calls Bright Eyes, and the brown ones with little round heads that smell so delicious. Oh, it is beautiful up there, and if you sit down among them you never want to get up again, everything looks and smells so lovely!"

Heidi's eyes sparkled with the remembrance of what she was describing; she was longing herself to see it all again, and Clara caught her enthusiasm and looked back at her with equal longing in her soft blue eyes.

"Grandmamma, do you think I could get up there? Is it possible for me to go?" she asked eagerly. "If only I could walk, climb about everywhere with you, Heidi!"

"I am sure I could push you up, the chair goes so easily," said Heidi, and in proof of her words, she sent the chair at such a pace round the corner that it nearly went flying down the mountain-side. Grandmamma being at hand, however, stopped it in time.

The grandfather, meantime, had not been idle. He had by this time put the table and extra chairs in front of the seat, so that they might all sit out here and eat the dinner that was preparing inside. The milk and the cheese were soon ready, and then the company sat down in high spirits to their mid-day meal.

Grandmamma was enchanted, as the doctor had been, with their dining-room, whence one could see far along the valley, and far over the mountains to the farthest stretch of blue sky. A light wind blew refreshingly over them as they sat at table, and the rustling of the fir trees made a festive accompaniment to the repast.

"I never enjoyed anything as much as this. It is really superb!" cried Grandmamma two or three times over; and then suddenly in a tone of surprise,

"Do I really see you taking a second piece of toasted cheese, Clara!"

There, sure enough, was a second golden-coloured slice of cheese on Clara's plate.

"Oh, it does taste so nice, Grandmamma—better than all the dishes we have at Ragatz," replied Clara, as she continued eating with appetite.

"That's right, eat what you can!" exclaimed Uncle. "It's the mountain air which makes up for the deficiencies of the kitchen."

And so the meal went on. Grandmamma and Alm-Uncle got on very well together, and their conversation became more and more lively. They were so thoroughly agreed in their opinions of men and things and the world in general that they might have been taken for old cronies. The time passed merrily, and then Grandmamma looked towards the west and said,—

"We must soon get ready to go, Clara, the sun is a good way down; the men will be here directly with the horse and sedan."

Clara's face fell and she said beseechingly, "Oh, just another hour, Grandmamma, or two hours. We haven't seen inside the hut yet, or Heidi's bed, or any of the other things. If only the day was ten hours long!"

"Well, that is not possible," said Grandmamma, but she herself was anxious to see inside the hut, so they all rose from the table and Uncle wheeled Clara's chair to the door. But there they came to a standstill, for the chair was much too broad to pass through the door. Uncle, however, soon settled the difficulty by lifting Clara in his strong arms and carrying her inside.

Grandmamma went all round and examined the household arrangements, and was very much amused and pleased at their orderliness and the cozy appearance of everything. "And this is your bedroom up here, Heidi, is it not?" she asked, as without trepidation she mounted the ladder to the hay loft. "Oh, it does smell sweet, what a healthy place to sleep in." She went up to the round window and looked out, and Grandfather followed up with Clara in his arms, Heidi springing up after them. Then they all stood and examined Heidi's wonderful hay-bed, and Grandmamma looked thoughtfully at it and drew in from time to time fragrant draughts of the hay-perfumed air, while Clara was charmed beyond words with Heidi's sleeping apartment.

"It is delightful for you up here, Heidi! You can look from your bed straight into the sky, and then such a delicious smell all round you! And outside the fir trees waving and rustling! I have never seen such a pleasant, cheerful bedroom before."

Uncle looked across at the grandmamma. "I have been thinking," he said to her, "that if you were willing to agree to it, your little granddaughter might remain up here, and I am sure she would grow stronger. You have brought up all kinds of shawls and covers with you, and we could make up a soft bed out of them, and as to the general looking after the child, you need have no fear, for I will see to that." Clara and Heidi were as overjoyed at these words as if they were two birds let out of their cages, and Grandmamma's face beamed with satisfaction.

"You are indeed kind, my dear Uncle," she exclaimed; "you give words to the thought that was in my own mind. I was only asking myself whether a stay up here might not be the very thing she wanted. But then the trouble, the inconvenience to yourself! And you speak of nursing and looking after her as if it was a mere nothing! I thank you sincerely, I thank you from my whole heart, Uncle." And she took his hand and gave it a long and grateful shake, which he returned with a pleased expression of countenance.

Uncle immediately set to work to get things ready. He carried Clara back to her chair outside, Heidi following, not knowing how to jump high enough into the air to express her contentment. Then he gathered up a whole pile of shawls and furs and said, smiling, "It is a good thing that Grandmamma came up well provided for a winter's campaign; we shall be able to make good use of these."

"Foresight is a virtue," responded the lady, amused, "and prevents many misfortunes. If we have made the journey over your mountains without meeting with storms, winds and cloud-bursts, we can only be thankful, which we are, and my provision against these disasters now comes in usefully, as you say."

The two had meanwhile ascended to the hay-loft and begun to prepare a bed; there were so many articles piled one over the other that when finished it looked like a regular little fortress. Grandmamma passed her hand carefully over it to make sure there were no bits of hay sticking out. "If there's a bit that can come through it will," she said. The soft mattress, however, was so smooth and thick that nothing could penetrate it. Then they went down again, well satisfied, and found the children laughing and talking together and arranging all they were going to do from morning till evening as long as Clara stayed. The next question was how long she was to remain, and first Grandmamma was asked, but she referred them to the grandfather, who gave it as his opinion that she ought to make the trial of the mountain air for at least a month. The children clapped their hands for joy, for they had not expected to be together for so long a time.

The bearers and the horse and guide were now seen approaching; the former were sent back at once, and Grandmamma prepared to mount for her return journey.

"It's not saying goodbye, Grandmamma," Clara called out, "for you will come up now and then and see how we are getting on, and we shall so look forward to your visits, shan't we, Heidi?"

Heidi, who felt that life this day had been crowded with pleasures, could only respond to Clara with another jump of joy.

Grandmamma being now seated on her sturdy animal, Uncle took the bridle to lead her down the steep mountain path; she begged him not to come far with her, but he insisted on seeing her safely as far as Dörfli, for the way was precipitous and not without danger for the rider, he said.

Grandmamma did not care to stay alone in Dörfli, and therefore decided to return to Ragatz, and thence to make excursions up the mountain from time to time.

Peter came down with his goats before Uncle had returned. As soon as the animals caught sight of Heidi they all came flocking towards her, and she, as well as Clara on her couch, were soon surrounded by the goats, pushing and poking their heads one over the other, while Heidi introduced each in turn by its name to her friend Clara.

It was not long before the latter had made the long-wished-for acquaintance of little Snowflake, the lively Greenfinch, and the well-behaved goats belonging to Grandfather, as well as of the many others, including the Grand Turk. Peter meanwhile stood apart looking on, and casting somewhat unfriendly glances towards Clara.

When the two children called out, "Good evening, Peter," he made no answer, but swung up his stick angrily, as if wanting to cut the air in two, and then ran off with his goats after him.

The climax to all the beautiful things that Clara had already seen upon the mountain came at the close of the day.

As she lay on the large soft bed in the hay loft, with Heidi near her, she looked out through the round open window right into the middle of the shining clusters of stars, and she exclaimed in delight,—

"Heidi, it's just as if we were in a high carriage and were going to drive straight into heaven."

"Yes, and do you know why the stars are so happy and look down and nod to us like that?" asked Heidi.

"No, why is it?" Clara asked in return.

"Because they live up in heaven, and know how well God arranges everything for us, so that we need have no more fear or trouble and may be quite sure that all things will come right in the end. That's why they are so happy, and they nod to us because they want us to be happy too. But then we must never forget to pray, and to ask God to remember us when He is arranging things, so that we too may feel safe and have no anxiety about what is going to happen."

The two children now sat up and said their prayers, and then Heidi put her head down on her little round arm and fell off to sleep at once, but Clara lay awake some time, for she could not get over the wonder of this new experience of being in bed up here among the stars. She had indeed seldom seen a star, for she never went outside the house at night, and the curtains at home were always drawn before the stars came out. Each time she closed her eyes she felt she must open them again to see if the two very large stars were still looking in, and nodding to her as Heidi said they did. There they were, always in the same place, and Clara felt she could not look long enough into their bright sparkling faces, until at last her eyes closed of their own accord, and it was only in her dreams that she still saw the two large friendly stars shining down upon her.

Chapter 21

How Life Went On At Grandfather's

The sun had just risen above the mountains and was shedding its first golden rays over the hut and the valley below. Alm-Uncle, as was his custom, had been standing in a quiet and, devout attitude for some little while, watching the light mists gradually lifting, and the heights and valley emerging from their twilight shadows and awakening to another day.

The light morning clouds overhead grew brighter and brighter, till at last the sun shone out in its full glory, and rock and wood and hill lay bathed in golden light.

Uncle now stepped back into the hut and went softly up the ladder. Clara had just opened her eyes and was looking with wonder at the bright sunlight that shone through the round window and danced and sparkled about her bed. She could not at first think what she was looking at or where she was. Then she caught sight of Heidi sleeping beside her, and now she heard the grandfather's cheery voice asking her if she had slept well and was feeling rested. She assured him she was not tired, and that when she had once fallen asleep she had not opened her eyes again all night. The grandfather was satisfied at this and immediately began to attend upon her with so much gentleness and understanding that it seemed as if his chief calling had been to look after sick children.

Heidi now awoke and was surprised to see Clara dressed, and already in the grandfather's arms ready to be carried down. She must be up too, and she went through her toilette with lightning-like speed. She ran down the ladder and out of the hut, and there further astonishment awaited her, for Grandfather had been busy the night before after they were in bed. Seeing that it was impossible to get Clara's chair through the hut-door, he had taken down two of the boards at the side of the shed and made an opening large enough to admit the chair; these he left loose so that they could be taken away and put up at pleasure. He was at this moment wheeling Clara out into the sun; he left her in front of the hut while he went to look after the goats, and Heidi ran up to her friend.

The fresh morning breeze blew round the children's faces, and every fresh puff brought a waft of fragrance from the fir trees. Clara drew it in with delight and lay back in her chair with an unaccustomed feeling of health and comfort.

It was the first time in her life that she had been out in the open country at this early hour and felt the fresh morning breeze, and the pure mountain air was so cool and refreshing that every breath she drew was a pleasure. And then the bright sweet sun, which was not hot and sultry up here, but lay soft and warm on her hands and on the grass at her feet. Clara had not imagined that it would be like this on the mountain.

"O Heidi, if only I could stay up here for ever with you," she exclaimed happily, turning in her chair from side to side that she might drink in the air and sun from all quarters.

"Now you see that it is just what I told you," replied Heidi delighted; "that it is the most beautiful thing in the world to be up here with Grandfather."

The latter at that moment appeared coming from the goat shed and bringing two small foaming bowls of snow-white milk—one for Clara and one for Heidi.

"That will do the little daughter good," he said, nodding to Clara; "it is from Little Swan and will make her strong. To your health, child! Drink it up."

Clara had never tasted goat's milk before; she hesitated and smelt it before putting it to her lips, but seeing how Heidi drank hers up without hesitating, and how much she seemed to like it, Clara did the same, and drank till there was not a drop left, for she too found it delicious, tasting just as if sugar and cinnamon had been mixed with it.

"Tomorrow we will drink two," said the grandfather, who had looked on with satisfaction at seeing her follow Heidi's example.

Peter now arrived with the goats, and while Heidi was receiving her usual crowded morning greetings, Uncle drew Peter aside to speak to him, for the goats, bleated so loudly and continuously in their wish to express their joy and affection that no one could be heard near them.

"Attend to what I have to say," he said. "From today be sure you let Little Swan go where she likes. She has an instinct where to find the best food for herself, and so if she wants to climb higher, you follow her, and it will do the others no harm if they go too; on no account bring her back. A little more climbing won't hurt you, and in this matter she probably knows better than you what is good for her; I want her to give as fine milk as possible. Why are you looking over there as if you wanted to eat somebody? Nobody will interfere with you. So now be off and remember what I say."

Peter was accustomed to give immediate obedience to Uncle, and he marched off with his goats, but with a turn of the head and roll of the eye that showed he had some thought in reserve. The goats carried Heidi along with them a little way, which was what Peter wanted. "You will have to come with them," he called to her, "for I shall be obliged to follow Little Swan."

"I cannot," Heidi called back from the midst of her friends, "and I shall not be able to come for a long, long time—not as long as Clara is with me. Grandfather, however, has promised to go up the mountain with both of us one day."

Heidi had now extricated herself from the goats and she ran back to Clara. Peter doubled his fists and made threatening gestures towards the invalid on her couch, and then climbed up some distance without pause until he was out of sight, for he was afraid Uncle might have seen him, and he did not care to know what Uncle might have thought of the fists.

Clara and Heidi had made so many plans for themselves that they hardly knew where to begin. Heidi suggested that they should first write to Grandmamma, to whom they had promised to send word every day, for Grandmamma had not felt sure whether it would in the long run suit Clara's health to remain up the mountain, or if she would continue to enjoy herself there. With daily news of her granddaughter she could stay on without anxiety at Ragatz, and be ready to go to Clara at a moment's notice.

"Must we go indoors to write?" asked Clara, who agreed to Heidi's proposal but did not want to move from where she was, as it was so much nicer outside. Heidi was prepared to arrange everything. She ran in and brought out her school-book and writing things and her own little stool. She put her reading book and copy book on Clara's knees, to make a desk for her to write upon, and she herself took her seat on the stool and sat to the bench, and then they both began writing to Grandmamma.

But Clara paused after every sentence to look about her; it was too beautiful for much letter writing. The breeze had sunk a little, and now only gently fanned her face and whispered lightly through the fir trees. Little winged insects hummed and danced around her in the clear air, and a great stillness lay over the far, wide, sunny pasture lands. Lofty and silent rose the high mountain peaks above her, and below lay the whole broad valley full of quiet peace. Only now and again the call of some shepherd-boy rang out through the air, and echo answered softly from the rocks. The morning passed, the children hardly knew how, and now Grandfather came with the mid-day bowls of steaming milk, for the little daughter, he said, was to remain out as long as there was a gleam of sun in the sky. The mid-day meal was set out and eaten as yesterday in the open air. Then Heidi pushed Clara's chair under the fir trees, for they had agreed to spend the afternoon under their shade and there tell each other all that had happened since Heidi left Frankfurt. If everything had gone on there as usual in a general way, there were still all kinds of particular things to tell Heidi about the various people who composed the Sesemann household, and who were all so well known to Heidi.

So they sat and chatted under the trees, and the more lively grew their conversation, the more loudly sang the birds overhead, as if wishing to take part in the children's gossip, which evidently pleased them. So the hours flew by and all at once, as it seemed, the evening had come with the returning Peter, who still scowled and looked angry.

"Good night, Peter," called out Heidi, as she saw he had no intention of stopping to speak.

"Good night, Peter," called out Clara in a friendly voice. Peter took no notice and went surlily on with his goats.

As Clara saw the grandfather leading away Little Swan to milk her, she was suddenly taken with a longing for another bowlful of the fragrant milk, and waited impatiently for it.

"Isn't it curious, Heidi," she said, astonished at herself, "as long as I can remember I have only eaten because I was obliged to, and everything used to seem to taste of cod liver oil, and I was always wishing there was no need to eat or drink; and now I am longing for Grandfather to bring me the milk."

"Yes, I know what it feels like," replied Heidi, who remembered the many days in Frankfurt when all her food used to seem to stick in her throat. Clara, however, could not understand it; the fact was that she had never in her life before spent a whole day in the open air, much less in such high, life-giving mountain air. When Grandfather at last brought her the evening milk, she drank it up so quickly that she had emptied her bowl before Heidi, and then she asked for a little more. The grandfather went inside with both the children's bowls, and when he brought them out again full he had something else to add to their supper. He had walked over that afternoon to a herdsman's house where the sweetly-tasting butter was made, and had brought home a large pat, some of which he had now spread thickly on two good slices of bread. He stood and watched with pleasure while Clara and Heidi ate their appetising meal with childish hunger and enjoyment.

That night, when Clara lay down in her bed and prepared to watch the stars, her eyes would not keep open, and she fell asleep as soon as Heidi and slept soundly all night—a thing she never remembered having done before. The following day and the day after passed in the same pleasant fashion, and the third day there came a surprise for the children. Two stout porters came up the mountain, each carrying a bed on his shoulders with bedding of all kinds and two beautiful new white coverlids. The men also had a letter with them from Grandmamma, in which she said that these were for Clara and Heidi, and that Heidi in future was always to sleep in a proper bed, and when she went down to Dörfli in the winter she was to take one with her and leave the other at the hut, so that Clara might always know there was a bed ready for her when she paid a visit to the mountain. She went on to thank the children for their long letters and encouraged them to continue writing daily, so that she might be able to picture all they were doing.

So the grandfather went up and threw back the hay from Heidi's bed on to the great heap, and then with his help the beds were transported to the loft. He put them close to one another so that the children might still be able to see out of the window, for he knew what pleasure they had in the light from the sun and stars.

Meanwhile Grandmamma down at Ragatz was rejoicing at the excellent news of the invalid which reached her daily from the mountain. Clara found the life more charming each day and could not say enough of the kindness and care which the grandfather lavished upon her, nor of Heidi's lively and amusing companionship, for the latter was more entertaining even than when in Frankfurt with her, and Clara's first thought when she woke each morning was, "Oh, how glad I am to be here still."

Having such fresh assurances each day that all was going well with Clara, Grandmamma thought she might put off her visit to the children a little longer, for the steep ride up and down was somewhat of a fatigue to her.

The grandfather seemed to feel an especial sympathy for this little invalid charge, for he tried to think of something fresh every day to help forward her recovery. He climbed up the mountain every afternoon, higher and higher each day, and came home in the evening with a large bunch of leaves which scented the air with a mingled fragrance as of carnations and thyme, even from afar. He hung it up in the goat shed, and the goats on their return were wild to get at it, for they recognised the smell. But Uncle did not go climbing after rare plants to give the goats the pleasure of eating them without any trouble of finding them; what he gathered was for Little Swan alone, that she might give extra fine milk, and the effect of the extra feeding was shown in the way she flung her head in the air with ever-increasing frolicsomeness, and in the bright glow of her eye.

Clara had now been on the mountain for three weeks. For some days past the grandfather, each morning after carrying her down, had said, "Won't the little daughter try if she can stand for a minute or two?" And Clara had made the effort in order to please him, but had clung to him as soon as her feet touched the ground, exclaiming that it hurt her so. He let her try a little longer, however, each day.

It was many years since they had had such a splendid summer among the mountains. Day after day there were the same cloudless sky and brilliant sun; the flowers opened wide their fragrant blossoms, and everywhere the eye was greeted with a glow of colour; and when the evening came the crimson light fell on mountain peaks and on the great snow-field, till at last the sun sank in a sea of golden flame.

And Heidi never tired of telling Clara of all this, for only higher up could the full glory of the colours be rightly seen; and more particularly did she dwell on the beauty of the spot on the higher slope of the mountain, where the bright golden rock-roses grew in masses, and the blue flowers were in such numbers that the very grass seemed to have turned blue, while near these were whole bushes of the brown blossoms, with their delicious scent, so that you never wanted to move again when you once sat down among them.

She had just been expatiating on the flowers as she sat with Clara under the fir trees one evening, and had been telling her again of the wonderful light from the evening sun, when such an irrepressible longing came over her to see it all once more that she jumped up and ran to her grandfather, who was in the shed, calling out almost before she was inside,—

"Grandfather, will you take us out with the goats tomorrow? Oh, it is so lovely up there now!"

"Very well," he answered, "but if I do, the little daughter must do something to please me: she must try her best again this evening to stand on her feet."

Heidi ran back with the good news to Clara, and the latter promised to try her very best as the grandfather wished, for she looked forward immensely to the next day's excursion. Heidi was so pleased and excited that she called out to Peter as soon as she caught sight of him that evening,—

"Peter, Peter, we are all coming out with you tomorrow and are going to stay up there the whole day."

Peter, cross as a bear, grumbled some reply, and lifted his stick to give Greenfinch a blow for no reason in particular, but Greenfinch saw the movement, and with a leap over Snowflake's back she got out of the way, and the stick only hit the air.

Clara and Heidi got into their two fine beds that night full of delightful anticipation of the morrow; they were so full of their plans that they agreed to keep awake all night and talk over them until they might venture to get up. But their heads had no sooner touched their soft pillows than the conversation suddenly ceased, and Clara fell into a dream of an immense field, which looked the colour of the sky, so thickly inlaid was it with blue bell-shaped flowers; and Heidi heard the great bird of prey calling to her from the heights above, "Come! Come! Come!"

Chapter 22

Something Unexpected Happens

Uncle went out early the next morning to see what kind of a day it was going to be. There was a reddish gold light over the higher peaks; a light breeze springing up and the branches of the fir trees moved gently to and fro the sun was on its way.

The old man stood and watched the green slopes under the higher peaks gradually growing brighter with the coming day and the dark shadows lifting from the valley, until at first a rosy light filled its hollows, and then the morning gold flooded every height and depth—the sun had risen.

Uncle wheeled the chair out of the shed ready for the coming journey, and then went in to call the children and tell them what a lovely sunrise it was.

Peter came up at this moment. The goats did not gather round him so trustfully as usual, but seemed to avoid him timidly, for Peter had reached a high pitch of anger and bitterness, and was laying about him with his stick very unnecessarily, and where it fell the blow was no light one. For weeks now he had not had Heidi all to himself as formerly. When he came up in the morning the invalid child was always already in her chair and Heidi fully occupied with her. And it was the same thing over again when he came down in the evening. She had not come out with the goats once this summer, and now today she was only coming in company with her friend and the chair, and would stick by the latter's side the whole time. It was the thought of this which was making him particularly cross this morning. There stood the chair on its high wheels; Peter seemed to see something proud and disdainful about it, and he glared at it as at an enemy that had done him harm and was likely to do him more still today. He glanced round—there was no sound anywhere, no one to see him. He sprang forward like a wild creature, caught hold of it, and gave it a violent and angry push in the direction of the slope. The chair rolled swiftly forward and in another minute had disappeared.

Peter now sped up the mountain as if on wings, not pausing till he was well in shelter of a large blackberry bush, for he had no wish to be seen by Uncle. But he was anxious to see what had become of the chair, and his bush was well placed for that. Himself hidden, he could watch what happened below and see what Uncle did without being discovered himself. So he looked, and there he saw his enemy running faster and faster down hill, then it turned head over heels several times, and finally, after one great bound, rolled over and over to its complete destruction. The pieces flew in every direction—feet, arms, and torn fragments of the padded seat and bolster—and Peter experienced a feeling of such unbounded delight at the sight that he leapt in the air, laughing aloud and stamping for joy; then he took a run round, jumping over bushes on the way, only to return to the same spot and fall into fresh fits of laughter. He was beside himself with satisfaction, for he could see only good results for himself in this disaster to his enemy. Now Heidi's friend would be obliged to go away, for she would have no means of going about, and when Heidi was alone again she would come out with him as in the old days, and everything would go on in the proper way again. But Peter did not consider, or did not know, that when we do a wrong thing trouble is sure to follow.

Heidi now came running out of the hut and round to the shed. Grandfather was behind with Clara in his arms. The shed stood wide open, the two loose planks having been taken down, and it was quite light inside. Heidi looked into every corner and ran from one end to the other, and then stood still wondering what could have happened to the chair. Grandfather now came up.

"How is this, have you wheeled the chair away, Heidi?"

"I have been looking everywhere for it, Grandfather; you said it was standing ready outside," and she again searched each corner of the shed with her eyes.

At that moment the wind, which had risen suddenly, blew open the shed door and sent it banging back against the wall.

"It must have been the wind, Grandfather," exclaimed Heidi, and her eyes grew anxious at this sudden discovery. "Oh! If it has blown the chair all the way down to Dörfli we shall not get it back in time, and shall not be able to go."

"If it has rolled as far as that it will never come back, for it is in a hundred pieces by now," said the grandfather, going round the corner and looking down. "But it's a curious thing to have happened!" he added as he thought over the matter, for the chair would have had to turn a corner before starting down hill.

"Oh, I am sorry," lamented Clara, "for we shall not be able to go today, or perhaps any other day. I shall have to go home, I suppose, if I have no chair. Oh, I am so sorry, I am so sorry!"

But Heidi looked towards her grandfather with her usual expression of confidence.

"Grandfather, you will be able to do something, won't you, so that it need not be as Clara says, and so that she is not obliged to go home?"

"Well, for the present we will go up the mountain as we had arranged, and then later on we will see what can be done," he answered, much to the children's delight.

He went indoors, fetched out a pile of shawls, and laying them on the sunniest spot he could find set Clara down upon them. Then he fetched the children's morning milk and had out his two goats.

"Why is Peter not here yet?" thought Uncle to himself, for Peter's whistle had not been sounded that morning. The grandfather now took Clara up on one arm, and the shawls on the other.

"Now then we will start," he said; "the goats can come with us."

Heidi was pleased at this and walked on after her grandfather with an arm over either of the goats' necks, and the animals were so overjoyed to have her again that they nearly squeezed her flat between them out of sheer affection. When they reached the spot where the goats usually pastured they were surprised to find them already feeding there, climbing about the rocks, and Peter with them, lying his full length on the ground.

"I'll teach you another time to go by like that, you lazy rascal! What do you mean by it?" Uncle called to him.

Peter, recognising the voice, jumped up like a shot. "No one was up," he answered.

"Have you seen anything of the chair?" asked the grandfather.

"Of what chair?" called Peter back in answer in a morose tone of voice.

Uncle said no more. He spread the shawls on the sunny slope, and setting Clara upon them asked if she was comfortable.

"As comfortable as in my chair," she said, thanking him, "and this seems the most beautiful spot. O Heidi, it is lovely, it is lovely!" she cried, looking round her with delight.

The grandfather prepared to leave them. They would now be safe and happy together, he said, and when it was time for dinner Heidi was to go and fetch the bag from the shady hollow where he had put it; Peter was to bring them as much milk as they wanted, but Heidi was to see that it was Little Swan's milk. He would come and fetch them towards evening; he must now be off to see after the chair and ascertain what had become of it.

The sky was dark blue, and not a single cloud was to be seen from one horizon to the other. The great snow-field overhead sparkled as if set with thousands and thousands of gold and silver stars. The two grey mountains peaks lifted their lofty heads against the sky and looked solemnly down upon the valley as of old; the great bird was poised aloft in the clear blue air, and the mountain wind came over the heights and blew refreshingly around the children as they sat on the sunlit slope. It was all indescribably enjoyable to Clara and Heidi. Now and again a young goat came and lay down beside them; Snowflake came oftenest, putting her little head down near Heidi, and only moving because another goat came and drove her away. Clara had learned to know them all so well that she never mistook one for the other now, for each had an expression and ways of its own. And the goats had also grown familiar with Clara and would rub their heads against her shoulder, which was always a sign of acquaintanceship and goodwill.

Some hours went by, and Heidi began to think that she might just go over to the spot where all the flowers grew to see if they were fully blown and looking as lovely as the year before. Clara could not go until Grandfather came back that evening, when the flowers probably would be already closed. The longing to go became stronger and stronger, till she felt she could not resist it.

"Would you think me unkind, Clara," she said rather hesitatingly, "if I left you for a few minutes? I should run there and back very quickly. I want so to see how the flowers are looking—but wait—" for an idea had come into Heidi's head. She ran and picked a bunch or two of green leaves, and then took hold of Snowflake and led her up to Clara.

"There, now you will not be alone," said Heidi, giving the goat a little push to show her she was to lie down near Clara, which the animal quite understood. Heidi threw the leaves into Clara's lap, and the latter told her friend to go at once to look at the flowers as she was quite happy to be left with the goat; she liked this new experience. Heidi ran off, and Clara began to hold out the leaves one by one to Snowflake, who snoozled up to her new friend in a confiding manner and slowly ate the leaves from her hand. It was easy to see that Snowflake enjoyed this peaceful and sheltered way of feeding, for when with the other goats she had much persecution to endure from the larger and stronger ones of the flock. And Clara found a strange new pleasure in sitting all alone like this on the mountain side, her only companion a little goat that looked to her for protection. She suddenly felt a great desire to be her own mistress and to be able to help others, instead of herself being always dependent as she was now. Many thoughts, unknown to her before, came crowding into her mind, and a longing to go on living in the sunshine, and to be doing something that would bring happiness to another, as now she was helping to make the goat happy. An unaccustomed feeling of joy took possession of her, as if everything she had ever known or felt became all at once more beautiful, and she seemed to see all things in a new light, and so strong was the sense of this new beauty and happiness that she threw her arms round the little goat's neck, and exclaimed, "O Snowflake, how delightful it is up here! if only I could stay on for ever with you beside me!"

Heidi had meanwhile reached her field of flowers, and as she caught sight of it she uttered a cry of joy. The whole ground in front of her was a mass of shimmering gold, where the cistus flowers spread their yellow blossoms. Above them waved whole bushes of the deep blue bell-flowers; while the fragrance that arose from the whole sunlit expanse was as if the rarest balsam had been flung over it. The scent, however, came from the small brown flowers, the little round heads of which rose modestly here and there among the yellow blossoms. Heidi stood and gazed and drew in the delicious air. Suddenly she turned round and reached Clara's side out of breath with running and excitement. "Oh, you must come," she called out as soon as she came in sight, "it is more beautiful than you can imagine, and perhaps this evening it may not be so lovely. I believe I could carry you, don't you think I could?" Clara looked at her and shook her head. "Why, Heidi, what can you be thinking of! you are smaller than I am. Oh, if only I could walk!"

Heidi looked round as if in search of something, some new idea had evidently come into her head. Peter was sitting up above looking down on the two children. He had been sitting and staring before him in the same way for hours, as if he could not make out what he saw. He had destroyed the chair so that the friend might not be able to move anywhere and that her visit might come to an end, and then a little while after she had appeared right up here under his very nose with Heidi beside her. He thought his eyes must deceive him, and yet there she was and no mistake about it.

Heidi now looked up to where he was sitting and called out in a peremptory voice, "Peter, come down here!"

"I don't wish to come," he called in reply.

"But you are to, you must; I cannot do it alone, and you must come here and help me; make haste and come down," she called again in an urgent voice.

"I shall do nothing of the kind," was the answer.

Heidi ran some way up the slope towards him, and then pausing called again, her eyes ablaze with anger, "If you don't come at once, Peter, I will do something to you that you won't like; I mean what I say."

Peter felt an inward throe at these words, and a great fear seized him. He had done something wicked which he wanted no one to know about, and so far he had thought himself safe. But now Heidi spoke exactly as if she knew everything, and whatever she did know she would tell her grandfather, and there was no one he feared so much as this latter person. Supposing he were to suspect what had happened about the chair! Peter's anguish of mind grew more acute. He stood up and went down to where Heidi was awaiting him.

"I am coming and you won't do what you said."

Peter appeared now so submissive with fear that Heidi felt quite sorry for him and answered assuringly, "No, no, of course not; come along with me, there is nothing to be afraid of in what I want you to do."

As soon as they got to Clara, Heidi gave her orders: Peter was to take hold of her under the arms on one side and she on the other, and together they were to lift her up. This first movement was successfully carried through, but then came the difficulty. As Clara could not even stand, how were they to support her and get her along? Heidi was too small for her arm to serve Clara to lean upon.

"You must put one arm well around my neck so, and put the other through Peter's and lean firmly upon it, then we shall be able to carry you."

Peter, however, had never given his arm to any one in his life. Clara put hers in his, but he kept his own hanging down straight beside him like a stick.

"That's not the way, Peter," said Heidi in an authoritative voice. "You must put your arm out in the shape of a ring, and Clara must put hers through it and lean her weight upon you, and whatever you do, don't let your arm give way; like that. I am sure we shall be able to manage."

Peter did as he was told, but still they did not get on very well. Clara was not such a light weight, and the team did not match very well in size; it was up one side and down the other, so that the supports were rather wobbly.

Clara tried to use her own feet a little, but each time drew them quickly back.

"Put your foot down firmly once," suggested Heidi, "I am sure it will hurt you less after that."

"Do you think so?" said Clara hesitatingly, but she followed Heidi's advice and ventured one firm step on the ground and then another; she called out a little as she did it; then she lifted her foot again and went on, "Oh, that was less painful already," she exclaimed joyfully.

"Try again," said Heidi encouragingly.

And Clara went on putting one foot out after another until all at once she called out, "I can do it, Heidi! Look! Look! I can make proper steps!" And Heidi cried out with even greater delight, "Can you really make steps, can you really walk? Really walk by yourself? Oh, if only Grandfather were here!" and she continued gleefully to exclaim, "You can walk now, Clara, you can walk!"

Clara still held on firmly to her supports, but with every step she felt safer on her feet, as all three became aware, and Heidi was beside herself with joy.

"Now we shall be able to come up here together every day, and go just where we like; and you will be able all your life to walk about as I do, and not have to be pushed in a chair, and you will get quite strong and well. It is the greatest happiness we could have had!"

And Clara heartily agreed, for she could think of no greater joy in the world than to be strong and able to go about like other people, and no longer to have to lie from day to day in her invalid chair.

They had not far to go to reach the field of flowers, and could already catch sight of the cistus flowers glowing gold in the sun. As they came to the bushes of the blue bell flowers, with sunny, inviting patches of warm ground between them, Clara said, "Mightn't we sit down here for a while?"

This was just what Heidi enjoyed, and so the children sat down in the midst of the flowers, Clara for the first time on the dry, warm mountain grass, and she found it indescribably delightful. Around her were the blue flowers softly waving to and fro, and beyond the gleaming patches of the cistus flowers and the red centaury, while the sweet scent of the brown blossoms and of the fragrant prunella enveloped her as she sat. Everything was so lovely! so lovely! And Heidi, who was beside her, thought she had never seen it so perfectly beautiful up here before, and she did not know herself why she felt so glad at heart that she longed to shout for joy. Then she suddenly remembered that Clara was cured; that was the crowning delight of all that made life so delightful in the midst of all this surrounding beauty. Clara sat silent, overcome with the enchantment of all that her eye rested upon, and with the anticipation of all the happiness that was now before her. There seemed hardly room in her heart for all her joyful emotions, and these and the ecstasy aroused by the sunlight and the scent of the flowers, held her dumb.

Peter also lay among the flowers without moving or speaking, for he was fast asleep. The breeze came blowing softly and caressingly from behind the sheltering rocks, and passed whisperingly through the bushes overhead. Heidi got up now and then to run about, for the flowers waving in the warm wind seemed to smell sweeter and to grow more thickly whichever way she went, and she felt she must sit down at each fresh spot to enjoy the sight and scent. So the hours went by.

It was long past noon when a small troop of goats advanced solemnly towards the plain of flowers. It was not a feeding place of theirs, for they did not care to graze on flowers. They looked like an embassy arriving, with Greenfinch as their leader. They had evidently come in search of their companions who had left them in the lurch, and who had, contrary to all custom, remained away so long, for the goats could tell the time without mistake. As soon as Greenfinch caught sight of the three missing friends amid the flowers she set up an extra loud bleat, whereupon all the others joined in a chorus of bleats, and the whole company came trotting towards the children. Peter woke up, rubbing his eyes, for he had been dreaming that he saw the chair again with its beautiful red padding standing whole and uninjured before the grandfather's door, and indeed just as he awoke he thought he was looking at the brass-headed nails that studded it all round, but it was only the bright yellow flowers beside him. He experienced again a dreadful fear of mind that he had lost in this dream of the uninjured chair. Even though Heidi had promised not to do anything, there still remained the lively dread that his deed might be found out in some other way. He allowed Heidi to do what she liked with him, for he was reduced to such a state of low spirits and meekness that he was ready to give his help to Clara without murmur or resistance.

When all three had got back to their old quarters Heidi ran and brought forward the bag, and proceeded to fulfil her promise, for her threat of the morning had been concerned with Peter's dinner. She had seen her grandfather putting in all sorts of good things, and had been pleased to think of Peter having a large share of them, and she had meant him to understand when he refused at first to help her that he would get nothing for his dinner, but Peter's conscience had put another interpretation upon her words. Heidi took the food out of the bag and divided it into three portions, and each was of such a goodly size that she thought to herself, "There will be plenty of ours left for him to have more still."

She gave the other two their dinners and sat down with her own beside Clara, and they all three ate with a good appetite after their great exertions.

It ended as Heidi had expected, and Peter got as much food again as his own share with what Clara and Heidi had over from theirs after they had both eaten as much as they wanted. Peter ate up every bit of food to the last crumb, but there was something wanting to his usual enjoyment of a good dinner, for every mouthful he swallowed seemed to choke him, and he felt something gnawing inside him.

They were so late at their dinner that they had not long to wait after they had finished before Grandfather came up to fetch them. Heidi rushed forward to meet him as soon as he appeared, as she wanted to be the first to tell him the good news. She was so excited that she could hardly get her words out when she did get up to him, but he soon understood, and a look of extreme pleasure came into his face. He hastened up to where Clara was sitting and said with a cheerful smile, "So we've made the effort, have we, and won the day!"

Then he lifted her up, and putting his left arm behind her and giving her his right to lean upon, made her walk a little way, which she did with less trembling and hesitation than before now that she had such a strong arm round her.

Heidi skipped along beside her in triumphant glee, and the grandfather looked too as if some happiness had befallen him. But now he took Clara up in his arms. "We must not overdo it," he said, "and it is high time we went home," and he started off down the mountain path, for he was anxious to get her indoors that she might rest after her unusual fatigue.

When Peter got to Dörfli that evening he found a large group of people collected round a certain spot, pushing one another and looking over each other's shoulders in their eagerness to catch sight of something lying on the ground. Peter thought he should like to see too, and poked and elbowed till he made his way through.

There it lay, the thing he had wanted to see. Scattered about the grass were the remains of Clara's chair; part of the back and the middle bit, and enough of the red padding and the bright nails to show how magnificent the chair had been when it was entire.

"I was here when the men passed carrying it up," said the baker who was standing near Peter. "I'll bet any one that it was worth twenty-five pounds at least. I cannot think how such an accident could have happened."

"Uncle said the wind might perhaps have done it," remarked one of the women, who could not sufficiently admire the red upholstery.

"It's a good job that no one but the wind did it," said the baker again, "or he might smart for it! No doubt the gentleman in Frankfurt when he hears what has happened will make all inquiries about it. I am glad for myself that I have not been seen up the mountain for a good two years, as suspicion is likely to fall on any one who was about up there at the time."

Many more opinions were passed on the matter, but Peter had heard enough. He crept quietly away out of the crowd and then took to his heels and ran up home as fast as he could, as if he thought some one was after him. The baker's words had filled him with fear and trembling. He was sure now that any day a constable might come over from Frankfurt and inquire about the destruction of the chair, and then everything would come out, and he would be seized and carried off to Frankfurt and there put in prison. The whole picture of what was coming was clear before him, and his hair stood on end with terror.

He reached home in this disturbed state of mind. He would not open his mouth in reply to anything that was said to him; he would not eat his potatoes; all he did was to creep off to bed as quickly as possible and hide under the bedclothes and groan.

"Peter has been eating sorrel again, and is evidently in pain by the way he is groaning," said Brigitta.

"You must give him a little more bread to take with him; give him a bit of mine tomorrow," said the grandmother sympathisingly.

As the children lay that night in bed looking out at the stars Heidi said, "I have been thinking all day what a happy thing it is that God does not give us what we ask for, even when we pray and pray and pray, if He knows there is something better for us; have you felt like that?"

"Why do you ask me that tonight all of a sudden?" asked Clara.

"Because I prayed so hard when I was in Frankfurt that I might go home at once, and because I was not allowed to

I thought God had forgotten me. And now you see, if I had come away at first when I wanted to, you would never have come here, and would never have got well."

Clara had in her turn become thoughtful. "But, Heidi," she began again, "in that case we ought never to pray for anything, as God always intends something better for us than we know or wish for."

"You must not think it is like that, Clara," replied Heidi eagerly. "We must go on praying for everything, for everything, so that God may know we do not forget that it all comes from Him. If we forget God, then He lets us go our own way and we get into trouble; Grandmamma told me so. And if He does not give us what we ask for we must not think that He has not heard us and leave off praying, but we must still pray and say, I am sure, dear God, that Thou art keeping something better for me, and I will not be unhappy, for I know that Thou wilt make everything right in the end."

"How did you learn all that?" asked Clara.

"Grandmamma explained it to me first of all, and then when it all happened just as she said, I knew it myself, and I think, Clara," she went on, as she sat up in bed, "we ought certainly to thank God tonight that you can walk now, and that He has made us so happy."

"Yes, Heidi, I am sure you are right, and I am glad you reminded me; I almost forgot my prayers for very joy."

Both children said their prayers, and each thanked God in her own way for the blessing He had bestowed on Clara, who had for so long lain weak and ill.

The next morning the grandfather suggested that they should now write to the grandmamma and ask her if she would not come and pay them a visit, as they had something new to show her. But the children had another plan in their heads, for they wanted to prepare a great surprise for Grandmamma. Clara was first to have more practice in walking so that she might be able to go a little way by herself; above all things grandmamma was not to have a hint of it. They asked the grandfather how long he thought this would take, and when he told them about a week or less, they immediately sat down and wrote a pressing invitation to Grandmamma, asking her to come soon, but no word was said about there being anything new to see.

The following days were some of the most joyous that Clara had spent on the mountain. She awoke each morning with a happy voice within her crying, "I am well now! I am well now! I shan't have to go about in a chair, I can walk by myself like other people."

Then came the walking, and every day she found it easier and was able to go a longer distance. The movement gave her such an appetite that the grandfather cut his bread and butter a little thicker each day, and was well pleased to see it disappear. He now brought out with it a large jugful of the foaming milk and filled her little bowl over and over again. And so another week went by and the day came which was to bring Grandmamma up the mountain for her second visit.

Chapter 23

"Goodbye Till We Meet Again"

Grandmamma wrote the day before her arrival to let the children know that they might expect her without fail. Peter brought up the letter early the following morning. Grandfather and the children were already outside and the goats were awaiting him, shaking their heads frolicsomely in the fresh morning air, while the children stroked them and wished them a pleasant journey up the mountain. Uncle stood near, looking now at the fresh faces of the children, now at his well-kept goats, with a smile on his face, evidently well pleased with the sight of both.

As Peter neared the group his steps slackened, and the instant he had handed the letter to Uncle he turned quickly away as if frightened, and as he went he gave a hasty glance behind him, as if the thing he feared was pursuing him, and then he gave a leap and ran off up the mountain.

"Grandfather," said Heidi, who had been watching him with astonished eyes, "why does Peter always behave now like the Great Turk when he thinks somebody is after him with a stick; he turns and shakes his head and goes off with a bound just like that?"

"Perhaps Peter fancies he sees the stick which he so well deserves coming after him," answered Grandfather.

Peter ran up the first slope without a pause; when he was well out of sight, however, he stood still and looked suspiciously about him. Suddenly he gave a jump and looked behind him with a terrified expression, as if some one had caught hold of him by the nape of the neck; for Peter expected every minute that the police-constable from Frankfurt would leap out upon him from behind some bush or hedge. The longer his suspense lasted, the more frightened and miserable he became; he did not know a moment's peace.

Heidi now set about tidying the hut, as Grandmamma must find everything clean and in good order when she arrived.

Clara looked on amused and interested to watch the busy Heidi at her work.

So the morning soon went by, and Grandmamma might now be expected at any minute. The children dressed themselves and went and sat together outside on the seat ready to receive her.

Grandfather joined them, that they might see the splendid bunch of blue gentians which he had been up the mountain to gather, and the children exclaimed with delight at the beauty of the flowers as they shone in the morning sun. The grandfather then carried them indoors. Heidi jumped up from time to time to see if there was any sign of Grandmamma's approach.

At last she saw the procession winding up the mountain just in the order she had expected. First there was the guide, then the white horse with Grandmamma mounted upon it, and last of all the porter with a heavy bundle on his back, for Grandmamma would not think of going up the mountain without a full supply of wraps and rugs.

Nearer and nearer wound the procession; at last it reached the top and Grandmamma was there looking down on the children from her horse. She no sooner saw them, however, sitting side by side, than she began quickly dismounting, as she cried out in a shocked tone of voice, "Why is this? why are you not lying in your chair, Clara? What are you all thinking about?" But even before she had got close to them she threw up her hands in astonishment, exclaiming further, "Is it really you, dear child? Why, your cheeks have grown quite round and rosy! I should hardly have known you again!" And she was hastening forward to embrace her, when Heidi slipped down from the seat, and Clara leaning on her shoulder, the two children began walking along quite coolly and naturally. Then indeed Grandmamma was surprised, or rather alarmed, for she thought at first that it must be some unheard-of proceeding of Heidi's devising.

But no—Clara was actually walking steadily and uprightly beside Heidi—and now the two children turned and came towards her with beaming faces and rosy cheeks. Laughing and crying she ran to them and embraced first Clara and then Heidi, and then Clara again, unable to speak for joy. All at once she caught sight of Uncle standing by the seat and looking on smiling at the meeting. She took Clara's arm in hers, and with continual expressions of delight at the fact that the child could now really walk about with her, she went up to the old man, and then letting go Clara's arm she seized his hands.

"My dear Uncle! My dear Uncle! How much we have to thank you for! It is all your doing! It is your caring and nursing——"

"And God's good sun and mountain air," he interrupted her, smiling.

"Yes, and don't forget the beautiful milk I have," put in Clara. "Grandmamma, you can't think what a quantity of goat's milk I drink, and how nice it is!"

"I can see that by your cheeks, child," answered Grandmamma. "I really should not have known you; you have grown quite strong and plump, and taller too; I never hoped or expected to see you look like that. I cannot take my eyes off you, for I can hardly yet believe it. But now I must telegraph without delay to my son in Paris, and tell him he must come here at once. I shall not say why; it will be the greatest happiness he has ever known. My dear Uncle, how can I send a telegram; have you dismissed the men yet?"

"They have gone," he answered, "but if you are in a hurry I will fetch Peter, and he can take it for you."

Grandmamma thanked him, for she was anxious that the good news should not be kept from her son a day longer than was possible.

So Uncle went aside a little way and blew such a resounding whistle through his fingers that he awoke a responsive echo among the rocks far overhead. He had not to wait many minutes before Peter came running down in answer, for he knew the sound of Uncle's whistle. Peter arrived, looking as white as a ghost, for he quite thought Uncle was sending for him to give him up. But as it was he only had a written paper given him with instructions to take it down at once to the post-office at Dörfli; Uncle would settle for the payment later, as it was not safe to give Peter too much to look after.

Peter went off with the paper in his hand, feeling some relief of mind for the present, for as Uncle had not whistled for him in order to give him up it was evident that no policeman had yet arrived.

So now they could all sit down in peace to their dinner round the table in front of the hut, and Grandmamma was given a detailed account of all that had taken place. How Grandfather had made Clara try first to stand and then to move her feet a little every day, and how they had settled for the day's excursion up the mountain and the chair had been blown away. How Clara's desire to see the flowers had induced her to take the first walk, and so by degrees one thing had led to another. The recital took some time, for Grandmamma continually interrupted it with fresh exclamations of surprise and thankfulness: "It hardly seems possible! I can scarcely believe it is not all a dream! Are we really awake, and are all sitting here by the mountain hut, and is that round-faced, healthy-looking child my poor little, white, sickly Clara?"

And Clara and Heidi could not get over their delight at the success of the surprise they had so carefully arranged for Grandmamma and at the latter's continued astonishment.

Meanwhile Herr Sesemann, who had finished his business in Paris, had also been preparing a surprise. Without saying a word to his mother he got into the train one sunny morning and travelled that day to Basle; the next morning he continued his journey, for a great longing had seized him to see his little daughter from whom he had been separated the whole summer. He arrived at Ragatz a few hours after his mother had left. When he heard that she had that very day started for the mountain, he immediately hired a carriage and drove off to Mayenfeld; here he found that he could if he liked drive on as far as Dörfli, which he did, as he thought the walk up from that place would be as long as he cared for.

Herr Sesemann found he was right, for the climb up the mountain, as it was, proved long and fatiguing to him. He went on and on, but still no hut came in sight, and yet he knew there was one where Peter lived half way up, for the path had been described to him over and over again.

There were traces of climbers to be seen on all sides; the narrow footpaths seemed to run in every direction, and Herr Sesemann began to wonder if he was on the right one, and whether the hut lay perhaps on the other side of the mountain. He looked round to see if any one was in sight of whom he could ask the way; but far and wide there was not a soul to be seen or a sound to be heard. Only at moments the mountain wind whistled through the air, and the insects hummed in the sunshine or a happy bird sang out from the branches of a solitary larch tree. Herr Sesemann stood still for a while to let the cool Alpine wind blow on his hot face. But now some one came running down the mountainside—it was Peter with the telegram in his hand. He ran straight down the steep slope, not following the path on which Herr Sesemann was standing. As soon as the latter caught sight of him he beckoned to him to come. Peter advanced towards him slowly and timidly, with a sort of sidelong movement, as if he could only move one leg properly and had to drag the other after him. "Hurry up, lad," called Herr Sesemann, and when Peter was near enough, "Tell me," he said, "is this the way to the hut where the old man and the child Heidi live, and where the visitors from Frankfurt are staying?"

A low sound of fear was the only answer he received, as Peter turned to run away in such precipitous haste that he fell head over heels several times, and went rolling and bumping down the slope in involuntary bounds, just in the same way as the chair, only that Peter fortunately did not fall to pieces as that had done. Only the telegram came to grief, and that was torn into fragments and flew away.

"How extraordinarily timid these mountain dwellers are!" thought Herr Sesemann to himself, for he quite believed that it was the sight of a stranger that had made such an impression on this unsophisticated child of the mountains.

After watching Peter's violent descent towards the valley for a few minutes he continued his journey.

Peter, meanwhile, with all his efforts, could not stop himself, but went rolling on, and still tumbling head over heels at intervals in a most remarkable manner.

But this was not the most terrible part of his sufferings at the moment, for far worse was the fear and horror that possessed him, feeling sure, as he did now, that the policeman had really come over for him from Frankfurt. He had no doubt at all that the stranger who had asked him the way was the very man himself. Just as he had rolled to the edge of that last high slope above Dörfli he was caught in a bush, and at last able to keep himself from falling any farther. He lay still for a second or two to recover himself, and to think over matters.

"Well done! Another of you come bumping along like this!" said a voice close to Peter, "and which of you tomorrow is the wind going to send rolling down like a badly-sewn sack of potatoes?" It was the baker, who stood there laughing. He had been strolling out to refresh himself after his hot day's work, and had watched with amusement as he saw Peter come rolling over and over in much the same way as the chair.

Peter was on his feet in a moment. He had received a fresh shock. Without once looking behind him he began hurrying up the slope again. He would have liked best to go home and creep into bed, so as to hide himself, for he felt safest when there. But he had left the goats up above, and Uncle had given him strict injunctions to make haste back so that they might not be left too long alone. And he stood more in awe of Uncle than any one, and would not have dared to disobey him on any account. There was no help for it, he had to go back, and Peter went on groaning and limping. He could run no more, for the anguish of mind he had been through, and the bumping and shaking he had received, were beginning to tell upon him. And so with lagging steps and groans he slowly made his way up the mountain.

Shortly after meeting Peter, Herr Sesemann passed the first hut, and so was satisfied that he was on the right path. He continued his climb with renewed courage, and at last, after a long and exhausting walk, he came in sight of his goal. There, only a little distance farther up, stood the grandfather's home, with the dark tops of the fir trees waving above its roof.

Herr Sesemann was delighted to have come to the last steep bit of his journey, in another minute or two he would be with his little daughter, and he pleased himself with the thought of her surprise. But the company above had seen his approaching figure and recognised who it was, and they were preparing something he little expected as a surprise on their part.

As he stepped on to the space in front of the hut two figures came towards him. One a tall girl with fair hair and pink cheeks, leaning on Heidi, whose dark eyes were dancing with joy. Herr Sesemann suddenly stopped, staring at the two children, and all at once the tears started to his eyes. What memories arose in his heart! Just so had Clara's mother looked, the fair-haired girl with the delicate pink-and-white complexion. Herr Sesemann did not know if he was awake or dreaming.

"Don't you know me, papa?" called Clara to him, her face beaming with happiness. "Am I so altered since you saw me?"

Then Herr Sesemann ran to his child and clasped her in his arms.

"Yes, you are indeed altered! How is it possible? Is it true what I see?" And the delighted father stepped back to look full at her again, and to make sure that the picture would not vanish before his eyes.

"Are you my little Clara, really my little Clara?" he kept on saying, then he clasped her in his arms again, and again put her away from him that he might look and make sure it was she who stood before him.

And now Grandmamma came up, anxious for a sight of her son's happy face.

"Well, what do you say now, dear son?" she exclaimed. "You have given us a pleasant surprise, but it is nothing in comparison to what we have prepared for you, you must confess," and she gave her son an affectionate kiss as she spoke. "But now," she went on, "you must come and pay your respects to Uncle, who is our chief benefactor."

"Yes, indeed, and with the little inmate of our own house, our little Heidi, too," said Herr Sesemann, shaking Heidi by the hand. "Well? Are you still well and happy in your mountain home? But I need not ask, no Alpine rose could look more blooming. I am glad, child, it is a pleasure to me to see you so."

And Heidi looked up with equal pleasure into Herr Sesemann's kind face. How good he had always been to her! And that he should find such happiness awaiting him up here on the mountain made her heart beat with gladness.

Grandmamma now led her son to introduce him to Uncle, and while the two men were shaking hands and Herr Sesemann was expressing his heartfelt thanks and boundless astonishment to the old man, Grandmamma wandered round to the back to see the old fir trees again.

Here another unexpected sight met her gaze, for there, under the trees where the long branches had left a clear space on the ground, stood a great bush of the most wonderful dark blue gentians, as fresh and shining as if they were growing on the spot. She clasped her hands, enraptured with their beauty.

"How exquisite! What a lovely sight!" she exclaimed. "Heidi, dearest child, come here! Is it you who have prepared this pleasure for me? It is perfectly wonderful!"

The children ran up.

"No, no, I did not put them there," said Heidi, "but I know who did."

"They grow just like that on the mountain, Grandmamma, only if anything they look more beautiful still," Clara put in; "but guess who brought those down today," and as she spoke she gave such a pleased smile that the grandmother thought for a moment the child herself must have gathered them. But that was hardly possible.

At this moment a slight rustling was heard behind the fir trees. It was Peter, who had just arrived. He had made a long round, having seen from the distance who it was standing beside Uncle in front of the hut, and he was trying to slip by unobserved. But Grandmamma had seen and recognised him, and suddenly the thought struck her that it might be Peter who had brought the flowers and that he was now trying to get away unseen, feeling shy about it; but she could not let him go off like that, he must have some little reward.

"Come along, boy; come here, do not be afraid," she called to him.

Peter stood still, petrified with fear. After all he had gone through that day he felt he had no longer any power of resistance left. All he could think was, "It's all up with me now." Every hair of his head stood on end, and he stepped forth from behind the fir trees, his face pale and distorted with terror.

"Courage, boy," said Grandmamma in her effort to dispel his shyness, "tell me now straight out without hesitation, was it you who did it?"

Peter did not lift his eyes and therefore did not see at what Grandmamma was pointing. But he knew that Uncle was standing at the corner of the hut, fixing him with his grey eyes, while beside him stood the most terrible person that Peter could conceive—the police-constable from Frankfurt.

Quaking in every limb, and with trembling lips he muttered a low, "Yes."

"Well, and what is there dreadful about that?" said Grandmamma.

"Because—because—it is all broken to pieces and no one can put it together again." Peter brought out his words with difficulty, and his knees knocked together so that he could hardly stand.

Grandmamma went up to Uncle. "Is that poor boy a little out of his mind?" she asked sympathisingly.

"Not in the least," Uncle assured her, "it is only that he was the wind that sent the chair rolling down the slope, and he is expecting his well-deserved punishment."

Grandmamma found this hard to believe, for in her opinion Peter did not look an entirely bad boy, nor could he have any reason for destroying such a necessary thing as the chair. But Uncle had only given expression to the suspicion that he had from the moment the accident happened. The angry looks which Peter had from the beginning cast at Clara, and the other signs of his dislike to what had been taking place on the mountain, had not escaped Uncle's eye. Putting two and two together he had come to the right conclusion as to the cause of the disaster, and he therefore spoke without hesitation when he accused Peter. The lady broke into lively expostulations on hearing this.

"No, no, dear Uncle, we will not punish the poor boy any further. One must be fair to him. Here are all these strangers from Frankfurt who come and carry away Heidi, his one sole possession, and a possession well worth having too, and he is left to sit alone day after day for weeks, with nothing to do but brood over his wrongs. No, no, let us be fair to him; his anger got the upper hand and drove him an act of revenge—a foolish one, I own, but then we all behave foolishly when we are angry." And saying this she went back to Peter, who still stood frightened and trembling. She sat down on the seat under the fir trees and called him to her kindly,—

"Come here, boy, and stand in front of me, for I have something to say to you. Leave off shaking and trembling, for I want you to listen to me. You sent the chair rolling down the mountain so that it was broken to pieces. That was a very wrong thing to do, as you yourself knew very well at the time, and you also knew that you deserved to be punished for it, and in order to escape this you have been doing all you can to hide the truth from everybody. But be sure of this, Peter: that those who do wrong make a mistake when they think no one knows anything about it. For God sees and hears everything, and when the wicked doer tries to hide what he has done, then God wakes up a little watchman that He places inside us all when we are born and who sleeps on quietly till we do something wrong. And the little watchman has a small goad in his hand, And when he wakes up he keeps on pricking us with it, so that we have not a moment's peace. And the watchman torments us still further, for he keeps on calling out, 'Now you will be found out! Now they will drag you off to punishment!' And so we pass our life in fear and trouble, and never know a moment's happiness or peace. Have you not felt something like that lately, Peter?"

Peter gave a contrite nod of the head, as one who knew all about it, for Grandmamma had described his own feelings exactly.

"And you calculated wrongly also in another way," continued Grandmamma, "for you see the harm you intended has turned out for the best for those you wished to hurt. As Clara had no chair to go in and yet wanted so much to see the flowers, she made the effort to walk, and every day since she has been walking better and better, and if she remains up here she will in time be able to go up the mountain every day, much oftener than she would have done in her chair. So you see, Peter, God is able to bring good out of evil for those whom you meant to injure, and you who did the evil were left to suffer the unhappy consequences of it. Do you thoroughly understand all I have said to you, Peter? If so, do not forget my words, and whenever you feel inclined to do anything wrong, think of the little watchman inside you with his goad and his disagreeable voice. Will you remember all this?"

"Yes, I will," answered Peter, still very subdued, for he did not yet know how the matter was going to end, as the police constable was still standing with the Uncle.

"That's right, and now the thing is over and done for," said Grandmamma. "But I should like you to have something for a pleasant reminder of the visitors from Frankfurt. Can you tell me anything that you have wished very much to have? What would you like best as a present?"

Peter lifted his head at this, and stared open-eyed at Grandmamma. Up to the last minute he had been expecting something dreadful to happen, and now he might have anything that he wanted. His mind seemed all of a whirl.

"I mean what I say," went on Grandmamma. "You shall choose what you would like to have as a remembrance from the Frankfurt visitors, and as a token that they will not think any more of the wrong thing you did. Now do you understand me, boy?"

The fact began at last to dawn upon Peter's mind that he had no further punishment to fear, and that the kind lady sitting in front of him had delivered him from the police constable. He suddenly felt as if the weight of a mountain had fallen off him. He had also by this time awakened to the further conviction that it was better to make a full confession at once of anything he had done wrong or had left undone, and so he said, "And I lost the paper, too."

Grandmamma had to consider a moment what he meant, but soon recalled his connection with her telegram, and answered kindly,—

"You are a good boy to tell me! Never conceal anything you have done wrong, and then all will come right again. And now what would you like me to give you?"

Peter grew almost giddy with the thought that he could have anything in the world that he wished for. He had a vision of the yearly fair at Mayenfeld with the glittering stalls and all the lovely things that he had stood gazing at for hours, without a hope of ever possessing one of them, for Peter's purse never held more than a halfpenny, and all these fascinating objects cost double that amount. There were the pretty little red whistles that he could use to call his goats, and the splendid knives with rounded handles, known as toad-strikers, with which one could do such famous work among the hazel bushes.

Peter remained pondering; he was trying to think which of these two desirable objects he should best like to have, and he found it difficult to decide. Then a bright thought occurred to him; he would then be able to think over the matter between now and next year's fair.

"A penny," answered Peter, who was no longer in doubt.

Grandmamma could not help laughing. "That is not an extravagant request. Come here then!" and she pulled out her purse and put four bright round shillings in his hand and, then laid some pennies on top of it. "We will settle our accounts at once," she continued, "and I will explain them to you. I have given you as many pennies as there are weeks in the year, and so every Sunday throughout the year you can take out a penny to spend."

"As long as I live?" said Peter quite innocently.

Grandmamma laughed more still at this, and the men hearing her, paused in their talk to listen to what was going on.

"Yes, boy, you shall have it all your life—I will put it down in my will. Do you hear, my son? And you are to put it down in yours as well: a penny a week to Peter as long as he lives."

Herr Sesemann nodded his assent and joined in the laughter.

Peter looked again at the present in his hand to make sure he was not dreaming, and then said, "Thank God!"

And he went off running and leaping with more even than his usual agility, and this time managed to keep his feet, for it was not fear, but joy such as he had never known before in his life, that now sent him flying up the mountain. All trouble and trembling had disappeared, and he was to have a penny every week for life.

As later, after dinner, the party were sitting together chatting, Clara drew her father a little aside, and said with an eagerness that had been unknown to the little tired invalid,—

"O papa, if you only knew all that Grandfather has done for me from day to day! I cannot reckon his kindnesses, but I shall never forget them as long as I live! And I keep on thinking what I could do for him, or what present I could make him that would give him half as much pleasure as he has given me."

"That is just what I wish most myself, Clara," replied her father, whose face grew happier each time he looked at his little daughter. "I have been also thinking how we can best show our gratitude to our good benefactor."

Herr Sesemann now went over to where Uncle and grandmamma were engaged in lively conversation. Uncle stood up as he approached, and Herr Sesemann, taking him by the hand said,—

"Dear friend, let us exchange a few words with one another. You will believe me when I tell you that I have known no real happiness for years past. What worth to me were money and property when they were unable to make my poor child well and happy? With the help of God you have made her whole and strong, and you have given new life not only to her but to me. Tell me now, in what way can I show my gratitude to you? I can never repay all you have done, but whatever is in my power to do is at your service. Speak, friend, and tell me what I can do?"

Uncle had listened to him quietly, with a smile of pleasure on his face as he looked at the happy father.

"Herr Sesemann," he replied in his dignified way, "believe me that I too have my share in the joy of your daughter's recovery, and my trouble is well repaid by it. I thank you heartily for all you have said, but I have need of nothing; I have enough for myself and the child as long as I live. One wish alone I have, and if that could be satisfied I should have no further care in life."

"Speak, dear friend, and tell me what it is," said Herr Sesemann entreatingly.

"I am growing old," Uncle went on, "and shall not be here much longer. I have nothing to leave the child when I die, and she has no relations, except one person who will always like to make what profit out of her she can. If you could promise me that Heidi shall never have to go and earn her living among strangers, then you would richly reward me for all I have done for your child."

"There could never be any question of such a thing as that, my dear friend," said Herr Sesemann quickly. "I look upon the child as our own. Ask my mother, my daughter; you may be sure that they will never allow the child to be left in any one else's care! But if it will make you happier I give you here my hand upon it. I promise you: Heidi shall never have to go and earn her living among strangers; I will make provision against this both during my life and after. But now I have something else to say. Independent of her circumstances, the child is totally unfitted to live a life away from home; we found out that when she was with us. But she has made friends, and among them I know one who is at this moment in Frankfurt; he is winding up his affairs there, that he may be free to go where he likes and take his rest. I am speaking of my friend, the doctor, who came over here in the autumn and who, having well considered your advice, intends to settle in this neighbourhood, for he has never felt so well and happy anywhere as in the company of you and Heidi. So you see the child will henceforth have two protectors near her— and may they both live long to share the task!"

"God grant it indeed may be so!" added Grandmamma, shaking Uncle's hand warmly as she spoke, to show how sincerely she echoed her son's wish. Then putting her arm round Heidi, who was standing near, she drew the child to her.

"And I have a question to ask you too, dear Heidi. Tell me if there is anything you particularly wish for."

"Yes, there is," answered Heidi promptly, looking up delightedly at Grandmamma.

"Then tell me at once, dear, what it is."

"I want to have the bed I slept in at Frankfurt with the high pillows and the thick coverlid, and then Grandmother will not have to lie with her head down hill and hardly able to breathe, and she will be warm enough under the coverlid not to have to wear her shawl in bed to prevent her freezing to death."

In her eagerness to obtain what she had set her heart upon Heidi hardly gave herself time to get out all she had to say, and did not pause for breath till she reached the end of her sentence.

"Dearest child," answered Grandmamma, moved by Heidi's speech, "what is this you tell me of Grandmother! You are right to remind me. In the midst of our own happiness we forget too often that which we ought to remember before all things. When God has shown us some special mercy we should think at once of those who are denied so many things. I will telegraph to Frankfurt at once! Fräulein Rottenmeier shall pack up the bed this very day, and it will be here in two days' time. God willing, Grandmother shall soon be sleeping comfortably upon it."

Heidi skipped round Grandmamma in her glee, and then stopping all of a sudden, said quickly, "I must make haste down and tell Grandmother, and she will be in trouble too at my not having been to see her for such a long time." For she felt she could not wait another moment before carrying the good news down to Grandmother, and, moreover, the recollection came to her of the distress the old woman was in when she last saw her.

"No, no, Heidi, what can you be thinking of," said her grandfather reprovingly. "You can't be running backwards and forwards like that when you have visitors."

But Grandmamma interfered on Heidi's behalf. "The child is not so far wrong, Uncle," she said, "and poor Grandmother has too long been deprived of Heidi for our sakes. Let us all go down to her together. I believe my horse is waiting for me and I can ride down from there, and as soon as I get to Dörfli the message shall be sent off. What do you think of my plan, son?"

Herr Sesemann had not yet had time to speak of his travelling plans, so he begged his mother to wait a few moments that he might tell her what he proposed doing.

Herr Sesemann had been arranging that he and his mother should make a little tour in Switzerland, first ascertaining if Clara was in a fit state to go some part of the way with them. But now he would have the full enjoyment of his daughter's company, and that being so he did not want to miss any of these beautiful days of later summer, but to start at once on the journey that he now looked forward to with such additional pleasure. And so he proposed that they should spend the night in Dörfli and that next day he should come and fetch Clara, then they would all three go down to Ragatz and make that their starting point.

Clara was rather upset at first at the thought of saying good bye like this to the mountain; she could not help being pleased, however, at the prospect of the journey, and no time was allowed her to give way to lamentation.

Grandmamma had already taken Heidi by the hand, preparatory to leading the way, when she suddenly turned. "But what is to become of Clara?" she asked, remembering all at once that the child could not yet take so long a walk. She gave a nod of satisfaction as she saw that Uncle had already taken Clara up in his arms and was following her with sturdy strides. Herr Sesemann brought up the rear, and so they all started down the mountain.

Heidi kept jumping for joy as she and Grandmamma walked along side by side, and Grandmamma asked all about Grandmother, how she lived, and what she did, especially in the winter when it was so cold. And Heidi gave her a minute account of everything, for she knew all that went on at Grandmother's, and told her how Grandmother sat crouching in her corner and trembling with cold. She was able to give her exact particulars of what Grandmother had and had not to eat. Grandmamma listened with interest and sympathy until they came to Grandmother's. Brigitta was just hanging out Peter's second shirt in the sun, so that he might have it ready to put on when he had worn the other long enough. As soon as she saw the company approaching she rushed indoors.

"The whole party of them are just going past, mother, evidently all returning home again," she informed the old woman. "Uncle is with them, carrying the sick child."

"Alas, is it really to be so then?" sighed the grandmother. "And you saw Heidi with them? Then they are taking her away. If only she could come and put her hand in mine again! If I could but hear her voice once more!"

At this moment the door flew open and Heidi sprang across to the corner and threw her arms round Grandmother.

"Grandmother! Grandmother! My bed is to be sent from Frankfurt with all the three pillows and the thick coverlid; Grandmamma says it will be here in two days." Heidi could not get out her words quickly enough, for she was impatient to see Grandmother's great joy at the news. The latter smiled, but said a little sadly,—

"She must indeed be a good kind lady, and I ought to be glad to think she is taking you with her, but I shall not outlive it long."

"What is this I hear? Who has been telling my good grandmother such tales?" exclaimed a kindly voice, and Grandmother felt her hand taken and warmly pressed, for Grandmamma had followed Heidi in and heard all that was said. "No, no, there is no thought of such a thing! Heidi is going to stay with you and make you happy. We want to see her again, but we shall come to her. We hope to pay a visit to the Alm every year, for we have good cause to offer up especial thanks to God upon this spot where so great a miracle has been wrought upon our child."

And now Grandmother's face was lighted up with genuine happiness, and she pressed Frau Sesemann's hand over and over again, unable to speak her thanks, while two large tears of joy rolled down her aged cheeks. And Heidi saw the glad change come over Grandmother's face, and she too now was entirely happy.

She clung to the old woman, saying, "Hasn't it all come about, Grandmother, just like the hymn I read to you last time? Isn't the bed from Frankfurt sent to make you well?"

"Yes, Heidi, and many, many other good things too, which God has sent me," said the grandmother, deeply moved. "I did not think it possible that there were so many kind people, ready to trouble themselves about a poor old woman and to do so much for her. Nothing strengthens our belief in a kind heavenly Father who never forgets even the least of His creatures so much as to know that there are such people, full of goodness and pity for a poor useless creature such as I am."

"My good grandmother," said Frau Sesemann, interrupting her, "we are all equally poor and helpless in the eyes of God, and all have equal need that He should not forget us. But now we must say goodbye, but only till we meet again, for when we pay our next year's visit to the Alm you will be the first person we shall come and see; meanwhile we shall not forget you." And Frau Sesemann took Grandmother's hand again and shook it in farewell.

But Grandmother would not let her off even then without more words of gratitude, and without calling down on her benefactress and all belonging to her every blessing that God had to bestow.

At last Herr Sesemann and his mother were able to continue their journey downwards, while Uncle carried Clara back home, with Heidi beside him, so full of joy of what was coming for Grandmother that every step was a jump.

But there were many tears shed the following morning by the departing Clara, who wept to say goodbye to the beautiful mountain home where she had been happier than ever in her life before. Heidi did her best to comfort her. "Summer will be here again in no time," she said, "and then you will come again, and it will be nicer still, for you will be able to walk about from the beginning. We can then go out every day with the goats up to where the flowers grow, and enjoy ourselves from the moment you arrive."

Herr Sesemann had come as arranged to fetch his little daughter away, and was just now standing and talking with Uncle, for they had much to say to one another. Clara felt somewhat consoled by Heidi's words, and wiped away her tears.

"Be sure you say goodbye for me to Peter and the goats, and especially to Little Swan. I wish I could give Little Swan a present, for she has helped so much to make me strong."

"Well, you can if you like," replied Heidi, "send her a little salt; you know how she likes to lick some out of Grandfather's hand when she comes home at night."

Clara was delighted at this idea. "Oh, then I shall send a hundred pounds of salt from Frankfurt, for I want her to have something as a remembrance of me."

Herr Sesemann now beckoned to the children as it was time to be off. Grandmamma's white horse had been brought up for Clara, as she was no longer obliged to be carried in a chair.

Heidi ran to the far edge of the slope and continued to wave her hand to Clara until the last glimpse of horse and rider had disappeared.

And now the bed has arrived, and Grandmother is sleeping so soundly all night that she is sure to grow stronger.

Grandmamma, moreover, has not forgotten how cold the winter is on the mountain. She has sent a large parcel of warm clothing of every description, so that Grandmother can wrap herself round and round, and will certainly not tremble with cold now as she sits in her corner.

There is a great deal of building going on at Dörfli. The doctor has arrived, and, for the present, is occupying his old quarters. His friends have advised him to buy the old house that Uncle and Heidi live in during the winter, which had evidently, judging from the height of the rooms and the magnificent stove with its artistically-painted tiles, been a fine gentleman's place at one time. The doctor is having this part of the old house rebuilt for himself, the other part being repaired for Uncle and Heidi, for the doctor is aware that Uncle is a man of independent spirit, who likes to have a house to himself. Quite at the back a warm and well-walled stall is being put up for the two goats, and there they will pass their winter in comfort.

The doctor and Uncle are becoming better friends every day, and as they walk about the new buildings to see how they are getting on, their thoughts continually turn to Heidi, for the chief pleasure to each in connection with the house is that they will have the light-hearted little child with them there.

"Dear friend," said the doctor on one of these occasions as they were standing together, "you will see this matter in the same light as I do, I am sure. I share your happiness in the child as if, next to you, I was the one to whom she most closely belonged, but I wish also to share all responsibilities, concerning her and to do my best for the child. I shall then feel I have my rights in her, and shall look forward to her being with me and caring for me in my old age, which is the one great wish of my heart. She will have the same claims upon me as if she were my own child, and I shall provide for her as such, and so we shall be able to leave her without anxiety when the day comes that you and I must go."

Uncle did not speak, but he clasped the doctor's hand in his, and his good friend could read in the old man's eyes how greatly moved he was and how glad and grateful he felt.

Heidi and Peter were at this moment sitting with Grandmother, and the one had so much to relate, and the others to listen to, that they all three got closer and closer to one another, hardly able to breathe in their eagerness not to miss a word.

And how much there was to tell of all the events that had taken place that last summer, for they had not had many opportunities of meeting since then.

And it was difficult to say which of the three looked the happiest at being together again, and at the recollection of all the wonderful things that had happened. Mother Brigitta's face was perhaps the happiest of all, as now, with the help of explanation she was able to understand for the first time the history of Peter's weekly penny for life.

Then at last the grandmother spoke, "Heidi, read me one of the hymns! I can feel I can do nothing for the remainder of my life but thank the Father in Heaven for all the mercies he has shown us!"

<u>OTHER TITLES AVAILABLE IN THIS SERIES</u>

9 789352 762729

9 789352 762736

9 789352 763337

9 789352 763160

Other Titles Available In This Series

9 789352 762767

9 789352 762910

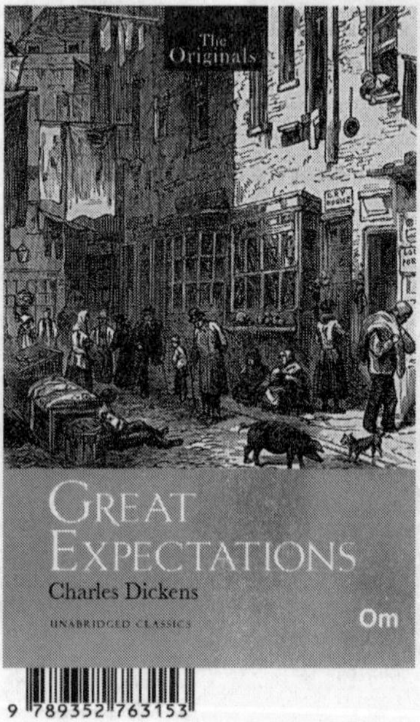

9 789352 763153

Other Titles Available In This Series

9 789352 763375

9 789352 763382

9 789352 763399